"I'm Kathleen Yardley."

"What are you doing with my daughter?" Booth demanded.

Kathleen glanced at the sleeping child. "Shh. She just fell asleep. Please lower your voice."

"Maybe I'm not making my questions clear enough," Booth muttered. "Let's try this. *Where's Mrs. Carmody?*"

At the sound of her name, Mavis Carmody entered the room, shaking her head at him. "Booth, do you have to bluster like a prison warden? You should be thanking Kathleen instead of yelling at her as if she were some common criminal."

Kathleen's face paled.

Booth, trying to quiet Lisa again, merely said, "I was not yelling."

"Yes, you were. Just like you used to when you were a little boy and didn't get your own way."

Kathleen smiled at the older woman. "I wonder why I'm not surprised that Mr. Rawlings was a difficult child. Just an observation, of course."

"You don't know me well enough to make an observation," he countered, "but we could easily remedy that."

ABOUT THE AUTHOR

Dee Holmes, a much-published author of both fiction and nonfiction, won her first major award, a RITA, in 1991 for her first novel, *Black Horse Island*. She has been writing steadily ever since.

Dee's books often feature the picturesque setting of New England, which isn't surprising, since she is a longtime resident of Rhode Island. She has a grown son and daughter.

Books by Dee Holmes

HARLEQUIN SUPERROMANCE
699—HIS RUNAWAY SON
732—PROTECTING MOLLY McCULLOCH

Don't miss any of our special offers. Write to us at the following address for information on our newest releases.

Harlequin Reader Service
U.S.: 3010 Walden Ave., P.O. Box 1325, Buffalo, NY 14269
Canadian: P.O. Box 609, Fort Erie, Ont. L2A 5X3

IT TAKES A BABY
Dee Holmes

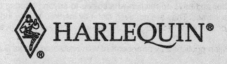

HARLEQUIN®

TORONTO • NEW YORK • LONDON
AMSTERDAM • PARIS • SYDNEY • HAMBURG
STOCKHOLM • ATHENS • TOKYO • MILAN • MADRID
PRAGUE • WARSAW • BUDAPEST • AUCKLAND

ISBN 0-373-70801-7

IT TAKES A BABY

IT TAKES A BABY

PROLOGUE

KATHLEEN HANES knew that returning to the house for the forgotten box of her mother's treasures and sheet music was stupid and dangerous. But as drunk and raging as her husband had been when she'd fled a few hours ago, she was fairly certain he would be passed out on the floor.

Steve was nothing if not predictable. Drink, rage, drink some more and then pass out. She'd witnessed the pattern too often to believe this time would be any different.

When she turned the car into the long road that led to the Wyoming ranch, her pulse sped up and she slowed to a stop before the final bend. She was some distance from the house, but she felt less exposed here. She parked so that she could drive straight out, and she left the engine running. The old Buick could be cantankerous at times, and she didn't want to take any chances.

For more than a year, her life had become a series of preparations, of ways of calculating escape, while still hoping that Steve would change. Then had come the terrifying realization, over the past few days, that if she stayed he would kill her, and maybe himself.

Kathleen drew closer to the house. The late-afternoon sun burned red in the western sky. The sheriff's car and a pickup truck were parked behind Steve's patrol car. The truck looked like Cory's— one of the deputies Kathleen liked. Most of the men who worked in the Rodeo, Wyoming, sheriff's office were like backroom-poker pals. If you weren't an insider, then what you said or did meant nothing to them. She'd learned that when she'd called the sheriff after Steve had beaten her. His attitude had been one of patient boredom. The unspoken message was "Cops stick together—we don't rat on one of our guys."

At that point, Kathleen had lost any illusions about "service and honor and protection,"—those impassioned words spoken at parades by elected officials. Steve, her husband of five years, was one of Rodeo's deputies.

At noon today, he'd awakened and started drinking. Kathleen had left him with his bottle and methodically packed her things in the car. When he'd come weaving into the bedroom and realized she was leaving, he'd hit her, then had gone to get his revolver. Kathleen had managed to get to the car, but not before he'd fired two shots at her.

Now, four hours later, all she wanted was her sheet music and the ivory-and-gold cameo. They were the only tangible links she had to her mother, and she couldn't leave them for Steve to destroy. He'd already done that to her trust and her hope and all her ideals about love and marriage and children. Besides, if he was busy with his buddies, she could get in and get out without him even knowing.

Drawing closer to the front door, she heard voices in the living room. A radio played rock music—Steve's favorite. Cory was probably trying to get Steve sober enough to go to work.

She made her way around to the back door and very quietly opened it, walked through the kitchen and down the hallway to the bedroom. She barely glanced at the double bed with its wedding-ring quilt or at Steve's messy dresser. She went to the closet and took out a flat cardboard blouse box from Shelly's Dress Shop. She made her way back to the kitchen.

The door between the kitchen and living room had been opened wider, and for a few seconds Kathleen feared she would be noticed. She stood, counting to twenty, as the voices resumed. They were coming from the living room. She inched along the wall, then paused to glance into the living room to make sure the men weren't looking in her direction. They weren't.

Cory and the sheriff, Buck Faswell, stood near Steve. He lay crumpled on the floor. Passed out, Kathleen thought. Then she saw the blood.

She stared, her eyes widening in horror before she clamped her hand over her mouth to stop the gasp.

What had happened? He'd been drunk and out of control when she'd fled the house, but he had also been very much alive. Had he shot himself?

"So what's your guess?" Cory asked.

"A couple of hours. I talked to him this morning."

Kathleen was about to come forward and say he'd been alive four hours ago.

But before she took a step, Cory said, "No, not when. I meant your guess on who did this."

"A no-brainer. His wife."

"Kathleen?"

"Who has a better motive? She claimed he beat her. She went off to that safe house a couple of times. They had an argument just two days ago. I also heard she bought a gun."

She stood glued in place, her chest swelling painfully to keep down the shout of "No!" She couldn't move.

"Kathleen kill him? No way."

Oh, Cory, thank you, she thought, but the sheriff's next words chilled her to the bone.

"Got it straight from Steve."

"Steve told you she planned to kill him?"

"Just this morning."

Liar! Steve had slept until noon. He'd been off duty the night before, played poker down at the old Palace Saloon until 3:00 a.m., then come home drunk and fallen into bed. Which was where he'd been until noon when he started drinking again.

Cory took off his hat and scratched his head. "Gotta say, it's pretty unbelievable. Kathleen didn't strike me as the violent type. Remember how she played all that classical stuff on the piano?"

"No doubt her prints are on the murder weapon," the sheriff said, ignoring Cory's words. Faswell reached down, slid a table knife through the trigger guard and lifted the pistol, placing it in a plastic bag.

"Hey, shouldn't we be dusting that first?"

"Do it back in town." Faswell walked around the body, stooped down, rolled it a bit and reached beneath it. A few seconds later, he stood. In his hand was a blood-smeared note. "She planned to leave him, or so this note says. Seems pretty clear. He caught her before she left, tried to make her change her mind. She refused, so he threatened her or something like that, and she got this here gun and shot him."

"I don't know. Steve wasn't some dunderhead. He had his own weapon. Hard to believe she'd be able to train a gun on him before he moved on *her*."

"Well, you work on how she did it," Faswell told Cory as if a good story was more important than the truth. "No wide-eyed babe is gonna screw me up. You just make sure the arrest warrant is issued and that when she's brought in, we got a case with no holes."

Cory looked stunned.

"You got a problem, kid?"

"You're going to frame Kathleen for Steve's murder."

"Frame? No one has to frame the guilty person."

"But you don't know if Kathleen did this.

There've been no charges yet, no trial, no witnesses.''

The sheriff ignored that, turning to another deputy, who stood in the shadows. ''Find her. Get on the radio, and get some roadblocks set up. I want her brought in, and I want a confession. We owe it to Steve's family to get this little bitch locked up and put away for the rest of her life.''

Somehow, Kathleen got outside safely. Escape. She had to escape. Clutching the box, she darted to her left, making a wide sweep to stay clear of the windows at the front of the house. She didn't have time to think, to figure out what had happened or who killed Steve, and why.

She got to the Buick, slid inside, put it in gear and drove out the long driveway. Her one hope was back roads. It would take twice as long, but she would avoid the highway.

She kept glancing in her rearview mirror, expecting flashing lights and sirens. But the road behind her stretched empty and silent.

The relief should have been sweet, but what about tomorrow? Next week? Next month?

My God. She was a fugitive—on the run for something she didn't do. And the police were the enemy.

CHAPTER ONE

KILLER! SHE'S A KILLER. She should burn in hell!

Kathleen Yardley Hanes tossed, her body damp. She heard the voices shouting, screaming. Then the crying.

The voices faded, but the crying wouldn't stop.

She turned over in the double bed, wrapping the pillow around her head to block the noise invading her subconscious. Her dream seemed so real. She was standing in the concert-hall wings, dressed in a white-trimmed lavender dress, about to walk on stage to play a grand piano before a sellout crowd. But there were the shouts of police after her, and the crowd was yelling, "Killer!"

Then silence. Followed by more cries from a wailing baby. The faraway sounds kept breaking through her consciousness until finally she awoke.

The early morning hours in Crosby, Connecticut, in July were warm and usually silent. She lay still for a few seconds, banishing the too-familiar nightmare, and listened. It was 1:25 a.m., according to the clock radio. The crying was coming from an upstairs apartment. She wondered if the parents were immune or if they believed in that silly theory about letting a child cry itself to sleep.

Don't interfere, an inner voice cautioned. Just as quickly, another voice reminded her of all the horrid scenarios on the evening news where no one had cared enough to get involved.

Kathleen knew about needing help and having no one to count on, no one to trust. It had been many weeks since she'd fled Wyoming, and she felt no more free or safe now than she had when she'd overheard the plan to frame her for her husband's murder.

She rubbed her eyes with her fists, closing out the lurking demons. She had to make sure the baby was all right; otherwise she'd never get back to sleep.

Quickly Kathleen pulled on cotton shorts beneath her nightie, added a lightweight sweatshirt and slipped her feet into canvas sandals. She found her keys, locked the apartment door and climbed the stairs to the second floor.

There were only two apartments upstairs. Leaning against the hall wall of the closest one was a cardboard carton with a toy box on the front. The crying had ebbed to an exhausted sobbing.

The door was slightly ajar, and Kathleen tried to shake off a sense of foreboding. This was nuts, she thought. She had no idea what she was walking into. Suicide. Murder. Someone badly beaten and incapable of tending the child? Still, she couldn't turn away. She had to find the baby.

She stepped inside. The apartment was dim except for the soft light from a floor lamp beside a rocking chair. Someone obviously loved clocks, for there was a collection of miniature ones displayed on a rolltop desk. The assembled toy box sat nearby, a pink jungle-print quilt tossed across the cushioned top. Newspapers were neatly bundled by the door for recycling. The crying came from a darkened room to her right.

Kathleen started forward, past a green plaid couch, then jumped when she caught sight of the elderly woman stretched out on it, her face turned sideways.

Was she dead? Was that why she hadn't heard the infant? Kathleen was about to approach her when she heard a snore. Relief rushed through her. The woman might be hurt, but she was alive. Right now, though, Kathleen had to check on the baby.

She followed its wail, knowing she would forever hear it in her dreams. In the nursery, a teddy bear nightlight glowed beside the change table, incongruous, somehow, under the circumstances.

She moved to a wooden-spindle crib that looked like a family heirloom. The child, who appeared to be about a year old, sat in the middle, nose running, hiccuping, sobbing sporadically. When Kathleen reached down and lifted the baby, she felt its flushed warmth and dampness.

"Shh. It's okay now. You're okay," she whispered. She held the chubby little body close, inhaling the sweet scent of skin and lotion, rubbing its back and murmuring against its ear. The child quieted. Kathleen switched on a lamp and laid the baby on the change table.

Blinking and skewering up its face at the invasion of light, it didn't appear to be hurt, just frustrated that all its crying hadn't brought attention sooner. In a few moments the child stilled, staring up at Kathleen and smiling.

"What a charmer you are. I'll bet a lot of that noise was because you need to be changed, don't you?" The baby followed Kathleen's motions as she quickly got the wet disposable off, then cleaned, powdered and put on a dry diaper. "Now, that has to feel better, doesn't it?"

The baby girl smiled again, reaching for Kathleen's silver bracelet. She gripped the wide band and tugged. "I bet you'll have this right in your mouth if I give it to you, won't you? I see a few teeth, and I bet there are more coming." The baby grinned, then giggled aloud. Kathleen's heart was captured. Suddenly her apprehension fled. The older woman had simply fallen asleep; this was no abused child.

"You are a precious bundle, you know that?" She brushed her fingers down the soft cheek, and was rewarded with another smile. "Is that your grandma out there on the couch? Mommy and Daddy are out, I'll bet. Maybe on a long-deserved night by themselves?" She lifted the baby, holding her securely, and walked back out to the living room. The woman awakened. She shrank back against the couch, her eyes pools of fear when she saw Kathleen.

"Who are you and what are you doing with Lisa?" the woman asked.

"Lisa has been crying for a long time."

"Crying?" She raised her hand to the side of her head.

"Yes. Babies have a habit of doing that when they're uncomfortable. And if no one comes, they tend to cry louder." Kathleen knew she sounded short and too sarcastic, but what good was a baby-sitter who didn't tend to the baby?

"But where did you come from?"

"Downstairs. Her crying woke me up. And the door was unlocked."

"Oh, dear. I must have fallen asleep wrong." The older woman rose to her feet, straightening a cotton print dress, her hands moving to her silver hair. Kathleen noted an elaborate ring with multi-colored stones, and hands with fingernails that had been recently manicured. She stared for a few seconds. The last manicure she'd had was before her wedding. How innocent she'd been in her Virgin Rose nail polish with her wide-eyed hope for the future.

The woman walked toward Kathleen and patted Lisa. "Oh, honey, I'm so sorry. All that crying probably made you hungry. I'll fix a bottle for you."

"You said something about falling asleep wrong?" Kathleen asked, putting aside her regrets.

"What? Oh, yes. That's why I didn't hear her crying."

Obviously, Kathleen wanted to say. Instead she changed tactics. "Are you Lisa's grandmother?"

"Oh, no. That would be Janet. She and her husband, Doug, went to the Cape for the week. He's retired. Used to be Crosby's police chief. Janet and I are bridge partners. Been playing every Thursday since the late fifties. I don't usually keep Lisa, but Darlene—she's Booth's sister, and just between you and me, a bit flighty—can't seem to settle down and find herself a husband. Do you know she's been engaged three times to three different men? Anyway, poor thing came down with one of those dreadful summer colds, and she was afraid she'd pass the germs on to little Lisa, so I was a last-minute fill-in."

Kathleen blinked, her mind scrambling to put all the relationships together. Obviously this woman was a well-intentioned gossip, but Kathleen did catch two pieces of pertinent information. Lisa's mother was absent from the list of relatives and Lisa's grandfather was once the police chief. The latter sent a shiver through her.

"What's your name, my dear?" the woman asked. "I'm Mavis Carmody, by the way."

"Kathleen Yardley."

"What a pretty name. Well, Kathleen, I know Booth will want to thank you for coming to Lisa's rescue."

"No need to thank me, but—"

"I can't believe I didn't hear little Lisa," she said, shaking her head in self-reproach. She chattered on again, this time fluffing the couch pillows, then picking up the newspaper and folding it. "I have total deafness in one ear. I swear it's because Eric—he's my son, by the way—used to play that pounding rock music so loud it would have turned Bach in his grave. The doctor has no idea what caused it—the deafness, I mean—which makes one wonder why medical care is so expensive when they can't come up with a reason for deafness. I mean, it's not like I expect perfect hearing, but..." She prattled on about the doctors she'd seen, a visit to a Boston specialist and money wasted on hearing aids. "Anyway, I fell asleep on my good ear," she said, finishing at last.

Kathleen was exhausted just listening. Lisa had closed her eyes, drifting off to sleep. "That explains it, then."

The woman nodded, clearly regretting her carelessness. "I try never to do that. I mean, I've missed a few important phone calls, but Lisa crying and not being heard, well, that's inexcusable. I'm so glad you awakened and were concerned enough to come up."

"I am, too. She's a beautiful little girl."

Mavis went to the kitchen, switching on lights, then prepared a bottle for Lisa. Kathleen liked cuddling the child in her arms, but she knew she really should return to her own apartment.

As Mavis took the baby back, Lisa immediately

awakened and began to cry again. "Oh, dear, I think she's still annoyed with me for not hearing her," Mavis said. "Well, I can hardly blame her. She's been upset enough tonight. Would you mind holding her while she has her bottle? She seems secure with you."

"I'd love to." Kathleen took the bottle, which the baby immediately grabbed and put in her mouth. When Mavis suggested the rocking chair, Kathleen settled there with Lisa. Then she asked, "Are her parents out for the evening?"

"Her father is working, but her mother..." Mavis's expression clouded with sadness. "She died shortly after Lisa was born."

Kathleen's eyes widened. "How awful."

"Angie and Booth had been so excited about the baby. They'd been married a number of years, and Angie had waited to have a child because she had the responsibility of an ailing father. The pregnancy wasn't difficult, but Angie unexpectedly developed an aneurysm. Lisa was delivered healthy and squalling, but Angie didn't make it."

To Kathleen's surprise, her eyes stung with tears—empathy for Angie who would never hold her sweet baby, and for Lisa who would never know her mother. "Some things in life just aren't fair, are they?"

Mavis agreed. "Booth was devastated, as you would expect, but to his credit he has managed wonderfully. Although I wish I didn't have to be here when he finds out I went to sleep and let his daughter scream her poor lungs out.''

"Is he the violent type?"

"Only when it comes to Lisa. If anything happened to her..." Mavis shuddered. She patted Lisa and said, "I'm going to freshen up and then straighten the kitchen. She should sleep after the feeding. Oh, dear, she should be changed.''

"I already did that.''

Mavis smiled. "You're way ahead of me, Kathleen." She lifted the quilt from the toy box. "This is the reason she was crying. She woke up and couldn't find her blanket. She'd been sitting with me and fell asleep. I put her to bed and forgot all about the quilt.'' She handed it to Kathleen.

The older woman went into the bathroom, and Kathleen rocked while Lisa drank her bottle. Minutes passed, and Kathleen felt a pleasant contentment drift over her. The sleepy baby in her arms, the gentle motion of the rocking chair... If she closed her eyes, she could almost believe that this was where she would be safe, where she could let down her guard, where she'd never have to run again.

BOOTH RAWLINGS slammed the door of his black Explorer and winced at the noise. He had a roaring headache. His frustration over three missing fourteen-year-old girls had turned what should have been a night of catching up on paperwork into a fruitless questioning of family members who were so clueless he'd wanted to shake them.

No, he corrected himself. Not clueless. Just incapable of believing that their daughters had methodically planned to disappear. He'd been diplomatic and sympathetic in his attempt to keep them focused on this issue, but they'd been more concerned about blaming themselves.

Booth had little use for the current psychobabble. Blaming parents for ill-conceived juvenile behaviors wasted time and accomplished little. From the pieces Booth had put together, these kids had gone by choice, and unless something significantly bizarre turned up, they'd undoubtedly come home by choice, as well.

He thought of Lisa, and vowed right then that he would make it a point to know who her friends were and what she was doing. Simplistic, sure, but he saw too many kids drift into trouble out of boredom or lack of attention.

His own interest in troubled teens had been nurtured by his father, who strongly believed that kids needed role models. Doug Rawlings had been one, both at work and at home. Booth could only hope to emulate him.

Because of his own heads-up work with troubled teenage boys, he'd gotten a promotion in March to detective in the juvenile division of the Crosby Police Department.

Crosby was much smaller than New London to the south, and Booth carried the responsibility of staying in close touch with parents as well as being available for the kids. He liked his job, and working nights had given heft to Crosby's commitment to keep juvenile crime under control.

To Booth's knowledge, no other detective had actually requested night shifts. Booth had good reason for his preference—his daughter. He wanted to spend time with her during the day as well as make sure she had consistent care at night. So far, his decision had been the right one, he decided as he climbed the stairs to his apartment.

But when he pushed open the door and saw the young woman holding Lisa, he was temporarily confused. Then, dragging his hand down his face, he realized he was witnessing an idealized scene; one he'd created almost a year ago during the last days of Angie's pregnancy—coming home, and seeing Angie holding Lisa to her breast. Angie waiting for him. His wife, his daughter, his family.

The scene had never materialized, yet here it was, as wonderful as he'd always fantasized it would be. He shook away the image. His headache, coupled with his lingering frustration, brought him back to reality.

"Who the hell are you?"

CHAPTER TWO

SHE LOOKED UP, startled, holding Lisa tightly against her.

Booth took a breath. "Well?"

"I'm Kathleen Yardley." She shrank back as though wishing she could disappear.

"What are you doing with my daughter?"

She swallowed, appearing to get her bearings, and looked at him for a long, unblinking moment. Then she glanced back down at Lisa. "Shh. Your daughter just fell asleep. Please lower your voice or she'll start crying again."

Booth noticed that her voice remained calm even while his had risen. He also noted that she was pretty in an unassuming way, with dark blond hair that was smooth and fine, unlike the heavy, lush curls Angie had had. Nor was this woman's body as ripe. Yet it was her eyes that captivated him. Wide-spaced and blue and finely lashed, they were eyes that were intensely on guard, eyes that held deeply hidden secrets, eyes that would darken like indigo fire when she was aroused....

Good God, Booth thought, what was he thinking?

Clearing away his disturbing thoughts, he deliberately made his voice gruffer. "You still haven't told me what you're doing with my daughter."

Holding Lisa so as not to jar her, the woman slowly rose to her feet. He watched her as she moved toward him. "Lisa's tummy is full, and if you take her carefully she shouldn't wake up."

She eased Lisa into his arms, and he felt the slight brush of her hands against his shirt. Then she handed him the pink quilt Angie had made during her pregnancy. Lisa had slept with it tucked around her since birth. The woman pulled away, but the feel of her fingers stayed with him. Lisa continued to sleep.

"Maybe I'm not making my questions clear enough," he muttered, as disturbed by his reaction to this stranger as he was by finding her holding his daughter. He shifted Lisa, and tucked her closer to him. "Let's try this. Where's Mrs. Carmody?"

"Mavis is in the kitchen."

"Mavis?" Booth arched his eyebrows. "I've never called her Mavis in my life."

"Really? Oh, well, if you'll excuse me."

"Wait a minute. Where did you come from and why are you here?" For reasons that mystified him, he couldn't understand why he needed to ask such obvious questions. The woman should be falling all over herself to explain. This was his apartment, his baby, and it was two o'clock in the morning. Lisa stirred and began to fuss, and he tried to settle her back down.

Mavis entered the room, planted her hands on her

hips and shook her head at him in a scolding manner. "Booth, for pity's sake, do you have to bluster like a prison warden? You should be on your knees thanking Kathleen instead of yelling at her as if she were some common criminal."

Kathleen's face paled.

Booth, trying to quiet Lisa, merely said, "I was not yelling."

"Yes, you were. Just like you used to when you were a little boy and didn't get your way." She gave Kathleen a knowing look as if she would understand the antics of small boys. "Then he would hold his breath, practically turning blue and frightening us all to death while we waited for what seemed like forever for him to breathe again."

Kathleen smiled. "One of my brothers used to do that, and my father would toss cold water in his face. It's called a temper tantrum." She eyed Booth with an odd look he couldn't quite pin down. "I wonder why I'm not surprised that Mr. Rawlings was a difficult child."

"You're a big help," Booth grumbled.

"Just an observation."

"You don't know me well enough to make an observation," he countered, amused and fascinated by her.

"My misfortune, I'm sure," she murmured.

He raised an eyebrow. "We could easily find a remedy for that."

"I think not."

Their eyes met, and a laser of tension shot between them. Booth took a deep breath. She was quick with comebacks if sufficiently irritated. It had been a while since he'd had a conversation with a woman that didn't involve feedings, baby-sitting and pediatricians. "Okay, I'll talk in a whisper. What has Kathleen done that I should be thanking her?"

"Thanking me on your knees," Kathleen added.

"You're enjoying this, aren't you?"

"As a matter of fact, I am."

"Don't push it."

"And if I do?"

She was too damn quick, and Booth couldn't deny that he was enjoying the sparring. "You always have to have the last word?"

"It's been a long time, Mr. Rawlings, and I have to say, it has a nice feel to it."

"Far be it from me to mess up the roll you're on."

She smiled. "Thank you."

"Okay, you two," Mavis interjected. "It's late, and I want to go home. But first, Booth, you need to hear exactly what happened."

Mavis explained about falling asleep on her good ear, Kathleen coming up when she heard Lisa crying and how Lisa had taken to her immediately. That, of course, explained why Kathleen had been feeding her when he came home.

"I'm so sorry, Booth. Truly, I am. I just feel so terrible and inadequate. I mean, if anything had happened, I would never have forgiven myself."

Booth almost said he wouldn't have forgiven her, either, but he didn't. Lisa was fine.

"I do owe you my gratitude," Booth said to Kathleen.

"It turned out to be a pleasant interruption. I had a chance to meet your daughter, and she's beautiful."

His mouth twitched. "Yeah, we agree on that, at least."

Mavis Carmody started to say good-night when the phone rang. Suddenly Lisa stiffened, opened her eyes, took one look at Booth and began to scream.

He patted her and whispered soothing words, but she was having none of it. Mavis answered the phone and called to Booth, who juggled and jounced his daughter in an attempt to stop her crying.

At that moment someone banged on the door, yelling about a baby keeping him awake all night.

"Alfred from downstairs," Booth said to Kathleen above Lisa's crying. "I should remind him of how loud he keeps his TV set on when I'm trying to sleep."

Mavis yawned, and opened the door to Alfred.

"Booth, do you need me to stay?" she asked, but clearly she wanted to leave, so he indicated she should go on home and went to the phone. Mavis put on her sweater, took her car keys from her purse, and said good-night.

Alfred Spottswood, a retired antique dealer, was left standing in the doorway in a nightshirt. He was scowling so hard his eyebrows came together in one long bushy shelf. "Booth, you must find a way to keep that baby from crying all night."

"I'm working on it, Alfred." Booth gratefully handed the still-wailing Lisa to Kathleen. Then, as if someone had thrown an invisible switch, the baby stopped crying.

"You're an angel of mercy, my dear," Alfred said. "How much would I have to bribe you to take up full residence with Lisa?"

Kathleen laughed. "You're very kind."

"No, just used to eight hours of sleep." He glanced at Booth. "Figure out a way to hire her, Booth. The entire building will be forever grateful." And with that he turned and went back to his own apartment.

Booth and Kathleen stood less than six feet apart as he held the phone and she held the child.

And the silence was suddenly filled with an odd new tension that coiled and sparked with an energy Booth didn't want to put a name to.

KATHLEEN REALIZED she should have made her exit when Booth came home. Now she lowered her eyes to break the hold he seemed to have on her. He turned his back to speak to the person on the phone, and Kathleen let out the breath she'd been holding.

There was no question that she'd felt a strange, indescribable rush when she'd glanced up and seen him standing a few feet from her. She wanted to attribute the unusual feeling to the dearth of men in

her life—a choice, she now reminded herself, that
was her own. But in the case of Booth, she sus-
pected her inner response to him was something
more complicated. Like curiosity and admiration—
despite his rudeness to her. Even for that she could
hardly blame him. He'd come home to find a
stranger holding his daughter. Kathleen decided she
was probably fortunate that crankiness had been his
only reaction.

She was amazed at how quickly her instincts had
taken his measure. He was obviously devoted to his
daughter. He had a quick sense of timing and humor that energized her. If she believed in Karma,
or fate, or the perfect alignment of planets, her reaction could easily be explained. But Kathleen
didn't put stock in mystical forces or divine inter-
vention. She trusted herself and her own determi-
nation to survive.

For too long her life had been a garish true-to-
life nightmare, without hope, without anyone. And
since she had to be so careful that no one learned
who she was, a lonely life seemed her destiny.
She'd become so accustomed to being suspicious
of everyone and everything, she feared she was losing perspective on the most innocent of events.

That deep loneliness, born of her fear of being
found, had churned inside her for so long that Kathleen was now like a dry sponge that had suddenly
been plunged into a pail of water. As wonderful as
they felt, she knew that these feelings for Lisa and,
yes, even for Booth, were an emotional minefield.

What was particularly puzzling and scary was that Booth seemed so perfectly in tune with her, as if he'd known her for a very long time.

And he was so attractive.... No, more than that, he was sexy and disturbing, which was a whole different thing. How strange that she would so easily take note of his physical appearance in a positive way. Her husband's physical appearance always struck her with its power, with his desire to conquer, to make sure she knew who was boss.

Kathleen rubbed Lisa's back, reminding herself of the baby's true connection with Booth. Lisa had made her think positively of Booth. How could she not, when his child so obviously ruled his heart?

She glanced over at him. He'd anchored the phone on his shoulder and was speaking in a low voice while he made some notes on a pad. His hair was a dark sable brown that was somewhat long without being shaggy. He wore snug faded jeans and a denim jacket over a cotton sports shirt with both collars flipped up; his clothes fit his tall lean body as if they'd been designed for him.

Booth straightened, covered the mouthpiece and said, "Would you mind putting her to bed for me? I'm afraid to touch her."

"It is puzzling that she reacted so strongly."

"She's a wise child. She knows a soft touch when she sees one."

Kathleen grinned. "Very wise."

"Brilliant, in fact."

"And beautiful."

"That, too. But brilliant beats beautiful any day."

"What an interesting comment. A man who values brains over beauty. You finish your call. I'll put Miss Brilliant to bed."

Booth chuckled and turned away.

Kathleen went into the nursery, changed Lisa again and started to lay her down in the crib when she saw the framed photo on the dresser. It was of Booth and a woman. Angie, no doubt. She was very pregnant, and Booth had both arms around her, clowning in such a way that Kathleen could almost hear him say, "See, I can still get my arms around you." They were both laughing, and judging from the background elements, it looked as if the picture had been taken at a family or community gathering.

Kathleen stared, an unexpected envy rushing through her. Envy of Angie, who had had a man who obviously adored her, and of their happiness and their sense of belonging. Her own loneliness darkened her spirit, so she made herself do what she'd been doing since she'd fled Wyoming. She gritted her teeth and reminded herself that she was alive, she was safe, she had her best friend, Gail Morgan, she had her music and her mother's cameo, and—

But this time, here with Lisa, surrounded by all the trappings of a normal life, she squeezed her eyes closed, shuddering. Her life *wasn't* normal; it never would be as long as the police in Rodeo wanted to charge her with killing her husband. She wished she had the money and the contacts to hire an investigator to find the real murderer. But that would mean returning to Rodeo, and that meant being arrested. It was a circle she couldn't break.

Here in Connecticut, she was safe. But safe for how long? She could never be sure. My God, would there ever come a time when she didn't have to look over her shoulder in suspicion? Gauge the actions and motives of every stranger? Answer every phone call with a millisecond of hesitation? Wake up and wonder if today she would be found?

Wyoming was almost two thousand miles from Connecticut, a million miles from her other life.

She carefully laid the sleeping Lisa in her crib, her pink quilt clutched in her hands. She stood for a long moment, thinking how often she'd dreamed of having children. Sadly, she couldn't even allow herself a "perhaps someday" scenario. Maybe Booth would allow her to come up and visit with Lisa— She cut off the possibility in midthought.

She couldn't do that. What was wrong with her? Getting to know Lisa meant getting to know Booth, and she had no desire to have a man around who would inevitably ask questions she couldn't answer.

She straightened, slipping her hands into her shorts pockets. "Sweet dreams, little one," she whispered.

She turned to leave, only to find Booth lounging in the doorway, watching her.

"You have the magic touch," he said softly.

"At least for tonight."

"So who are you?"

"I think we covered that, didn't we?"

"I know your name and that you rescue crying babies in the middle of the night."

"Which is probably enough." With Booth blocking the doorway, she felt uneasy, almost trapped. She needed to exert some authority here, and now was as good a time as any if his intention was intimidation. In fact, she imagined he was very good at intimidation when he chose to be.

She moved toward the door, hoping he'd merely step aside.

He didn't.

"I'd like a few answers," he said.

"Why?"

"Well, let's see, I believe it's called 'conversation,'—an exchange of ordinary information that's warranted under the circumstances."

Kathleen took a deep breath and reminded herself he knew nothing about her, wouldn't know anything unless she revealed it. Conversely, she was making herself more interesting and more mysterious by being evasive. And he was right. Given the circumstances, his desire for information was quite natural.

"All right," she said. "But let's go into the other room. Lisa's had enough excitement for one night, and I don't think you want her to wake up again."

"On that you're right."

He stepped aside without really moving away, and Kathleen had no choice but to walk very close to him to pass. She was about to make a comment about him crowding her when he crossed the room and settled on the couch, stretching his legs out and indicating she was welcome to the rocking chair.

"This won't take long," she said, not taking the offered seat. "I really need to get back to bed."

Booth nodded. "So are you a professional baby-sitter? And if you answer yes, I want to take Alfred's advice and hire you no matter how much you charge."

It was a joke, of course, and she laughed at the look of sincere desperation on his face.

"I believe there are professional baby-sitters."

"Nannies and day care are out."

"Oh."

"Nothing personal. Hell, maybe it is personal because it involves my daughter. I've lost her mother, and I have no intention of putting her into the care of strangers, no matter how qualified and well-intentioned."

"But I'm a stranger."

"Not when you call Mrs. Carmody 'Mavis' and have her eating out of your hand. Never heard anyone but my mother and her friends use her first name."

"She was embarrassed and upset that she'd fallen asleep, so we dispensed with the formalities."

Booth looked as if that explanation was the mere tip of the endorsement. "Believe me, she's a tough bird. Maybe she didn't look like it tonight, but it's not too often that anyone catches her at a disadvantage. Tell me, did she chatter on about all the Rawlings until you were totally confused?"

"As a matter of fact, she did remark that your parents were on the Cape and that your sister was sick."

"And she didn't mention that Darlene is a steady customer for engagement rings at the local jewelry store?"

Kathleen grinned. "Yes, as a matter of fact, she did."

Booth chuckled. "My sister is looking for Prince Charming. When the poor guy turns out to be a mere mortal, she freaks and breaks the engagement."

"Maybe the men have deceived her. Broken expectations can be jarring and painful."

Booth looked at her for a long time. "An odd choice of words."

"I merely meant that when men present themselves as one thing, and once you get to know them you learn they're something else—well, that can be disappointing."

"They all seemed like good guys to me."

Kathleen shrugged. "But you aren't marrying them."

He nodded, started to say something, then scowled. "Hey, wait a minute. We're supposed to be talking about you, not Darlene's engagements."

"I'm not half as interesting."

"I doubt that." He glanced at her left hand. "Married?"

She couldn't contain the flinch. And she knew he'd seen it. "No."

"Divorced?"

"I really don't want to talk about it."

"Which means you probably had a bad time of it."

She didn't want to reply to that, but he was looking at her with such empathy that she responded anyway. "It was difficult, yes."

In a soft voice that drew her like a summer rain after a drought, asked, "Is it okay if I say he was an ingrate and an idiot?"

She lowered her head, wanting to agree but feeling unable to bring herself to offer even that much. Besides, she guessed he would be asking different questions if he knew the real details.

"I'll take your silence as a yes." When she still said nothing, he added, "Kathleen, look, I'm not going to pry. Hell, it's not my business, but whatever happened doesn't change the fact that my daughter thinks you're the best thing since a bottle of milk and her jungle blanket."

Kathleen smiled, her heart swelling at his efforts to reassure her. She braced herself for more questions—or worse, some show of sympathy that would have her releasing the icy distance and control she had wrapped around her life and marriage to Steve Hanes. Gail knew, of course, but Kathleen had told no one else in Crosby.

The very fact that Booth was making it far too easy to blurt out her past terrified her. Sure, he was being patient and understanding, but if he knew the truth, she doubted he'd be so kind and he certainly wouldn't want her near his daughter.

To her relief he dropped the subject and asked, "You live in this building? Where?"

"I'm staying with Gail Morgan."

"That sounds temporary."

"It is. I'm looking for my own apartment. In fact I probably wouldn't have been here tonight if Gail's mother hadn't suddenly taken ill. Gail had to fly out to Missouri. She asked me to stay on and cover for her at a volunteer job she has at the youth center on Powell Street."

Booth nodded. "I know the place. They do some good work with messed-up kids."

"Mostly they're just kids who've had limited advantages. I've been amazed at some of the potential I've seen, as well as the strides a few have made." She raised her hand to cover a yawn. "I really need to go. I have a busy day tomorrow—uh, I mean in a few hours."

"Where do you work?"

"I waitress over at the Silver Lining Restaurant."

"Not a bad place. The owners are good friends."

"They've been wonderful."

"So what's your shift?"

She scowled. "Why?"

"Because a lot of guys I work with eat there, and

they tip well. Or are you independently wealthy from your divorce?''

Kathleen stiffened and started for the door.

"Wait," Booth said. "That was a nasty comment, but you seem so suspicious of the most innocent questions.''

"There's no such thing as an innocent question when one person is doing all the asking.''

He spread his arms in an open gesture. "Ask away.''

She managed a small smile. "Another time.'' Then, as if acknowledging that his questions were as innocent as he claimed, she said, "I work the dinner shift. Four to eight. Sometimes it feels like twice those hours when it's super busy, but the tips are very generous, and I have my days free.''

He looked at her for a long time. "Can I say something? Will you promise not to take offense?''

She felt her insides freeze. She hated ominous questions more than she did nosy ones. "That depends,'' she said warily.

"You don't look like a waitress. Not that I have anything against them. My sister was a waitress all through college. But you look like…'' He paused, tipping his head a bit sideways.

Like I'm wanted for killing my husband? Like I'm running from the police who want to frame me for a crime I didn't commit?

"Like a dancer. Slender and long-legged. Delicate.''

His answer was so off the mark, so weirdly wonderful, that she laughed aloud. "Delicate? Me? Oh, Booth, what a lovely thing to say, but the last dancing I did was in college. Now, I really do have to go."

He followed her to the door. "Oh, and by the way, I admire your bravery."

"Bravery?"

"Yeah, coming up to a strange apartment in the middle of the night. Could have been a trap or God knows what kind of mess."

"I did think of that but I couldn't ignore Lisa's crying."

"Bet you were relieved when Mrs. Carmody told you I was a cop."

Kathleen had just turned away from him. Now she swung back, instantly alert. "You're a police officer?"

"She didn't tell you?"

Kathleen took a deep breath. Her pulse raced, and she suddenly felt hot and claustrophobic.

Booth frowned, drawing closer. "You okay? You look as if I'd told you I was a serial killer."

"I'm sorry—it's just— Never mind. Mavis said you worked nights, but she never said doing what."

"Look, you want me to get you a drink? You really do look rattled."

"I'm fine. Really, I am." She held up her hand to ward off any attempt he might make to get closer to her, to stop her from leaving.

"At the risk of insulting you, you look as if I'd condemned you to hell."

God, she had to get out of here before she said something really stupid.

He reached out to take her arm, and she shrank back. ''Don't touch me.''

He backed up a step, and Kathleen rushed from the apartment, hurrying down the stairs, not stopping until she was through her own door and it was securely locked behind her.

She sank down onto the floor and wrapped her arms around herself to stop the shaking. She'd seen his confusion, his curiosity— No, he'd been more than curious.

Cops never stopped at "curious."

The wheels of his mind were turning already, and speculating with seasoned efficiency because he was a cop. Her husband had demonstrated all too well that a cop had built-in radar when it came to detecting suspicious behavior.

Damn! Why hadn't she been prepared? Mavis had said his father was a former police chief. She should have considered the implications.

He was a cop. She couldn't ignore that, nor did she want to. No way. She'd already been married to one cop. She could never chance getting even marginally involved with another one. Her freedom and future depended on it.

CHAPTER THREE

THREE NIGHTS LATER, at 7:50 p.m., Booth walked into the Silver Lining Restaurant. Located in Crosby's south end, it was a popular eating place for families. An adjacent video arcade drew the kids, and the inexpensive food attracted the parents.

Crosby was a town struggling from recent layoffs at Electric Boat down in Groton. Caught in the escalating move to high technology, many workers found themselves unemployable at the salaries they'd been accustomed to making. As a result there were more than a few disgruntled patrons reading the classifieds at the Silver Lining.

Booth received a few smiles and nods, but for the most part the patrons all went back to their burgers, beers and the Red Sox game blaring from a TV set anchored above the bar.

He liked the friendliness, although the close-knit community did have its drawbacks. Gossip was rampant. Most everyone was related either by blood, marriage or length of time living in Crosby. A true native of the town had to be born there. Even if you'd arrived inside the town limits thirty seconds after your birth, you were considered a carpetbagger.

Booth was the latter. His mother had made the mistake of visiting her sister a month before her due date, and Booth had been born in a hospital near Putnam. By arriving early, Booth had established his roguish reputation for blowing away the status quo. In so doing, he'd become the only Rawlings in five generations not to have been born in Crosby.

He chose a table, aware of Norge Varden at the end of the bar. He was the father of one of the three missing girls in the case Booth had been assigned to investigate. The gossip was that Varden had been drinking heavily. Booth sympathized on a father-to-father level, but at the same time, it was hard to understand how getting crocked every night was helpful.

He glanced around, hoping to spot Kathleen, when Porky Fife, the owner, approached. Porky was short, apple round and had withered pink skin that gathered even more wrinkles when he smiled. At sixty, his wife Nell wanted him to retire so they could move out west where her sister owned a dude ranch. So far, Porky had stubbornly resisted.

"Hey, Booth, haven't seen you in a while," Porky said.

"Fatherhood keeps me close to home."

The two men shook hands.

"Ah, yes, I remember it well," Porky said. "You shoulda brought her."

"My parents are showing her off to some visiting relatives, so I ducked out."

"You look beat. She's a handful, huh?"

"An understatement. She's independent, with a mind of her own, lungs that could be heard in Carnegie Hall without a microphone, and she hates green beans. About an hour ago, I was wearing her dinner."

Porky smiled with a "Been there" gleam in his eye. "Do I hear the rattle of frustration?"

Booth sat back and sighed. "I think she's the one who gets frustrated with me. She seems to know what she wants, and how and when she wants it. It's me who gets it all confused. Plus, I don't think she cares that I'm the one who's supposed to be in charge. She runs my life instead of the other way around."

"Baby girls can tie a papa up in knots, can't they?" Porky mused, obviously remembering his own experience with two daughters. "Well, enjoy it now. This is a picnic. Wait till the boys start sniffing around."

"Boys?" Booth scowled.

Porky patted him on the shoulder. "Don't worry. You got a few years before you have to deal with that."

"Not gonna happen."

"That's what we all say." They were both quiet for a moment. Then they each spoke at the same time.

"Porky, is Kathleen around?"

"What can I get for you?"

Both men chuckled. "Just coffee," Booth said. "You know Kathleen?"

"She lives in my building."

"Yeah? Hey, ain't that a coincidence. You're single and so's she." Porky was quiet for a moment, then, in a sadder voice, he added, "A real tragedy you losin' Angie like you did, then selling that nice house. Too many memories, huh?"

Not wanting to rehash painful details, Booth said, "Yeah. Too many memories."

Actually, it hadn't been the house but a particular neighbor's obsession with Lisa that Booth had believed wasn't healthy. But before Porky went off on a tangent about houses versus apartments, he quickly said, "To be honest, the apartment is more central and it's easier to keep clean."

God, he thought, he sounded like some fussy housekeeper. All Booth wanted to do was see Kathleen, not discuss the variables of his life—past or present. He said, "You were talking about Kathleen living in my apartment building."

"Oh, yeah. She's staying with Gail Morgan until she finds her own place. But you probably know that. Guess she plans to buy a piano and wants a place big enough to hold it." Porky peered at him. "Did you know she's quite a piano player? Offered her a chance to play for a friend who owns a nightclub, but she refused. Sort of strange that she would want to hustle trays when she could just sit and tickle the ivories, maybe get noticed by someone important. Then, you know, she could move on to the big time—New York or Vegas. But hey, I'm the winner, so I ain't complainin'."

"Maybe she doesn't play professionally. Just for her own enjoyment."

"But if you can make money doin' what you enjoy, ain't that the ideal way?"

"You've got a point," Booth said. But he also tucked away this new piece of information about Kathleen. That she played the piano somehow suited her much better than waitressing.

"Kathleen is a good worker," Porky said. "Been here about three weeks and already she has the customers askin' for her. Dinner rush has really picked up."

"What do you know about her?" Booth asked casually, trying not to sound like an interrogator.

Porky shrugged. "That she's increased my business. That's all I need to know. You know I don't ask nosy questions." He peered closely at Booth. "What are you gonna tell me? That's she's some female ax-murderer wanted by the feds?"

"Kathleen?" Booth nearly laughed. "Hardly. I was just curious about her."

Porky leaned down in an obvious posture of "just between us guys." "Now, Booth, you're a helluva good-looking man. And before you married Angie—God rest her soul—when you were lovin' them and leavin' them, I don't ever remember you asking around about some woman you were sizin' up. You just made the move. Even now I could name ten ladies who would be hikin' their skirts to keep your backside warm tonight. So what am I supposed to make of you comin' in here when I haven't seen you in months? Then askin' all these questions? Last time you quizzed me about a new woman in town, the broad turned out to be a con artist.''

Booth chuckled. "You remember that, do you? That was four years ago. Okay, I admit to being a little more than curious about Kathleen, but it's personal, not official.''

Porky folded his arms, nodding, smiling.

"Don't jump to any rash conclusions, okay?''

"Me?''

"You.''

"Wouldn't hurt none if you hooked up with a good woman. Little Lisa could use a full-time mother.''

Instead of what was turning out to be an unsteady stream of part-time baby-sitters, Booth reflected, but said nothing. Any thoughts he had about Kathleen were strictly in the baby-sitter role. At least, that was what he'd been telling himself for the past seventy-two hours.

Porky continued, "Gail Morgan brought Kathleen in after Gail spoke with Nell. You know Nell—anyone gives her a hard-luck story and the ole lady's drippin' tears while she's pressin' cash into their palms. Kathleen didn't want money, she wanted a job, and so I hired her. Don't know much beyond she's from out west somewhere—Missouri, I think, or is it Idaho? Never mind, don't matter. Anyway, she moved here after some messy breakup with a man. Now, mind you, Gail told me all this.

Something about the past being difficult for Kathleen to talk about. It sounded like the poor kid had a rough time. I figure it was either divorce or one of them live-together deals that blew up. I didn't ask because Gail said Kathleen was really touchy about it. I do know this—she's a damn good waitress."

Booth listened to all of this, concluding that he knew little more than he had before he came in. He'd learned that she played the piano, and the Missouri part made sense. Gail had gone there to be with her mother, so obviously Kathleen and Gail were friends from when they were kids. The divorce part fit, too, as did Kathleen's reluctance to say much about herself. Her overreaction to him being a cop, however, still pricked at him. And nothing Porky had said had explained that.

"You don't know where in Missouri, do you?" Booth asked.

"You can ask her yourself. Kathleen, come on over here. Got a big-tippin' customer for you. Bring him a mug of coffee on your way. Black."

Porky winked at Booth. "You can add your own sugar."

"Very funny," Booth said with a wry grin.

"Just tryin' to help." Porky stepped away from where he'd effectively been preventing Booth and Kathleen from seeing each other.

Kathleen glanced up, her hand stilling over the clean mug she was about to fill. Booth studied her. Slender, wary like a fawn poised to run. To his annoyance, he felt that same lurch in his heart he'd experienced a few nights ago. He reminded himself that he needed a full-time baby-sitter, not a woman.

His celibacy had been more because of exhaustion than disinterest in sex. Grief over losing Angie had waned in the past few months, although he couldn't imagine being serious about another woman. Then there was his work, Lisa, moving, lining up sitters—all had weighed heavily on him. Usually, by the time he got into bed, sleep claimed him immediately.

Until he'd come home the other night and seen Kathleen holding Lisa. But, of course, she'd caught him at a vulnerable moment. The thought of a courtship process interested him not at all. For damn sure, it was much too soon for Angie's friends to be seeing Booth dating some new woman in town.

In Crosby, Angie's name had always been spoken with the reverence usually reserved for saints, and her tragic death had canonized her in the eyes of many. That was both a blessing and a curse. A blessing because of the endless kindness and offers of help Booth had received for Lisa and himself, but as the months had passed, he'd also felt trapped by that very kindness.

Somewhere deep down, despite his refusal to give those thoughts life, he wanted to break loose, make his life his own again. He'd considered that path with more deliberateness since meeting Kathleen. Because she had no ties to Crosby, perhaps.

All he wanted from Kathleen was— The unfinished statement snarled his usually straightforward thinking. And that was the crux of his emotional interest; she complicated his thoughts—and other parts of him, as well.

Now, she moved slowly toward him and set the mug of coffee down. Wearing the restaurant's standard uniform of short black skirt, white cotton shirt with an open placket and a Silver Lining logo sewn on the left side just above the swell of her breast, she still didn't look like a waitress to him.

"Hi," he said.

"Hello."

He waited for more, but she remained silent, turning to leave.

"Kathleen, come on, don't run off."

"What are you doing here?" she asked, clearly suspicious.

"I wanted to talk to you."

"About what?"

He chuckled. "You don't waste words, do you? Okay, how about the warm weather, Lisa, where you came from, how long you're staying and why you hate cops?"

She stiffened visibly. "Look, I don't mean to be rude, but we don't know each other very well. I look up from my station and see you and Porky talking, and then he calls me over here. This isn't even one of my tables. I mean, it does seem strange, you just showing up for no reason."

"Would you think it was strange if I were a plumber instead of a cop?"

"A plumber wouldn't be asking questions of my employer or coming in here to rattle me."

"My intent wasn't to rattle you."

She thought for a few seconds, and he expected a lethal slam at cops. Instead she said softly, "Please, I don't know what you want or why, but whatever it is, I can't be what you're looking for."

The light in this particular area of the restaurant was dim, and her head was turned so that he couldn't catch her expression. It was an unusual comment—"I can't be what you're looking for." Not *won't,* but *can't.*

"Lisa misses you," he said simply.

For a moment, she appeared flustered, as if his comment was the last thing she expected.

Rallying to the offense, she said coolly, "Really, Booth, if that's a line, you should be ashamed of yourself."

"A line? Are you kidding?"

She turned to leave, and he grabbed her wrist to stop her. "Come on, lighten up. Talking to you is like playing dodgeball. I get hit no matter which way I move."

The moment she looked down at him, he knew he'd crossed some line, but frankly he was getting weary of trying to figure out just what in hell that line was.

"Excuse me?" His clasp on her wrist loosened slightly and she pulled free. "Just because you're a customer doesn't give you any right to touch me or come on to me.''

"Come on to you?" Booth felt something deep inside snap. "Babe, if I intended that, I wouldn't be playing games. I'm too old for that nonsense. Besides, using my daughter as bait would be contemptible.''

"I'm glad to hear you say that.''

"My God, don't tell me we actually agree on something.''

"A good place to leave this conversation, wouldn't you say?" She took a step back. "I'm off work in a few minutes, but if you want something to eat, Cassie will take care of you.''

Booth watched her turn and leave, irritated with himself. What should have been a simple conversational exchange felt more like a battle. He was frustrated by her dislike of him when he had no clue why, and he was furious with himself for giving a damn. At the same time his mind was progressing far beyond just being puzzled about Kathleen. She was so different from Angie. Not outgoing and colorful, but reserved and careful, and not a woman easily intrigued by a man.

Booth knew he could charm his way around most women—hell, he'd been doing it since he was sixteen with considerable success. But not Kathleen. That was why she fascinated him. And if coming here to see her had been to explore that fascination, she'd only presented him with a more interesting web of paths.

He shifted, suddenly aware of a familiar heaviness low in his body; a humming grip that twisted more pleasantly than it ached. Sipping the coffee, he came to an inevitable conclusion. His problem wasn't only curiosity about the mysterious Kathleen. He had another, much more basic one.

He needed a woman.

KATHLEEN PATTED her cheeks with a wet paper towel, cursing herself for not remaining cool as she'd promised herself she would. She knew she was uptight, too accustomed to being suspicious, too conscious of looking over her shoulder. Both times she'd been around Booth, she'd acted bizarrely.

In a desperate attempt to keep herself aloof and not raise anyone's suspicions, she'd become a demon about raising red flags. But red flags at a cop, for heaven's sake? It was crazy and dangerous. What was really strange was that she didn't have this problem with anyone else in Crosby—from Porky to Cassie and the other girls she worked with here, to the staff and music students at the Powell Street Center.

Only with Booth. He made her edgy, and getting to know him in a personal way would be wholesale stupidity. Yes, she was careful about questions, but he always managed to ask her one or two that threw her off guard. Not only didn't she trust him because he was a cop, but he had access to computers and databases where she was sure she was listed as a fugitive. How often had Booth heard the "I'm innocent" excuse from those charged with a crime or someone he'd arrested? Probably all the time. But she had nothing except her word; she couldn't prove anything, she had no witnesses, and she couldn't expose herself for fear of being arrested. And whom would Booth believe? Her or the Rodeo police? A no-brainer, she concluded grimly.

Then, to make things more complicated, there were her unfathomable feelings for Booth—a disturbing warning that, on a personal level, she was drawn to him. She didn't want to like him; nor did she want to hate him. She wanted to feel nothing. Absolutely nothing.

She cleaned up her station, restocking for the next shift, keeping her hands busy so she wouldn't glance over at Booth. She really needed to make a serious effort to find an apartment, but even if one popped up tomorrow, she couldn't move until Gail returned. Gail's cat needed to be taken care of, and she'd promised Gail she'd stay.

What a dilemma she'd created by going to check on a crying baby. Yet she knew she'd do the same thing again. She took a deep breath. How hard was it to avoid one man she didn't want to see? Only as hard as she wanted to make it. What puzzled her was his interest in her. Was it because he was suspicious, or bored? She left "attracted to her" off her list of reasons. Kathleen had seen that photo of Angie. She'd been sexy and gorgeous—the kind of woman who made Kathleen fade into the shadows.

Perhaps it was Kathleen's interest in Lisa, or Booth's need for a permanent sitter that drew him. Both motives were innocent enough. Maybe *she* was the one inventing tangled webs of intrigue, when all Booth wanted was a baby-sitter.

She smiled to herself. It was funny; if Booth were a plumber, she would have jumped at the chance to take care of Lisa.

Ten minutes later, she made one last pass of her tables to make sure they were clean and set with clean silver. When she glanced at the table where Booth had been seated, he was gone.

Pleased, but at the same time disappointed he'd given up so easily, she sighed in self-disgust. *You don't know what you want, do you? Unless it's never to have met him. Then your insides would be much less restless and your life less complicated.* She wiped off the table and picked up his coffee mug.

As she did so, she saw the five-dollar bill tucked beneath it.

And on the bill, he'd written, "Lisa sends a new-tooth grin."

Kathleen pressed her hand against her mouth to stop the sudden trembling. *Booth, this is so unfair, and dammit, you know it.* She decided she was the world's biggest sap when it came to Lisa Rawlings. And maybe when it came to her father, too.

She finished up her duties, took off her apron, and asked Porky if there was anything else he needed done.

"You know, Kathleen, you're too good for business. You're going to spoil me." As she started to leave, he added, "Booth's a good guy. You could do worse."

Kathleen started to object and then closed her mouth. The less said, the better. "He certainly has a beautiful baby girl," she replied, smiling broadly. "See you tomorrow."

Kathleen said good-night to those at the bar, and made her way out into the parking lot. She'd sold the cantankerous Buick in Pennsylvania when the exhaust system had let go, and she'd been using Gail's Subaru. The lot was well lit, and Porky insisted that all his "girls," as he called them, park directly under the floodlights. Keys in hand, Kathleen was ready to unlock the car door, when she heard a noise behind her.

She twisted around, her purse in a position to swing, and then froze, her hand coming up to clutch her chest.

"My God, you scared me." She sank back against the car, her body trembling.

Booth kept his distance and Kathleen almost smiled. *He probably thinks I'm going to scream the place down.*

Still looming in the shadows, he finally spoke. "I have an idea. Why don't we start over?"

"Over?"

"Yes, as in introductions and no surprises."

Kathleen smiled then, reminding herself to be

cool and normal. "It has been pretty bad, hasn't it?"

"We can chalk it up to weird circumstances."

"I think that's a good idea."

"Great. My name is Booth Rawlings, I'm a cop." He paused for a moment, as if admitting to an ongoing vice, then looked relieved when she didn't rush off screeching like a banshee. He continued, "I'm a widower with an eleven-month-old daughter, and if you get close enough to me, you'll notice my aftershave is the newest scent, thanks to my daughter. It's green-bean spray."

Kathleen burst into laughter, the sound surprising even her with its naturalness. The laughs turned into giggles, and Booth tipped his head so he could see her face.

"Did I miss my calling as a comic?"

She giggled again. "I think I needed a good laugh."

"I didn't think it was so funny when I had to change clothes twice in a hour."

"What happened the other time?"

"A leaky diaper."

She laughed again, shaking her head.

"That better be in sympathy, and not because you're scared to tell me I don't know what in hell I'm doing." He leaned against the car, so that their shoulders touched. "Because I don't. One little girl—"

"With another tooth. I noticed quite a few the other night," Kathleen said.

Booth held up his right forefinger.

"Oh, no, she bit you?"

"I thought she had a peanut in her mouth—bad for babies, the pediatrician told me. Allergies and choking. So I tried to get it out, and, well, never mind."

"And she didn't want to let go of it."

"Something like that," he murmured.

In a natural, spontaneous way, Kathleen took his finger, rubbed her thumb over it and said, "Poor man, you're suffering the battle scars of fatherhood."

"Do we know each other well enough for me to ask you to kiss it and make it better?"

Kathleen assumed a thoughtful pose. "Not yet."

"Damn."

"Nice try, though." She frowned. "Aren't you supposed to be at work?"

"My night off. My parents are showing Lisa off to out-of-town relatives."

"And you're hanging around here?"

"I wanted to see you."

"Why? I haven't exactly been a barrel of laughs."

"Well, laughs I can get with the guys. You just interest me. I think because I met you at a time when not much beyond my daughter and my job intrigues me."

"I'll accept that as a compliment."

He grinned, the creases in his cheeks deepening. "Whew. For a minute I was afraid I'd said the wrong thing again. I'm beginning to wonder if I need to brush up on my approach. You're different, so I'm pretty much winging it, and doing even that badly.''

"I've been a little spacey myself."

"So can we consider this an official start-over point?"

She hesitated, retreating. "Booth, really, uh, I don't want to seem—''

"Uninterested?"

"No, it's not that. It's just that my life is pretty complicated right now, and I don't have time for... Okay, I'll be blunt. I'm not interested in any kind of continuing involvement."

"Like a relationship."

"Yes."

"Okay. How about friendship?"

She lowered her head.

"How about friendship because we live in the same apartment building and it's kind of nice to speak to a neighbor without getting uptight."

When she took a deep breath, he said, "How about this. I promise to keep my hands in my pockets, my zipper zipped and my thoughts chaste and pure."

"You're making this very hard for me."

"Is that a no?"

"Look, if this were any other time, and if my life weren't so—''

"Yeah, I know, complicated." He straightened, looking weary and ready to leave it where it was, which was no place. "Well, I guess that does it, then. Thanks again for rescuing my daughter. See you around." And with that he walked toward a black Explorer and climbed inside.

Kathleen got into her own car, started the engine and slowly drove out of the lot.

She should be pleased. She'd gotten rid of him. He'd probably never do any more than nod if he should see her. But she didn't feel relieved or pleased—she felt sad and angry that she couldn't let herself accept a simple offer of friendship. But he was a cop. *Dammit, Booth, why couldn't you have been a plumber?*

But he was the police, and at this point, that made him her sworn enemy.

Better to be sad than have him arrest her and return her to Rodeo. Better to be angry than go to prison for a murder she didn't commit.

CHAPTER FOUR

IN THE ROADKILL Café, a dimly lit saloon on the eastern border of Wyoming, two men sat opposite each other in a red vinyl booth that had darkened to maroon with age. One drank expensive whiskey. The other nursed a bottle of beer. Reba McEntire sang from the jukebox, and a couple slow-danced in the middle of a scuffed dance floor.

The whiskey drinker was a small man with carbon black eyes behind wraparound sunglasses. He wore a mocha-colored silk suit, white shirt and a butter yellow tie decorated with tiny sunflowers. He hardly fit in with the cowboy-country locals, but that didn't matter. Wherever he went, he was greeted with deference and a degree of fear. He'd brought a bonanza of cash into the local economy, and anyone who asked too many questions conveniently disappeared. No one knew his real name—he was known as "The Rainmaker," but he answered to the name "Mr. Smith." He got a kick out of using the phony moniker, a ploy that more than once had been taken as a bad joke, but the Rainmaker always had the last laugh.

He'd arrived in Wyoming about a year ago driving a Mercedes, and escorting a movie star from

Mexico known for her nude scenes and touchy temperament. She also had a heroin habit that the Rainmaker had quietly exploited to his own advantage for the past six months. He'd supplied her habit and given financial support to her love child; in return, she'd opened some previously closed doors to the higher echelon of drug traffickers.

The Rainmaker wanted to import on a daily basis; the traffickers wanted new outlets and airstrip access to the U.S. A deal had been struck and would be finalized when the Rainmaker found the required conduit into the United States. Establishing that connection would cost him time and money. He needed more than an inconspicuous chunk of land large enough to set a plane down. What he required was far dicier; he and the cartel needed mutual assurance that the drug-moving operation had protection.

The Rainmaker knew the best protectors were the police. He'd used his vast contacts to search out cops who would, for the right amount of cash, take a bribe. Plus, he'd wanted guaranteed leverage to keep them in his pocket once he had them there. What was necessary were greedy cops with messy private lives, and a department in a financial crunch. He'd ended his search in a flat dusty town that still had hitching posts in front of the sheriff's office. Rodeo, Wyoming's sheriff, Buck Faswell, and his deputy sheriff, Steve Hanes, had welcomed the Rainmaker and his endless stream of cash with the enthusiasm of two johns cruising through a bonanza of first-time whores. But then Hanes had gotten too drunk and too talkative.

"I trust that Mr. Hanes had a proper funeral," the Rainmaker said now to the man seated across from him. He dabbed at his mouth with a linen handkerchief.

The beer drinker, known as Pony, wore a once-white Harley T-shirt with sleeves rolled up to display a tattoo and impressive biceps. His jeans were as grimy as the gum stuck on the underside of the table. But on his feet were brand-new lizard boots. Those brought him whistles from the bartender and a broad wink from the busty waitress. A Chicago Cubs baseball cap was pulled low to shield his eyes—eyes that had witnessed more than a few gruesome murders without flinching.

He wiped the beer foam from his mouth with a beefy forearm, then lit a cigarette. "Yep, the town did itself proud. Flowers and a grave marker that makes old Stevie look better croaked than he did when he was breathin'."

"Good. And his parents? Are they getting past this?"

"His old lady is still weepin' and wailin', but the money made his old man smile."

"Yes, he thanked me for handling the funeral expenses, and the goodwill money for him and his wife."

"You're too good, Mr. Smith. Waving a couple hundred-dollar bills under old Roger Hanes's nose will make him do more tricks than a trail dog eyein' a big slab of pork ribs.''

"That will be enough, Pony. The man lost his son. He deserves some compensation. What is the status of Rodeo now?'' Implicit in his question was the state of the sheriff's office.

"Uh, things have quieted down. Sheriff is looking for someone to take Hanes's place.''

"An arrest yet?''

"No, sir.''

"Why not?''

"Well, sir, she seems to have disappeared.''

"'Seems to'?'' The Rainmaker focused on Pony with a probing intensity. "Either the cops know where she is or they don't.''

"They don't.''

"And you? You work for me. You don't need to follow rules.''

"Yes, sir. But me and the boys, we ain't had no luck, either.'' Pony's cigarette burned his fingers and he put it out, then leaned back as if expecting a palm across his cheek.

The Rainmaker sighed heavily. Pony was an idiot, which was what the Rainmaker got when he let his soft heart rule his good sense. If it weren't for his old partner being near death and the Rainmaker wanting to give his idiot nephew a chance... He sighed again. "What about her father? Her brothers?''

"They haven't seen her. Her old man said he hasn't talked to her in years. Not since his old lady took off with her when Kathleen was a kid. One brother is workin' on the farm, and the other one blew the place and took off for the bright lights of L.A. a few years ago. Last anyone heard, he had a boyfriend and a job doin' dog-food commercials.''

The Rainmaker had taken out a leather notebook and made some notations. ''The brother in California. That would be Clarke?''

''Yes, sir.'' Pony began to relax. He added a street address, and the Rainmaker jotted it down.

''Her friends?''

''Not many. Rose over at the general store, and a cripple the locals call Beethoven. He runs a music store. Talked to both of them and they don't know nothin'.''

''Perhaps they simply don't know that they have information.''

''Huh?''

''You didn't ask the right questions.'' He made another notation. ''Has this young woman had a lot of experience eluding either the police or the Mob?''

Pony blinked, looking confused by the question, then grinned. ''Hey, that's funny, Mr. Smith. She's a broad, and we all know what they got a lot of experience at, don't we?''

The Rainmaker didn't smile. He closed the notebook, slipped it inside his jacket, then leaned forward, his voice dropping. ''It appears that we have a bright young fugitive and a bunch of half-assed hunters who wouldn't know they were in a closet full of rattlers unless someone turned on the lights."

Pony shrank down in the booth. "Yes, sir."

"And since you can't find her, we have to assume she knows she's being hunted and therefore is hiding."

"But, sir—"

"And since the police want to arrest her for icing Hanes, then they are in the position to notify other departments across the country—I believe it's called an all-points bulletin?"

Even Pony didn't miss the sarcasm. "Yes, sir, they did that, but it's not like every cop in the country is focused on one broad who offed her old man. I mean, jeez, that happens about twenty times a day. Unless she does something that gets the attention of some cop—you know like a speeding ticket or an accident or gettin' hauled in on a DWI—" He ran out of breath, took one and finished, "You know, somethin' where they would have a reason to run a check on her. Otherwise, it's tough."

"Pardon me?"

Pony leaned forward and spoke a bit louder, as if the Rainmaker were getting deaf. "I said, it's tough. It's a big country, and she could be anywhere. Then again, I mean, hell, what's the big rush? I mean, she don't know nothin'. She was gone before Hanes got whacked. I mean, she might not even know she's wanted. We got lucky when she left him the same day the murder was planned. What with him knockin' her around all the time, it

was choice timing. And with her history of phonin'
up those abuse counselors and then goin' back to
Hanes to try again, she had a perfect motive. Perfect
timing, if you ask me.''

The Rainmaker brought his tassel loafer down on
Pony's lizard boot and moved his foot in a grinding
motion. Pony stiffened, his head popping up like a
jack-in-the-box, his eyes bulging circles of pain.

In a perfectly modulated voice that would have
chilled a polar bear, the Rainmaker replied, ''I don't
want to hear 'tough' or 'hard' or 'freaking impossible.' I don't want to hear about 'choice timing.' I
want to hear she's been arrested and charged and
is doing time for murder. You got it? You think she
doesn't know she's wanted? You're a bigger idiot
than your sheriff who swore no roadblocks were
needed on the secondary roads. She knows she's
being hunted for one simple reason—no one has
heard from her, and she's makin' damn sure no one
does. It's called brains, and unfortunately hers are
in her head, whereas yours are not.''

Pony's wince grew to a moan as the pressure on
his foot increased.

''But,'' said the Rainmaker, ''running gets tire-
some, and having no friends gets lonely. The longer
she's out there, free and desperate and lonely, the
bigger the chance she'll get herself a new best
friend who'll tell her to get an investigator on the
case—and then we're looking at some potential
problems. I, for one, don't intend to be a target for
some flat-footed, rumpled P.I. trying to be a hero.''

Pony hadn't moved since the Rainmaker had begun talking. He swallowed now, but the pain in his
foot had moved all the way up his leg.

The Rainmaker pushed his loafer harder.

"Mr. S-Smith, p-please." Beads of sweat dotted
Pony's forehead and upper lip.

"You're understanding the problem?"

"Y-yes, s-sir."

"And it will be taken care of swiftly with no
excuses?"

"Y-y-yes. S-s-sir."

"Good." The Rainmaker lifted his shoe and
Pony collapsed in relief against the back of the
booth.

Standing, the Rainmaker adjusted his dark
glasses. "I want a progress report with more on it
than the sweat on your upper lip. I'll be in touch,
and I suggest that all your news be exactly what I
want to hear."

He walked to the door, pressing a fifty-dollar bill
into the hand of the waitress, who grinned widely.
The bartender waved goodbye, shouting, "Always
good to see you, Mr. Smith."

Pony sat as still as a dead man until he saw the
Mercedes pull away from the building. Only then
did he reach down to rub at the permanent scuff
mark on his brand-new boot.

SIX DAYS AFTER her encounter with Booth at the
Silver Lining, Kathleen sat cross-legged and bare-
foot in the middle of her double bed. Above her a

ceiling fan moved the hot sticky July air in circles around her. She'd opened all the windows after she'd come home from getting her mail, then stripped out of her clothes and put on shorts and a loose cotton blouse. Beside her on the bedside table was a tall glass of iced tea and the portable phone. Scattered in front of her were articles that she'd poured from a large manila envelope. She sorted them by date, looking for some pattern or repetition of information. Like a clue-starved detective, she'd spent the past two hours reading, rereading, analyzing, searching the copies of articles from Wyoming newspapers for some hint of who killed Steve.

She'd concluded that she was being framed in order to get someone off the hook. Either Steve's death had been an encounter that had turned violent, or it had been a very deliberate murder. But why? There was no mention in the clippings of Cory and the sheriff being at the house when the body was found—only that Cory had called in to report the murder. Maybe it was an unimportant detail, but to Kathleen it loomed like a missing piece of the puzzle.

Kathleen sighed. What did it matter? All this information only raised more questions and offered no solutions, nor any possibility that the police were searching for anyone but her. That troubled her deeply. They had tried and convicted her—but based on what? The fact that she was an abused wife and the assumption that she'd retaliated?

She picked up the phone, held it against her chest

for a few seconds while she took deep breaths. Then, before she changed her mind, she pushed the buttons for a long distance number.

It rang and rang, and was finally picked up by a man with a Spanish accent.

"Is Clarke there?"

"Uno momento, señorita."

She waited, reaching for the paper that detailed events following Steve's death.

"Yeah? Who is it?"

"Clarke?"

"Kat?"

"Yes."

"Hold on a minute. I want to get some privacy here." She heard music and laughter and then a door closing. "A bunch of people are here celebrating with me. I got a part in a new movie project that promises to be a blockbuster."

"Oh, Clarke, that's wonderful. Maybe this is the big break you've been waiting for. Congratulations."

"Thanks. I expected to be saying that to you about your music, but that was before—"

Kathleen thought of her piano still in storage in Wyoming. Just this morning, she'd seen an old Baldwin in a used-furniture store. Her mother had given lessons on a Baldwin, and Kathleen's best memories of her were of when she had been playing her favorite classical pieces. Kathleen had stood staring at the instrument for so long that the owner, thinking a sale was imminent, had asked if she would like to try it out. The keys were yellow, it was out of tune and two of the ivories were missing, but for a few moments none of that had mattered. She was once again twelve years old, and playing "Greensleeves" while her mother predicted that someday she would play for the world. The whole "world" was a bit ambitious, but the "someday" was definitely doable.

Someday, she thought now with a grimace, when she didn't have to worry about being arrested for murder.

To Clarke, she said, "Sorry. Just having a flashback."

"It's okay."

"I got the envelope." Kathleen had taken a post-office box in a town a few miles north of Crosby. She'd only been to the Crosby post office three times, and already the postal worker remembered her. Kathleen didn't want to take any chances of being recalled as "that woman who got big envelopes from California." The town north of Crosby, although not a huge metropolis, was much larger, and she felt less visible.

"Tim got it all off the Internet," Clarke told her. "I didn't want to subscribe to local Wyoming newspapers or ask for back issues. This way, no one will find it curious and start asking me questions."

"Has anyone contacted you about me?"

"I haven't seen anyone. No one has called."

For some reason that didn't relieve her.

"Have you talked to Dad and Gary?"

"Yeah," he replied in disgust. "Long enough to be called a fag, a queer and a pervert."

"Oh, Clarke, I'm sorry."

"It was nothing they didn't say to my face before I left. Not my problem to deal with. It's theirs." He laughed self-consciously. "So how closely did you read the accounts? I mean, did you notice how vague the details were about Steve's murder? No exact time of death, no other suspects even considered, and someone telling the sheriff that they saw you driving away like a bat out of hell."

The article he referred to was one she'd read and reread. She, too, had wondered who the someone was. She hadn't wasted any time leaving, but if someone had seen her drive away the first time, would that give her an alibi? She doubted anyone had seen her when she returned to the house.

"Steve and I had argued so I left in a hurry." She didn't tell Clarke about going back. Then she'd have to admit that she'd known Steve was dead, and had seen his body and overheard the police. It just raised too many questions in her own mind, and the less Clarke knew, the less responsibility he'd have, should she be found and arrested. "What are you getting at?"

"You told me Steve waved his gun at you and threatened to kill you if you left him."

"He did."

"But you did leave. And you're alive and he's dead. What happened?"

Kathleen heard the accusatory tone and reminded herself that if her own brother had questions, she could expect a lot more suspicion from those who didn't know her.

To Clarke, she said, "He'd also been drinking, and that always made him nasty. I tried to stay calm and reasonable, but he was out of control. He threatened to shoot the tires of the car, so I drove off very fast, making a huge swell of dust so he couldn't see me. And it gave me the momentum to get away. The last time I saw him, he was standing there with his revolver in one hand and the whiskey bottle in the other."

"Then you're saying someone came in after that and killed him?"

"Yes." Maybe the same someone who claimed to have seen her drive away. Or an accomplice. That could mean someone had been waiting for her to leave, that Steve's murder had been timed for a precise moment. It was several hours before she'd returned for the treasured items, and by that time that "someone" was long gone. Kathleen scowled, new questions rushing through her mind.

"But why?" Clarke asked.

"Why was Steve murdered? I don't know why, or have the vaguest idea who would do it."

"So why are they trying to pin it on you? Someone out to get revenge against you? It could go down as an unsolved case. Wouldn't be the first time."

"But the first time a deputy sheriff has been murdered in Rodeo. From what I read in the papers you sent, the town was shocked and outraged. A dead deputy sheriff, and no arrest? The entire department could be fired for incompetence if someone isn't convicted.''

''But why you?''

''Maybe it's easier than tracking down the real killer. Maybe the real killer is someone the police want to protect.'' That seemed bizarre, but not unlikely. ''They need a credible suspect, and with all the domestic-abuse cases, a woman in a desperate situation killing a brutal husband isn't that uncommon.

''Steve had a problem, and for too long I tried to solve it by being the perfect wife. I finally realized it wasn't my responsibility to be perfect, it was his to stop beating me up. But the point is that I had a believable motive for killing him—one the town of Rodeo would believe. If the police don't look for other plausible suspects, my disappearance makes me look even guiltier. While the cops are chasing around trying to find me, the townspeople are feeling secure that the police are doing their job. The sheriff's office, meantime, can bask in the praise that they were quick, precise and professional carrying out their duty to identify Steve's killer.''

''So you're saying they don't care who did it, just that they make an arrest?''

''Yes.''

''And you're sure he was alive when you left?'' Clarke asked.

Kathleen caught her breath. "Wait a minute. What kind of question is that?"

"Nothing. Never mind—"

"You can't figure out why they want to frame me, so you assume I'm somehow responsible? You think I killed Steve and put it out of my mind? Denial?" She could feel a sickish feeling clog in her throat.

"Kat, the guy was a bastard to you. He probably deserved killing. But why did you stay and put up with the abuse? My God, you were married to him for more than five years!"

Kathleen gripped the phone so hard her hand ached. "I stayed because I loved him. Because I thought he would change. Because he kept telling me he wanted to change. Two days before I left, he tried to choke me after telling me that if I ever tried to leave him again he would kill me. I knew then that he was never going to change, so I made plans to go, and I went. There you have the five years in a nutshell. I'll spare you the pregnancy I never had, the friends I never made, the music I wasn't allowed to play."

Clarke was silent for a long moment, then said grimly, "If I'd been there I would've killed the son of a bitch."

Kathleen shuddered. "I don't want to talk about this anymore."

"Wait, Kat. Don't hang up. Listen to me. I don't give a flying frig who killed him, and if you did blow him away, I would never say anything to anyone, but I'm worried about you. I know what happens when you think the world is out to get you. Being a gay man has shown me how suspicious even ordinary things can seem. After a while, you get weird, you know, delusionary, and you're jumping at every move and always looking over your shoulder.''

"Paranoia?" she asked through gritted teeth.

"Yes."

Kathleen wanted to scream and she wanted to burst into tears. "What do you suggest, Clarke? That I call the local police and turn myself in?"

"Nothing is gonna happen to you," he assured her. "A good lawyer could get you off on that new domestic-violence defense. The way things are now, you're gonna be running the rest of your life."

"Ah, and the alternative is going to prison for a crime I didn't commit. Or if I'm very lucky, and get acquitted, I can just spend the rest of my life as a woman who killed her husband and got away with it. That sounds like a swell way to live."

"Better than what you have now, Kat."

"No, Clarke. Not being hunted, not having the cops trying to frame me for a murder I didn't commit, that is better than what I have now."

She glanced up to see Bosco, Gail's black-and-white cat, stroll into the room and leap gracefully onto the bed. He walked across the papers, nosing her knee before crawling across her legs. Then Kathleen heard another sound and looked toward the doorway.

Lisa Rawlings, wearing a pink gingham sunsuit and a sagging bow in her hair, was crawling through the doorway and headed right for Bosco.

"Sweetheart, where did you come from?" There was no sign of Booth or Mavis or anyone else.

Lisa pointed to Bosco, grinned and said something that sounded like "kitty."

"Got company?" Clarke asked.

"The little girl from upstairs. I have to go. Someone is no doubt looking for her."

"Want Tim to keep gathering stuff on this?"

"Yes. And tell him thanks from me."

"Oh, don't worry, he'll probably send you a bill. Research is how he makes his living."

"How fortunate for me," she said, feeling cranky and out-of-sorts. Clarke's solution had all the appeal of a tour of Sing Sing, and learning that his lover was going to stick her with a bill at God-knows-how-much per hour only added to her annoyance. She replaced the phone on its cradle and moved it to the nightstand.

Lisa had pulled herself to her feet, using the bedspread for handholds. Her small fingers grabbed at one of the pages, and Kathleen rescued it and Lisa before she fell. She swept the pages into a messy pile, gathered up the child, kissed her neck and settled her on the bed beside a purring Bosco.

"If you're here, then Daddy is either frantic or he left you with another careless baby-sitter." The plump baby wiggled and stretched to touch the cat. "Be gentle. Like this." Kathleen took Lisa's hand

and drew it across the cat's fur. The little girl squealed and did it again. Then she reached for Bosco's tail and Kathleen diverted her. "Kitties don't like to have their tails pulled. Can you hear him singing?" Lisa gave Kathleen a wide-eyed look when she placed a finger to her mouth in a shushing sound. "Listen." Bosco purred, his eyes half-closed, as both Kathleen and Lisa petted him.

"Lisa! Thank God." A very pale Booth came to a halt inside the doorway, then sagged against the jamb. "I thought I'd lost her."

"She followed Bosco."

"Bosco?" He looked at the cat, who eyed him with studied boredom. "Is it yours?"

"Gail's. And your daughter is fascinated."

"She'll have to get unfascinated. I don't like cats." He came forward, prepared to sweep his daughter into his arms.

"I think Bosco is offended."

"Let him use one of his nine useless lives to get over it."

"That's a horrid thing to say."

"Yeah, well, at the moment, I'm not feeling polite. I just went through hell when I looked up and she was gone."

"So you owe a debt of thanks to Bosco for coaxing her in here and not into the street. And another debt of thanks to me that I left the door ajar for Bosco to come in."

"The next mouse I run into, I'll send his way. As for you, Lisa and I will buy you dinner."

She eyed him skeptically. "That's a lot of thanks for one slightly ajar door."

"We're a generous and grateful pair."

Kathleen nuzzled the baby's neck. She should say thanks but no thanks, but she sensed Booth would become even more suspicious. For the time being she decided to say nothing. "So how did she escape you?"

Bosco leaped off the bed and scooted around the corner as Lisa struggled to get off the bed and follow. Kathleen distracted her by giving her a set of plastic keys Booth had pulled from his pocket.

"I came downstairs to get the mail, put her down while I sorted through it, then Alfred stopped to ask me about a house break-in on the next block." Alfred Spottswood was the elderly man Kathleen had met at Booth's that first night. "The next thing I knew, she was gone."

"She's very quick and curious, isn't she?" Kathleen glanced up at Booth. He was wearing a red T-shirt and old, faded jeans that fit him so well, Kathleen had to look away. She concentrated on Lisa.

"'Quick and curious' is an understatement. This morning I turned around and there she was, trying to climb up the kitchen drawers to get the cookies on the counter."

Kathleen laughed and straightened the bow in the baby's hair. "You're going to make your daddy gray."

"Already has."

"Really, Booth. It's hard to believe one full-grown adult male can't handle one little bundle of pink gingham.''

"Actually, in the kitchen I was distracted." He lifted Lisa up and settled her into his arms. "I was too busy watching a certain neighbor named Kathleen climb into her car wearing a sexy sundress, and she looks even sexier in the middle of her bed."

A rush of heat swelled inside her. Booth hadn't moved. Lisa was trying to put the plastic keys into his shirt pocket. While he held the baby firmly, his undivided attention was on Kathleen. All her senses tingled into one fluid melody that both enchanted and alarmed her. It had been a long time since she'd had such an impulsive arousal, and rather than shrink from it, she found herself wanting to hold on to it.

For so long she'd felt nothing with Steve and had even wondered if she'd been irretrievably burned by her marriage. Obviously she hadn't, but at the same time, Booth Rawlings created a real problem for her.

She slanted a look at him and found him watching her, his dark eyes smoky and serious; she couldn't miss a kind of patient anticipation that seemed to say, "It's only a matter of time. Me and you. Alone. Naked. Hot."

Kathleen wriggled a little, trying to separate herself from her own erotic images.

"Yeah," he murmured as if reading her thoughts.

"I can't," she whispered back, wincing because she'd been so quick to answer.

His gaze swept down her. "You want to."

She shook her head.

"Liar."

Before Kathleen could fashion a response, Bosco returned and leaped onto the bed.

Lisa began to squirm to get down, and the spell was broken. When Booth wouldn't release her, she started to howl. "Now what's wrong?"

"She wants to pet Bosco." Kathleen took the struggling Lisa, who immediately quieted and allowed Kathleen to take her hand and stroke the kitty.

Booth didn't move, watching with a kind of measured amusement. Lisa was enthralled with the cat, and when Kathleen reached behind her for her iced tea, Booth handed it to her. Their fingers brushed, and Kathleen felt the effect race through her like a jolt of electricity. She glanced away, and in that instant panic seized her. My God, the papers! All this time, the very thing she'd wanted to keep hidden was spread out like Thanksgiving dinner. Dumb. Dumb. Dumb.

She was sitting here having sexy thoughts about Booth, while he was probably reading enough of the scattered papers to send his curiosity into high gear.

Lisa had curled against her, thumb firmly in her mouth, sleepy now. "Could you take her?" Kathleen asked him.

"We could prop some pillows around her and leave her here. Let me get these papers out of the way."

Kathleen grabbed his wrist, and he swung around to look at her. Distract him. She had to distract him.

"What's the matter?" he asked.

She curled her hand around the back of his neck and stretched her body up to kiss him.

CHAPTER FIVE

BOOTH TOOK FULL ADVANTAGE. She tasted of sweet tea and summer heat, and if his daughter hadn't been wedged between them he would have eased her down on the bed and taken the kiss deeper.

"Very nice," he murmured when she pulled away.

"Impulse." She licked her lips, savoring him.

The gesture electrified him. He tried to shake off the disturbing feelings, which had far too much significance for such a short kiss. But the fact that the woman who hadn't even wanted a friendship a few days ago was now in his arms made the kiss even more pleasantly puzzling.

"I think we shouldn't be in the bedroom." She'd pulled herself together, the mask back in place, and if he couldn't still taste her, he might have thought he'd imagined the moment. She handed Lisa to him and got off the bed, tossing the papers to the floor on the far side.

Booth halted when she gestured toward the door. "Aren't you going to pick them up?"

"Later."

"Not important, huh?"

"No."

He didn't believe her. She'd been too succinct and definite; had given no explanation, no casual dismissal. Since he had no reason to expect her to explain, he blamed his overly suspicious mind. What bothered him was that suspicions about Kathleen were becoming more and more firmly entrenched.

In addition, she'd sparked a personal and intimate interest from the very beginning, which might be why he kept trying to find excuses for her odd behavior. But Booth had been a cop for too long to be sucked in by feminine gestures—impulsive or otherwise. Perhaps it was just as well she'd refused the baby-sitting offer. It was one thing to ponder a personal relationship with her, but taking any chances with Lisa was out of the question.

The truth was that Kathleen didn't fit the mold— whatever the hell the mold was—of an average woman, new in town and attempting to fit into the community. As for her unimportant mail—who fixed iced tea and settled with the phone in the middle of her bed just to surround herself with unimportant papers? He remembered his sister following a similar ritual when she got a letter from a boyfriend. Opening and reading it was an event that demanded privacy and atmosphere, and woe to anyone who barged in at the wrong time.

In this case, though, that they were love letters was unlikely. There were too many pages, and they'd been reproduced by a printer. From the quick glance he'd had, the papers had looked more like a file of some sort, or a report. Then there was the fact that she'd turned the papers over when she'd swept them aside. Had she done that because she was naturally private or was she deliberately hiding them?

Neither was a crime, he reminded himself, forcing his thoughts away from asking questions he guessed she wouldn't answer anyway. Then again, if he could get a look at just one of those pages... He damned himself for not looking more closely when he'd had the chance.

"It was nice to see Lisa again. Now, if you'll excuse me, I have some things to do." She went back and pulled the bedroom door firmly closed. Then she took her iced-tea glass to the kitchen and returned. She gave him an exasperated look when she saw he still hadn't moved.

"You're a puzzlement, Kathleen Yardley."

"A woman's prerogative."

"No relationship, not even a friendship, and then that kiss. Very curious."

"It didn't mean anything, you know." She straightened a stack of paperback books, fixed a window shade and opened the door for Bosco.

"Really." He shifted Lisa into a more comfortable position. She'd fallen asleep. "Then why are you still thinking about it and fluttering around like you're not sure what to do next?"

"I am not fluttering. I'm waiting until you leave."

He laid Lisa on the couch, then picked up a small

trio of pictures from a bookcase. The snapshots had been taken on a farm or ranch of a man and woman and three children, one of them a little girl. Before Kathleen snatched it from his hand, he thought he saw some cattle in the background.

"It's Gail's family. Your investigative nose is too obvious."

"And you, my mysterious Kathleen, always seem to give me something new to think about."

"And what, pray tell, have I done now?"

He lifted an eyebrow.

"The kiss?" She laughed, giving a dismissive shrug. "Please, no analysis. You're very attractive and, well, I just wondered what kissing you would be like. Now, can we stop talking about it? My goodness, it's been discussed far longer than it lasted." She turned her back to indicate she didn't expect a response.

Booth remained silent and instead, stepped into the common hallway for Lisa's stroller, which was exactly where he'd left it after returning from a walk the afternoon before. If he'd placed his daughter there while he'd been sorting his mail and talking to Alfred, she wouldn't have followed Bosco, and right now he'd be wending his way through his least favorite place—the grocery store. Which, he reminded himself grimly, he still had to endure.

He got the stroller, swept out the mail he'd tossed there before he'd gone looking for his daughter. He moved Lisa from the couch to the stroller, where she continued to sleep.

Kathleen had gotten a watering can and was giving a drink to a trailing plant with blotchy leaves. Then she straightened some magazines and put last night's newspaper into a wicker wastebasket. Booth watched her for a few minutes, guessing she was staying silent in the hopes that he would leave. Then again, if she could be unpredictable, so could he.

A small spinet piano stood in one corner of the apartment, and Booth took advantage of its presence to remark, "Porky said you played."

"What? Oh, the piano. Yes."

"Your friend Gail plays, too?" He assumed so, since this was her home.

"Yes. We were both music majors in college."

"Where was that?"

She placed her hands on her hips. "The Juilliard. And you're being nosy again."

"Every question isn't nosy, Kathleen. Perhaps I'm just interested in getting to know you."

She clasped her hands. "I'm sorry. I was being flip, and it wasn't the Juilliard. I just said that because it's where every music major dreams of going. I went to a Midwest college in Missouri."

He nodded. "Are you good?"

"I'm very good."

"Play something for me."

"Now?"

"Why not?" Booth settled onto the couch, stretched his legs out and said, "Unless you'd rather kiss me again. You're damn good at that, too."

She gave him a withering look as she slid onto the piano bench. "You're not going to let it go, are you?"

"My one sweet memory with you, sweets. I want to treasure it."

She plunged her fingers down on the keys. "For God's sake, Booth…"

He held up his palms, indicating he'd let it go. "Okay, okay, but it's tough to square a kiss like that with the fact that you didn't even want to be friends a few days ago."

For an instant she looked stricken, then she flexed her fingers, placing them on the keys again. "Maybe that was a little hasty," she murmured.

And before he could respond to that, she began to play. Booth settled back, relaxing, fingers tented, tucking her comment into the back of his mind to consider later.

He had no idea what the music was, aside from a vague recollection of something similar at a concert he'd gone to in junior high. At the time, he'd been more into the Rolling Stones than Bach or Beethoven. Then he'd been bored and itchy. Now he was drawn in as irresistibly as he would be if she crawled into his lap and kissed him again. Her piano selection was classical, complicated, and her skill at the keyboard far surpassed "very good." He listened, even closing his eyes for a few moments as the music rolled through him.

When she'd finished, and sat with her hands in her lap, he was struck by how relieved she seemed. As if playing had been some kind of catharsis.

"Magnificent."

"Thank you. My mother was very exacting when it came to piano lessons. She was a brilliant pianist."

"And she taught you?"

She nodded.

He stayed still, thinking, debating and soaking it all in while a random thought took told. He made a mental note to do some checking during the next few days.

He looked at Lisa, who was waking up, and then walked to the piano, where Kathleen was still seated. He noted the name Loretta Brown on the front of the sheet music Kathleen had just played.

He looked down at her and she glanced up, and then, as if fearful he'd see too much in her expression, she looked back down at the keyboard. Booth cupped her chin and tipped her head up. Her eyes were wide blue pools of naked vulnerability.

In that instant, he knew that what he'd just listened to was what she loved more than anything. Which again raised the question of why she wasn't playing professionally. She lowered her lashes and started to slide from the bench, but he stopped her. For the barest of seconds it felt as if she were fighting his hands.

Immediately he loosened his grip. "When Porky said you played, I assumed it was a few runs up and down the keys and Christmas carols for your family. You have an incredible talent."

"I've always loved the classics."

"So why aren't you playing professionally?" he asked bluntly.

"Someday I hope to."

"Why not now?"

"Because it's not possible now." She slid to the other end of the bench and stood. "Lisa is awake."

Booth was the first to reach Lisa who was trying to climb out of the stroller. He lifted her out and placed her on the floor. Kathleen had moved away from the piano, but Lisa headed straight for it. She pulled herself up, and stretched one hand out to press the keys. For a moment the two adults listened, sharing grimacing smiles.

"I have some shopping to do," Kathleen said when Lisa lost interest. She held the door for him and Lisa to leave.

Booth wasn't ready to end this. The kiss, the mysterious mail, her talent at the piano—they all bothered him and he wanted to know more, but at the same time he doubted he'd learn anything here in the apartment. She was much too guarded.

"Would you do me a huge favor?" he asked.

"I don't know. Depends on what it is." Then Lisa crawled over to her and put her arms out to be picked up. Kathleen hoisted his daughter onto her hip as if she did it every day. Lisa pointed to Bosco, who had wandered back in and was headed for the kitchen.

"I think you wore Bosco out, sweetheart." She glanced up at Booth. "What's the favor?"

"Come with us."

"Pardon me?"

"I have to go buy food—my least favorite chore. That's the favor. I could use a hand with Lisa."

"Why don't I keep Lisa while you go to the store?"

"I thought you said you had shopping, too."

"Just the drugstore."

"Then we're all set."

"Booth, really, I don't think—"

He slipped his hand around the back of her neck and dropped a kiss on her startled mouth. It lasted long enough for him to know that if he continued, she wouldn't stop him. She tipped her head sideways as though wanting to indulge for a few seconds. He felt the clamor of the pulse behind her ear.

"That wasn't fair," she said softly.

"Impulse."

She didn't smile, her eyes troubled. "Why are you doing this? Yes, I was too quick to say no to a friendship, but anything more... I don't want to get involved with you, and you need someone who's ready for a relationship, someone for Lisa. I have too much going on in my life, too many unresolved issues."

Booth said nothing, asked nothing and refused to even speculate. It was the first time she'd said so much voluntarily, and he felt as if he'd inadvertently touched on the secrets she held deep within her. He wondered what in hell they were.

"Kisses, babe, and especially the impulsive kind, definitely mean involvement. Then again, what's to worry about in a food store? Seduction in the produce aisle?"

He felt her relax and then she grinned. "Ice cream."

"What?"

"I like ice cream. Seduction should definitely take place near the ice cream."

He stared at her. "I don't think I'd better touch that," he said, his voice suddenly husky. "We could be in all sorts of interesting trouble."

"Exactly the reason I shouldn't go with you."

"Live dangerously."

"I already am," she murmured, then nodded. "All right, I'll go with you. Give me a few minutes to change."

In fifteen minutes she emerged wearing another sundress, sandals and the light scent of something flowery. She slid a straw bag onto her shoulder while Booth carried Lisa. When they reached the Explorer, he opened the back door and strapped Lisa into the infant carrier. Kathleen climbed into the front seat.

Booth slid behind the wheel, started the engine and pushed the air conditioning to high. He pulled out of the parking spot and headed toward the drug store. Kathleen picked up the items she needed and returned to the car. Then Booth drove to the shopping center. They parked and were in the process of going inside when a uniformed police officer approached.

Kathleen's steps slowed, her guard immediately in place, wariness evident. It was all too obvious that she didn't like cops. Was it dislike—or fear? With an eye on her, Booth said, "Hi, George. What's up?" George peered at Kathleen, nodded in silent greeting, then said to Booth, "Can I talk to you privately?"

Booth said to Kathleen, "Would you hold Lisa?"

She looked as if she were going to bolt, and for a moment he thought she would refuse to take the baby.

"George, give me a second here and I'll be right with you."

He took Kathleen's arm and urged her a few feet away, so that they were under the store canopy and out of the sun. "What in hell is wrong with you?" he asked in a low, irritated voice. He believed they'd made some progress just moments ago, and now this.

"Nothing."

"Bull. You're sweating, and you look as if someone's going to drag you off to an execution."

She turned, and Booth stopped her. "No, you're not. You're not running off. I want some answers."

She shook off his hand. "I don't owe you any answers."

Booth swore, kicking himself for shutting her down, then swore again.

Kathleen glared at him. "Not very nice language for your daughter to hear."

Lisa was looking back and forth between the two of them, her eyes wide, her thumb firmly in her mouth.

"We'll settle this later. Would you mind holding her while I find out what George wants? Or do you want to refuse and make George wonder what's wrong with you?"

She folded her arms and looked away. "You're not nearly as nice as everyone said you were."

"Ah, at last some insight. You've been asking around about me. A new topic for discussion. As for being nice, I'm not. I was amused, curious and patient. Now I'm just annoyed."

"Well, you don't have to be nice or patient or annoyed with me anymore, because I'm sick of your quizzes and your questions. You've asked the last ones today."

"One more."

"No," she snapped.

He asked it anyway. "Will you please hold Lisa while I find out what George wants?"

She took the baby, snuggling her close. "Did you hear what I said?"

"With you, Kathleen, I mostly hear what you don't say."

He'd started to walk away when she said, "I mean it, Booth."

He cursed again under his breath and hurried to where George was leaning against his patrol car. His insides churned, and he dug a roll of antacid tablets from his pocket, popping two into his mouth and crunching down hard.

He sure as hell didn't need the hassle. And for damn sure, forgetting about her meant he could quit thinking about all the unanswered questions. But he couldn't get past the sense that she was hiding something. The quick solution would be a police check, yet he resisted the impulse, afraid of stumbling across something he didn't want to know. Then again, his instincts were telling him to get it done and then deal with the results.

KATHLEEN TOOK A deep breath, got one of the grocery carts equipped with a baby seat and settled Lisa into it. Something had to give, and refusing to see Booth after today would go a long way toward relieving her anxiety.

She couldn't continue this charade with him. He was suspicious, and rightly so. She was doing weird things because she was trying so hard to appear normal. First there was the kiss, then her comment about the Juilliard. She smiled. She could only wish, but her answer, far-fetched as it was, had stopped the questions. Maybe that was what she should have been doing from the beginning. Making up stories and events that best fit the situation. As it was, she'd taken some basic measures against discovery. Using her mother's maiden name, keeping a low profile, renting the out-of-town post office box and taking a job where a lot of questions weren't asked. So many lies. An inner voice whispered, "And you know how much you hate lies."

Yet, if she had been totally truthful, she'd be arrested, returned to Wyoming and probably locked up for the rest of her life. She had a dilemma, no matter what she said or did.

How instantly her inner warning system had gone off at the approach of George. What did he want with Booth? Had he learned who she was and wanted to tell Booth privately? Had Booth started some process at the Crosby police station to find out about her? Maybe taking her to the store had been planned, and even while she stood here, Booth and George were deciding what to do.

Kathleen shuddered, rubbing at her suddenly chilled arms. Her brother was right; she was becoming paranoid. George's arrival was probably unrelated to her, but she had reacted nevertheless, and of course, Booth missed nothing.

She brushed Lisa's curls back from her cheeks. "You, sweetheart, are the cause of all of this, you know that?" Lisa giggled, tugging on Kathleen's earring. "On second thought, it's Mavis. If she'd heard you crying that night, then I would never have met your daddy."

Immediately Lisa said, "Dada."

"Yes, Daddy. Your too sexy, too good-looking, too curious daddy."

"Dada."

She said it again, pointing toward Booth, who even from this distance looked annoyed. *Get a grip,* she warned herself. *You barely know the man, and you're reading his body language?* Kathleen pushed the cart over to a bench of plants in need of watering. One had tiny yellow flowers that made her think of her mother's window box back on the farm. It had hung outside the kitchen window, and every spring she had gone to the nursery and bought flats of plants to fill it. She blinked away the moisture that suddenly filled her eyes.

"What an adorable little girl."

Kathleen glanced up at a tall lissome woman wearing a wide-brimmed straw hat and a billowy lime-sherbet-colored dress; she spoke with a slight Southern accent. She looked as if she belonged at a garden party, sipping a mint julep while harp music played.

"Yes, she is," Kathleen said.

"And she looks just like you, sugar. Pretty hair and that sweet smile. I'll bet she's Daddy's girl, isn't she?"

"Uh, yes, she is that."

"You must be very proud of her. Is she your first? Of course, she is. How silly of me. I have a granddaughter in Georgia just about her age." She pronounced it "Jawgia." "I usually spend summers up here in New England. I might be a Southerner, but the heat down there is just too much. Your accent doesn't sound New Englandy."

"I'm not from here originally."

"A Midwest cadence, I think," the woman said thoughtfully. "My Mason and I travel a lot and we hear all kinds of accents. Yours sounds like a friend from... Oh dear, now I can't remember. Never can keep them all straight."

"Accents are very different from state to state," Kathleen said, being deliberately vague. She reminded herself that this had nothing to do with her particular situation, only with the fact that this woman was indeed a stranger.

The woman didn't seem to notice her vagueness. "And you're clear over here on the East Coast. Why, I do declare, I bet you have a story, don't you? You know, we Southerners don't move a lot. And if we do, it's not very far. Is your husband from the Midwest, too?"

"I'm not married."

She looked at Lisa, then touched her fingers to her mouth. "Oh, I'm terribly sorry. How gauche of me. I just assumed—"

"We've set the wedding for next month," Booth said from behind her.

The Southern woman turned, her smile broadening, color flushing her cheeks, her voice coquettish. "Why, how wonderful." She lightly touched his arm. "My hubby tells me I ask too many questions."

"I've been told the same thing," Booth said, oozing charm. But he was looking at Kathleen. She glared at him, trying to decide whether to murder him here in broad daylight or wait for a private moment.

"Your daughter looks just like her mommy."

"Yes, she does."

"And both are beauties."

"That, too," Booth said, smiling while Kathleen fumed.

"Oh, there's my hubby with the car. I have to dash. It's been so wonderful chatting. You know a lot of New Englanders aren't as friendly as us Southerners. Your wife—oh, dear, your wife-to-be—even though she's from the Midwest—has been just delightful. Take care of that lovely baby, and I hope you have a lovely wedding."

The woman strode off, getting into a car that sat parked about five spaces away.

Kathleen glared at Booth. "She 'hopes we'll have a lovely wedding.'"

Booth took the handle of the cart, grinned at Lisa and turned to push it into the store. "Generally it's best to have Daddy married to Mommy."

"How ridiculous, Booth."

"Hey, I could have said you weren't her mommy and then she would have been even more embarrassed."

"You could have said nothing."

"And miss that murderous look on your face? Catching you wanting to strangle me is becoming an hourly occurrence." He winked. "Forget it. You'll never see her again, and I have to admit, Lisa does look a little like you."

Kathleen rolled her eyes.

He flung an arm around her shoulders, hugging her, then grinning. "Come on, let's get the food gig done."

At the deli counter, Booth asked to see the manager. The two women working there grinned and flirted, asking him if he wanted the usual order of sliced roast beef, shaved honey ham and pints of three different cold salads. He said he did, told them to give it to Kathleen and went through a door that said Keep Out.

Oscar Roanquist looked up, expectation filling his eyes when Booth closed the door.

"You found Pamela," the manager said, his words eager and hopeful.

"Wish I could say yes. But I do have something. I just spoke to one of my officers, and Pamela and five other kids were seen in a convenience store yesterday afternoon outside Hartford."

"Hartford. She doesn't know anyone there." Oscar sighed, dragging one hand down his face. "At least she's still in the state. How do you know it was Pamela?"

"They'd locked themselves out of the car they were riding in, and the clerk in the store told them they'd either have to call a cop or a lock expert. Obviously a cop would ask too many questions, so they called a lock expert. He had to have proof of ownership, and since the registration was locked in the car, he made the kid give him his license and wallet. Once he got the car opened and found the registration was in the kid's name, he was satisfied.''

"But how—"

"The lock expert notified the police. They usually do when they have to open up a car. Obviously they have no authority to do anything, but they get information from the registration, including the plate number. Hartford ran the plate, and the driver was Johnny Ellfort.''

"Pamela's old boyfriend,'' Oscar said. His eyes narrowed in disgust. "God, I couldn't stand that kid. He was too old for her. Mouthy and flip and always looking at Pamela like his greatest wish was to see her naked.''

"Probably was.''

"Now what?''

"We're looking for the car.''

"Did the lock expert say anything else? Like the three girls were being held against their will?''

"No.''

"Which is it?''

"He didn't mention anything out of the ordinary. Six teenagers hanging out in front of a convenience store is a pretty common sight. He got the car info and opened the door. They all piled in and drove away. Three girls and three guys.''

"Doing God knows what.''

"Look, Oscar,'' Booth said, understanding the man's frustration. He was feeling it himself. "Take the news we have as progress. The car will be spotted and stopped. Kids might think they're smart, but

there isn't a trick they can come up with that hasn't
been done a hundred times before." Booth glanced
at his watch. Twenty minutes had passed. "I have
to go. Someone is with Lisa and waiting for me.
I'll call the other two fathers and let them know
what's going on.

"Try not to worry too much. We'll get Pamela
home safe."

CHAPTER SIX

WHEN BOOTH RETURNED, Kathleen had put a number of items into the cart.

"What's all this stuff?" Booth asked.

"Food."

"But it's all raw."

"It's called fruits and vegetables. You can eat them as is or cook them."

"I don't do much cooking. Rita and Arlene take care of me," he said, gesturing to the two women working the deli counter.

"But you can't eat deli food all the time."

"Why not? I like it, I don't dirty dishes and it's quick."

Kathleen sighed. "What about a real meal with meat and potatoes and vegetables? Since it's summer, a steak on the grill, or maybe chicken? Potatoes baked on the coals."

Booth grinned. "I'm starving."

They made their way up the dessert aisle, where Booth grabbed a package of chocolate-chip cookies. Kathleen picked up a box of animal crackers for Lisa.

"I should think you would be hungry if all your

meals are processed foods and store-made side dishes.''

"It's not that bad. I go to my mother's for dinner once in a while.''

"Cooking steak and potatoes on the grill isn't difficult. And steamed zucchini. A great summer meal.''

"When do we eat?'' He opened the animal crackers, gave Lisa one and popped two into his mouth.

"We?''

"Sure. It's no fun eating alone, and if I'm going to buy steak, I'd like to share it with someone other than the beagle next door.''

She laughed. "I think I got myself into this one.''

"An interesting dilemma, wouldn't you say?'' he commented smugly.

"Wait a minute. All this food talk, and I almost forgot. Rita, or maybe it was Arlene, said that the manager's daughter ran away and you're looking for her? Her name's Pamela?''

"That at least changes the subject,'' Booth muttered. "Yeah, her name's Pamela Roanquist. She and two other girls took off some weeks back, and we've been trying to find them. George had some news—the first real break we've had—and I wanted to tell Pamela's father.''

"How odd, or maybe just coincidental. I met a young woman at the Powell Street Center named Pamela. She only came once. I don't think anyone else met her.''

Booth shrugged. "It's a common name."

"As I recall, she was short with curly red hair. She said she liked playing the guitar."

Booth looked at her closely. "Did she wear a nose ring?"

"Yes."

"Terrific," he muttered with a scowl. "We checked all the places she was known to hang out. No one mentioned the Powell Street Center."

"As I said, she was only there that one time. Maybe she never told anyone. Some of the boys quit coming because they got teased for doing sissy things."

"Music being sissy."

"Yes."

"So you're saying that Pamela went there secretly?"

"I think it was more like checking the place out, and for whatever reason, she chose not to come back. I went through the names of all the new enrollees just yesterday. Pamela's name wasn't on the list. I would have remembered, because their music interest is stated beside their name."

"I see she made an impression on you."

"We talked about making a career of music, and I told her how very competitive the field is. Like most teenagers, kids see these rappers or rock groups making millions and think they can do it, too. Pamela was more interested in country music, and she had a guitar at home. I told her to bring it in, that I'd love to hear her play. But I never saw her again."

Booth folded his arms. "This is amazing. All this time, you've known about Pamela, and I'm running up blind alleys."

"I didn't know I had information that was important."

He peered at her. "I have a feeling that you have a lot of important information if I could only figure out the right questions."

She busied herself looking for an animal cracker shaped like a lion for Lisa. "We were talking about Pamela."

"Hmm. Yes, we were, weren't we? Anything else you recall about her?"

"She mentioned she wanted to go to Nashville to see some friend named Diana whose brother worked at the Grand Ole Opry."

"Did she happen to give you a last name of this friend?" he asked, still astonished at how much information she had about Pamela Roanquist.

"Sorry."

He shook his head. "This is incredible, but a better lead than I've had since she took off with her girlfriends. I'm gonna go call this in so we can alert the police in Nashville. Be right back."

Kathleen continued down the condiment aisle and had just turned into the snack-foods section when Booth came back, plucked a bag of chips off the shelf and dropped it into the cart.

"All set," he said. "Now we wait."

Rearranging things so the chips didn't get crushed, she asked, "How long do you keep looking for someone who has run away?"

"It remains an open case. With these girls it will stay active because they're local, and the families want constant updates."

"Do you get a lot of runaway cases?"

"Local kids?"

"Anybody. I guess I'm wondering how much you take on? Say some Maine kids ran away."

"If they were declared runaways, we'd have them in the system. If we got a call from a police department in Maine saying they thought the kids were in the area, we'd pay closer attention. Otherwise, we depend on license checks, arrests, something that would directly involve the police. Their names would show up on a missing-kids database, or if they're wanted for something, even a minor traffic violation, their name would show up on a national computer system."

"Then how is it I read about people staying hidden for years?"

"As I said, they have to do something to draw attention to themselves. These kids locked themselves out of their car. We had an escaped fugitive once who was clear down in Texas. She went to a bar one night and got into a fistfight with another woman. The cops were called, ran a computer check on her and, bingo, she was arrested."

"She was stupid."

"Yep."

"So you're saying that if someone is smart, they can stay hidden for years."

"Depends on a hundred different circumstances, but, yeah. If a guy was careful, low-key and stayed out of trouble, he could probably hide for a long time. Most people mess up. They drive too fast, or like the woman in the Texas bar, they forget they're supposed to hiding and make a spectacle of themselves and get nailed."

Booth picked up a package from the meat counter. "So how about this one?"

Deep in thought, Kathleen blinked and then glanced at the chuck steak. "No, that's for pot roast. You want a sirloin steak, or a porterhouse. Here. This one looks fine."

"Not big enough."

"Booth, it's over a pound."

"But not enough for both of us. Now this one, there's a steak."

"My God, it costs almost as much as Gail's rent."

"So here's the deal," he said, dismissing the price. "I'll cook it if you come and help me eat it."

She started to refuse, and then almost instantly changed her mind. Why not? She liked him, she was weary of being suspicious and jumping at every unexpected word or event. Like George wanting to talk to Booth. Very routine and totally unrelated to her. Too many more of those over-the-top reactions, and she'd have only herself to blame if Booth learned the truth. Besides, she was tired of thinking only about her own situation. It had been many weeks since she'd fled Wyoming, and so far nothing had occurred to make her think the Rodeo police knew where she was.

Now Kathleen knew better than to do anything obvious. If the Rodeo police knew where she was or were actively searching for her in the area, Booth would be aware of it. She'd probably dropped way down on any priority list of fugitives—unless Sheriff Faswell had become a lot more energetic about his job than Kathleen remembered Steve saying he was. She was probably a lot safer than she'd ever allowed herself to believe. But that didn't mean she shouldn't be cautious. Her own carelessness could trip her up.

Still, this was one meal, not an intimate relationship, and she'd agreed to try being friends. She adored Booth's daughter. And frankly, she was getting tired of eating alone.

"All right," she finally replied.

Booth had folded his arms, and shaking his head, he said, "All that thinking just to say okay?"

Stay cool and light, she reminded herself. *This isn't serious, this is just fun.* "I'm just making sure I can handle your seduction techniques."

He raised an eyebrow. "'Techniques'? As in wine and dine you and then take you to bed?"

"That's one way."

"Not mine."

"Thank God."

"Interested in my way?"

Instantly, she wanted to say yes, but clamped her mouth shut. That would come under the category of flirting, or at the very least, teasing.

Then he looked at her in a way that made her feel he was reaching inside to all those feelings she wanted to hide.

In a voice so low she had to move closer to hear him, he said, "When we go to bed, you'll be just as eager as I am."

She shook her head. "My God, you're serious."

"Chemistry is serious stuff."

"But I don't love you. I don't even know you very well."

"That goes both ways. But love and a long acquaintance aren't the same as chemistry."

"You make it sound so uncontrollable. That scares me."

"You, babe, scare the hell out of me. I still love my wife. I have a daughter who needs to know who her mother was and how much she is missed. The distraction of serious sex is not my choice, believe me."

Serious sex? As opposed to casual sex? Was there a difference? Kathleen swallowed to relieve the dryness in her throat.

The sounds in the store slipped away, leaving a riveting tension throbbing between them and pulling at something dark and hot. He hadn't touched her, and yet he enfolded her; she could smell him and taste him and in some deep primal way, she felt as if they had connected centuries ago—not just in some ritual dance of desire, but by some eternal bond.

She looked away, shaking off the strange sensation. Centuries? Eternity? How ridiculous.

Second thoughts clamored through her. She needed to get her bearings and sort out her feelings before spending an evening with him. After the kind of day she'd had, she was feeling far too vulnerable.

"It can't be tonight," she said, hoping he wouldn't start probing.

"To sleep with me, eat with me or both?"

Kathleen blinked, then felt color flush her cheeks. "You are too quick, Booth Rawlings."

He grinned and gave her a brief one-arm hug. "I couldn't resist, babe. You walked right into that one."

"I'm going to have to work on my responses."

"No. I like them just as they are. Honest and straightforward."

Kathleen hated the deceit that was becoming far too entrenched in her. If there were two things she had not been with Booth, they were "honest" and "straightforward."

"As for getting together tonight," he said, "it's out for me, too. I have to work. In fact, I'm going to go in early and do some checking on this latest turn in the missing-girls case."

Perfect. She had breathing space.

"How about Wednesday night?" Booth asked.

"All right."

Booth walked over to a stack of sale items while Kathleen closed the almost empty box of animal crackers, letting Lisa hold the string handle.

She smiled at the pleasant turn of events. She had three days to anticipate something positive and fun. She felt almost buoyant, as though her life had taken a decisive turn. My God, had she been that lonely, that starved for a normal life? She winced. Of course she was starved for a normal life. She hadn't had one in years. Not since the first year of her marriage. Not since the doctor had told Steve that her inability to get pregnant might be *his* problem. Steve had refused to believe it, had blamed her, and from then on their marriage had deteriorated. For five years, she'd lived with Steve's abuse, the apologies, her own attempts to mend their relationship, when actually there had been nothing left to put back together.

Dammit, it was about time she put herself back together and started living again. Nothing wicked or wild that would get her into trouble. Just a summer night enjoying grilled steak with a friend, maybe some wine. She loved the idea. As for all his talk about sex and heat—well, she'd simply sidestep all that.

Feeling better than she had in months, she had to restrain herself from twirling around and flinging her hands in the air. Instead she put the steak he'd selected back into the meat case.

"What are you doing?" Booth asked, spilling cans into the cart.

"Since we're not going to eat until Wednesday, I'll come in and get the steak then." With her domestic instincts moving into high gear, she said, "They have some gorgeous fresh blueberries. Do you like cobbler?"

"If you're going to make it, I'll like it."

"What a sweet thing to say."

"Hey, we're making progress, aren't we?"

Lisa giggled and clapped her hands. Booth dropped an arm around Kathleen's neck. "I think she approves."

"She'll love my blueberry cobbler."

"I meant of us."

Automatically Kathleen started to protest, but then stopped herself. She didn't want to spoil such a happy moment.

"Why, Booth Rawlings, is that you? I don't believe what I'm seeing."

Kathleen felt him stiffen, then saw him paste a bland look on his face and turn to face the woman speaking to him.

She was short and lumpy in a mustard-colored dress with a lace collar, buttoned up so that her neck disappeared, giving the impression that her head sat directly on her shoulders. Kathleen guessed she was about seventy. Her face was pinched and grim, and the look in her eyes said her life was made up of gossip that she relished, even while she disapproved. Her arms clutched a white purse with frayed handles.

"Gladys."

"It is you," she said as if his crime was acknowledging it.

"How are you?"

Ignoring the question, she looked at Kathleen. "This isn't one of Angie's friends. I don't recall ever seeing her around your wife."

Despite her confrontational comments, Booth made the introductions, although it was obvious to Kathleen he would have preferred to take Lisa and her and walk away.

To Kathleen, he explained, "Gladys is a widow. She lived a few houses from Angie and me."

"I was like a mother to Angie," Gladys said earnestly. "I watched over her when she was pregnant, helped her when Booth was too busy working, even taught her how to knit. She promised me I could help take care of her baby just like I took care of her. And when she died, I volunteered to take care of the little angel."

"That was very generous of you, Mrs. Hucklebee," Kathleen said.

"Well, *he* didn't think so. Did he honor Angie's memory by doing what she wanted? No." She glared at Booth. "He refused. Then he moved away, and not once has he ever invited me to see Angie's baby."

Kathleen could feel the fury rolling off Booth, and thinking the best way was to humor Gladys, she offered, "Then this is your chance to meet her. Isn't she beautiful?"

Gladys moved a few steps closer, and Booth moved, too. No question his intent was to place himself between this woman and his daughter. Kathleen put her hand on his arm, giving him a look that said, "Indulge Gladys."

Booth narrowed his eyes, and Kathleen nodded, the meaning of their silent exchange clear.

"I don't want her near Lisa."

"I know. But nothing can happen here."

"I don't like it."

"I know that, too."

Lisa grinned when the older woman gently touched her tiny hand still clutching the animal-cracker box.

"She looks like Angie," Gladys said, her voice softer, growing nostalgic as she drew closer.

"Yes, she does."

And for a few seconds the woman's face softened in a grandmotherly way, her eyes focused on Lisa.

Then she straightened and gave Kathleen a wary look. "How do you know? You didn't know my Angie."

"Booth has told me about her, and I've seen pictures. She would be very proud of her daughter."

Then, just when Kathleen thought the woman had been satisfied, she turned to Booth. "So when do I get to baby-sit?"

Booth tugged the shopping cart closer, his restraint obvious.

Ease her out gently, Booth. Gently.

"That's not possible, Gladys."

Kathleen's heart sank.

Gladys drew herself up, mouth prim, chin lifted in haughtiness. Peering pointedly at Kathleen, the older woman made her feel as if she'd conspired with Booth to erase Angie's memory.

"She ain't been dead a year, Booth, and here you are out with some woman, letting her paw you and letting that poor child watch."

"Now wait a minute," he snapped.

"Does your mother know about her?"

Booth tried to guide Kathleen out of Gladys's reach, but Kathleen balked and pulled away. Booth taking her side was only going to fuel the woman's annoyance.

"Actually, Mrs. Hucklebee, I'm new in town. I live in the same building as Booth. Since we both had errands in the same direction, we decided to do them together."

Gladys ignored her. "I know about women taking up with men and making them forget their wives. Angie was sweet, wonderful and loving. She wanted me to help with the baby. We had plans. Booth knew all about them. And when my poor Angie died, he broke Angie's promise."

"I'm sure he had no intention—"

"The hell I didn't," Booth muttered under his breath.

"How do you know?" Gladys asked suspiciously. "You said you're new in town."

"Gladys, that's enough."

"I wanted to baby-sit with my grandchild."

"She's not your grandchild, and you're not going to baby-sit for her."

He nudged Kathleen ahead, then wheeled the cart around, moving away from Gladys, but not before she gave a parting shot.

"If you had loved my Angie, you wouldn't be whoring with another woman. You would be mourning and keeping her memory alive."

"Dammit!"

"Booth, don't," Kathleen said hurriedly.

But Gladys was already ambling away, mumbling something that neither heard.

Once again Booth swore, this time dragging a hand through his hair and closing his eyes for a few seconds. He drew in a long breath, then put his arm around Kathleen and pulled her close. "I'm sorry you had to witness that."

"Was she really as close to Angie as she said?"

"Angie felt sorry for her. She lives alone in a house packed with forty years' worth of junk, and she doesn't have any friends. Gladys and her husband once owned a yarn shop, but he took off with some stripper, leaving Gladys with the store, the bills and a very bitter anger against men. I was never particularly fond of her, but Angie had a soft spot for people not as fortunate as she."

"I wish I'd known her. She sounds wonderful."

"The best. Too damn good to Gladys, and this is what came of it." Booth sighed. "Anyway, when

Angie learned she was a reclusive neighbor, she recalled going to the yarn shop with her mother when she was a little girl. Gladys had always given her gingerbread cookies, and Angie never forgot it. One afternoon, she went to see Gladys, reminded her about the visits and the cookies. Gladys began to invite Angie in to see all 'her special things,' as she called them. In time they became friends."

"But surely Angie realized she was strange."

Booth shrugged. "Angie always thought the best of people, and Gladys adored her. The old lady was lonely, and Angie made a vague promise that she could help out with the baby."

"Where do you come in all this?"

"I didn't like Angie going over there. The woman is weird. Maybe harmless, but she gossips and spreads rumors and in general is a royal pain."

"Is she why you moved?"

"She was one reason. No way was I gonna let her take care of Lisa."

Kathleen agreed wholeheartedly, but she also still reeled from the name-calling and suddenly being thrust into the role of the woman who was taking Angie's place.

Now the teasing with Booth and the planned dinner together had taken on more serious implications. If Gladys was a gossip and she began to spread Kathleen's name around, she could not only make Booth look bad in the eyes of all those who loved Angie, but she could draw attention to Kathleen in a far-too-public way.

As she went through the checkout, holding Lisa while Booth handled the bags of groceries, Kathleen decided she had to stay away from him. The tricky part would be giving him an explanation he would believe.

They loaded the groceries into the car, got Lisa strapped into her seat in the back, and Kathleen slid into the front.

"You're awfully quiet," he said, starting the engine and the air conditioning. "Gladys get to you?"

She stared straight ahead. "I can't see you anymore, Booth."

"What?"

She took a shaky breath. "Look, nothing has really started between us. And we've both admitted that whatever there is isn't serious. I think it's best if we just leave things here."

He drummed his hand on the steering wheel. "You know, if I wasn't a cop and if I didn't have a daughter, I'd go and strangle that vindictive old lady."

"It's not just Gladys. Although, to be honest, any woman following Angie would get a tough time from people here in town. Just from the little I've heard, she was liked and respected by everyone. Gladys might be a bit rabid, but there are a lot of people who'd resent a new woman taking Angie's place."

"Has anyone else said anything to you?"

"No, but we haven't really been seen together."

He looked at her for a long time, saying nothing.

"I just think it's best if we don't start," she said softly.

"It stinks to hell and back."

He drove out of the parking lot, sliding his sunglasses over his eyes and never once glanced at her until they stopped in front of the apartment building.

He turned off the air conditioning and put all the windows down. Then, right in full view of Alfred, who was watering the rosebushes, and Mrs. Starkey, an across-the-street neighbor, Booth kissed her.

In fact he made it quite clear this wasn't any light brush across the lips. The kiss was full and deep and lingering, causing her senses to reel, making her forget he was doing this for an audience. Then, before she could draw a deep breath, he did it all over again, this time sliding his hand into her hair.

When Kathleen opened her eyes, Alfred's watering hose was drowning one of the bushes and Mrs. Starkey's poodle had wrapped his leash around her legs. Both spectators were staring in obvious astonishment.

"They want something to gossip about, that should keep the buzz up to speed for at least a week."

With that, he got out of the car, hauled the groceries into the building and returned for Lisa, while Kathleen sat in stunned silence, her mouth feeling bee-stung, her heart racing, her cheeks hot.

Oh, my God.

CHAPTER SEVEN

DAYS LATER, after managing to successfully avoid him, yet unable to forget his kiss, Kathleen found herself in an even more unexpected place—his apartment at nearly midnight. He looked disgruntled and edgy—and sexy.

"Well of course it's ridiculous," Kathleen said to Booth.

"How can you say that? She's stopped fussing."

"She's too young to have a preference for one person over another."

"Not one person, Kathleen. You."

Despite her disbelief, Kathleen was flattered and touched by the compliment. "Who's been staying with her?"

"My mother and my sister. My mother is exhausted and my sister told me to give her chocolate. Then again, her answer to any emergency is chocolate."

"With all due respect to your sister, I don't think Lisa is having chocolate withdrawal."

"Hey, look, all I know is that for the first time in three days she's not sobbing or fussing."

Lisa was indeed quiet, breathing in a contented rhythm, snuggled in Kathleen's arms. It gave Kathleen a whole new sense of rightness deep within, as if she'd finally come home. The baby made her feel wanted and needed and special.

It was Wednesday night, and just a half hour ago, she'd returned from a delightful dinner with Alfred, during which they'd discussed music and antiques and the highlight of his years in business—when he'd discovered a forgotten masterpiece in a boxed lot he'd bought from an estate.

She'd been about to undress and go to bed when Booth had called. Booth sounding desperate about anything struck her as odd, but there was no mistaking the edge of raw panic in his voice. She'd gone up to his apartment immediately.

Kathleen had noted his exhaustion and rumpled appearance the moment she walked in. Obviously he'd gotten very little sleep, and he looked as if he'd dressed in the dark. Jeans zipped but unsnapped. No shirt. No shoes. Beard-stubbled cheeks and uncombed hair. The look, although undoubtedly unintentional, sent a flurry of raw skips and jumps leaping through her tummy.

Clearly, from the irritated look on his face, he resented her outward calmness and control. It gave her a satisfied feeling that her avoidance of him had been the best decision, given the growing awareness between them.

That distance had been easier to keep since she'd begun hunting for a place of her own. Gail had called on Monday to say she'd be bringing her sister back for a visit. Since the apartment had only two bedrooms, an extra guest would make for tight living. In addition, Kathleen had had her work at the restaurant and the youth center. Consequently, she hadn't been home very much, which was fortunate. After the grocery-store debacle and Booth's public kiss, she felt exposed and frighteningly aware of how tenuous staying out of the limelight could be.

But tonight she felt invincible. For the first time since she'd met Booth, she felt more than equipped for anything he might toss her way. A sense of female power blossomed within her. It was indeed a heady feeling, knowing that Booth needed her.

"I've been calling you all evening."

"I was out," she replied, amused by his disgruntlement.

"Yeah, I figured that." His gaze swept down her dress all the way to her heeled sandals.

The baby's warm head pressed into her neck, her scent sweet and comforting. "I thought Wednesday was your night off."

"It was, and I planned to catch up on my sleep. Unfortunately Lisa wasn't cooperating."

"She is now. Shh. Let me put her down."

Kathleen carried her into the bedroom and slowly lowered her into the crib. The baby stirred, then settled. Kathleen put Lisa's jungle quilt over her, stroked her cheek and smoothed back her curls until she heard the even breathing of deep sleep.

When she returned to the living room, Booth had sprawled in an easy chair, a bottle of beer dangling from one hand, his expression grumpy. She resisted going to him, brushing her hand across his hair and whispering sympathy. He looked exhausted, but he seemed agonized, too. Lisa was growing and becoming a handful. No doubt that increased his feeling of loss for Angie. His daughter needed a full-time mother, rather than a long line of well-intentioned friends and relatives. Kathleen's erratic role—and she had no idea what that was beyond being a downstairs neighbor—had apparently been embraced by Lisa. She couldn't deny that she was deeply and profoundly moved by the baby's trust.

"So where were you?" Booth asked, raising the bottle and drinking. "It's close to midnight."

"Excuse me?"

"You heard me."

She touched a finger to her chin and tapped. "Let me see if I have this straight. You live up here and I'm a temporary guest in a downstairs apartment. I don't date you. You're not my father, my husband, my keeper or my conscience. Therefore it escapes me why you have the right to ask where I was."

"Humor me."

He was serious. He really expected her to account to him for her activities. "No."

He took a long swallow of beer. "So what's he have that I don't? A better line or was the chemistry just too strong to resist?"

Kathleen folded her arms and tilted one hip. "You have a hell of a nerve."

"Apparently I don't have much else when it

comes to you. Tell me, has this guy, whoever he is, been on the side all along? Is that why you've been so determined to avoid me? You could have explained. I don't cruise in private waters, babe, and being told the truth doesn't send me over the edge.''

She pressed her lips together to keep the smile back. The mental image of intimacy with Alfred, as delightfully warm and sweet as he was, struck her as ludicrous in the extreme. She had little use for jealousy in men, but Booth's reaction was transparent and endearingly cranky. ''Just because you can't get in touch with me whenever you want, you assume I'm sleeping with some guy?''

''If he's sleeping, he's dead.''

''I think that was a compliment.''

He shook his head, obviously aware he wasn't going to rattle her or get any answers. He scowled, waving the bottle to indicate the door. ''My apologies for being such a bastard. Blame it on exhaustion and confusion. Thanks for coming up. It hasn't been this quiet in days.''

Kathleen debated the course of action that floated through her mind. She weighed the potential consequences, reminded herself that she was too attracted to him to risk it. These weeks of ordinary living with kind people had too often made her past fade like an old photo in the sun. But that didn't change the fact that she was still in danger, and that Booth, because he was a cop, was the last man she should become involved with.

Yet her denials were weakening, her resolve lessening. Even the fear and panic of those early weeks had diminished. At the same time, this suddenly revisited decision felt right. More than that, she wanted to do it.

She pressed her hand to her mouth to cover her yawn, but also to give him the sense that what she was about to say was not a major reversal, merely a favor. "If you'd like, I'll take care of Lisa tomorrow so you can get some rest."

He stared at her as if he'd misunderstood. "Serious?"

"Yes."

"God, that sounds better than taking you to bed. I must be in a bad way."

She laughed. Then he grinned. She walked to the door. "What time?"

"About eight? Is that too early?"

"I'll be here at eight."

Later, as she crawled into bed and listened to the soft hum of the ceiling fan, Kathleen realized she could hardly wait for morning. She'd missed Lisa.

And she'd missed the volatile tension between her and Booth, too.

AT THE ROADKILL Café in Wyoming, the Rainmaker settled into the same booth he'd occupied the last time he'd met Pony here. Since then, there had been two weeks of frustration and dead ends. From the enthusiastic phone call from Pony, he assumed he'd finally made some progress. At the very least, Pony had better have located the woman.

Protecting his business and its cash flow was paramount. With cops all over the state looking for Kathleen Hanes, he'd had to sharply curtail the drug shipments coming in by air. The abandoned landing strip had already provoked some phone calls about unidentified lights; to continue his import activity now would heighten curiosity and get other cops nosing around. That he didn't need. Since the real killer was part of his very successful enterprise, the sooner an arrest was made, the sooner the heat of an investigation would cool and the Rainmaker could resume full operations. The bottom line was that as long as Kathleen Hanes was a fugitive, the investigation into Hanes's death would remain open and in the news. And the Rainmaker would be hampered from doing business.

The plan to pin this on the woman had been the Rainmaker's—she fit the mold of the desperate wife who would do anything to escape the next beating. Her general isolation from the townsfolk and her sudden and unexpected departure with a drunken Hanes waving a gun had been exquisitely fortuitous. She'd run, having no clue that what she was doing to keep herself safe was in fact making her look very guilty. It couldn't have gone more perfectly if he'd scripted events himself.

Using powerful binoculars, the Rainmaker had watched the twist in his own scenario unfold that dusty June afternoon from a hidden area a few hundred yards away. He'd been watching the daily routine of the Hanes household for over a week, assessing the right time for a permanent resolution to the problem of the deputy sheriff. The Rainmaker had never been particularly impressed by Hanes. The man's inability to control his drinking and his temper had posed risks from the get-go, but within the loop of cops willing to look the other way, Hanes had friends, thereby making an outright erasure tricky.

The Rainmaker had exercised patience until Hanes had shot off his mouth in a local saloon to a stranger who had turned out to be a retired DEA agent. The Rainmaker had had no choice then; the agent had to be taken down, and the arranged car accident had to be clean, swift and untraceable.

He'd blamed Hanes for the necessity of the agent's death, and the event had signaled Hanes's own elimination. The Rainmaker had the man to do the job—one who liked power trips and needed cash in a major way for his escalating gambling debts. The biggest hindrance was Hanes's wife.

Getting her away from the house would have been ideal, but she rarely left, and forcing her away would have created a whole new set of problems. The next best plan was to render her unconscious and deal with Hanes; then, when she awakened, she'd find him dead. Naturally, she'd be hysterical, call the cops and when they arrived, she'd have no alibi. Given her abusive history with Hanes, the killing would look as if she'd finally retaliated. She had few friends, was estranged from her family and had no money—all complications that would tie her up with a public defender for God knew how long. Her conviction wouldn't have been a sure thing, but it would stop any ongoing search for Steve's real killer.

But the lady had convicted herself and played unwittingly into the Rainmaker's hands when she fled the house with her cheap suitcase in her old car. All he would have to do was wait until she was arrested as a killer on the run. He'd been positively blissful about the entire operation, certain that an arrest would be made within hours.

Except she hadn't been arrested. Hanes's wife had escaped, and as long as she wasn't in jail, the case stayed open and his own operation was on hold. Days and weeks had passed with no sign of the woman, despite police searches and bulletins. He was losing money, irritating contacts and sending his own stress level into the danger zone.

It was then that the Rainmaker had dispatched his own people to find her—primarily Pony and his pals. Any meager confidence he'd had in the lizard-booted idiot had soon grown from frustration into brittle fury.

He wondered how long it had taken the Hanes woman to learn of her husband's death and find out she was wanted. It had to have been soon, for no one, legal or illegal, had had any luck in picking up her escape route.

Not only must she know she was a fugitive, but

she had to be the smartest broad on the planet. The
Rainmaker didn't like smart women, and he sure as
hell hadn't expected to find one on a desolate piece
of ground in Wyoming. Then again, if she was so
brilliant, why had she been married to an ass like
Hanes and living like some martyr? But at the same
time he couldn't see her as stupid. More than six
weeks had passed, and they were no closer to finding her than they'd been hours after Steve had been
eliminated.

He blamed Pony's incompetence, but he blamed
himself, too. Benevolence toward a dying partner
and protecting his own operation had not been com-
patible.

Now the Rainmaker glanced up as the door
opened. Pony sauntered in, arrogant and smug, his
tinny laugh making the Rainmaker wince. The waitress placed the Rainmaker's drink in front of him
while Pony got himself a beer and slipped into the
seat opposite.

"By the grin, can I presume your report is going
to make me happier than I've been the past few
weeks?"

"Man, you're gonna love what I got," Pony replied.

"Good. Spare me the preening and get to the
point."

"Her brother in California? You know the queer
one?"

"Let's dispense with the name-calling, Pony. I

spoke with Clarke, and he doesn't know where she is."

"He was lyin', man."

"Really. And how did you determine that?"

"Me and the boys beat the shit outta him."

The Rainmaker sipped his drink. Giving Pony a second opportunity to do the job had been a chance decision. He seemed more likely to screw up than a brain surgeon using a screwdriver, but perhaps, the Rainmaker thought, his benevolence had finally reaped some rewards. "No one saw this persuasive tactic, I presume. Witnesses would be a problem for you and your friends."

"Jeez, Mr. Smith. Give me some credit, huh?"

The Rainmaker raised an eyebrow. "I haven't had much cause to praise you for efficiency and getting to the heart of the problem in the past, Pony."

"This time we got the broad nailed."

"Very well. And just where have you nailed her?"

"In Ohio. Outside of Cleveland. Her brother said so."

"And?"

"I got the guys there and they're trackin' her down."

"An address?"

"The brother didn't have one. She's called him a few times, but he claimed she never said exactly where she was."

The Rainmaker sighed. "But he gave you a general area." Now that he thought about it, "idiot" was too kind a description. "'Outside of Cleveland' could mean any place from Youngstown to Buffalo."

"Ain't that in New York? I said she was in Ohio."

The Rainmaker rolled his eyes. "Why do you suppose she would have said even that much?"

"Cuz she's a dumb broad and trusts her pretty-faced brother," he said dismissively.

"No, Pony, we already established at our previous meeting that the lady was not dumb. Unlike you and your friends."

Pony choked on the beer he'd just swallowed. "Man, that ain't fair!" Coughing and wiping his mouth on his forearm, he added, "We know where she is, we just gotta pick her up."

"When exactly did you find out she was in the Cleveland area?"

"Uh, about a week ago. Lotta people live in Cleveland. It's gonna take some time."

The Rainmaker sighed. "I'm not interested in waiting for you to check out the entire population of Cleveland and its environment. My guess is that Clarke might have sent you on a merry chase so you'd quit beating him."

Pony shrugged. "Naw. We said we'd be back if he was lyin'."

The Rainmaker's benevolence drained out of him like sand through a sieve. Pony was simply not going to work out. Telling his old partner was going to be difficult, but the Rainmaker didn't want to waste any more time. His backup plan was now a necessity.

He raised a hand and signaled. Another man rose from two booths away and came forward. "Pony, I believe you know Max."

Pony stared, swallowed and then not surprisingly, he began to shake. "Oh, my God. Please, Mr. S-Smith, p-please, you ain't gonna do th-this to me."

The Rainmaker said to Max, "He apparently knows your reputation."

Max smiled confidently. He was tall, sleek and handsome enough to make most women look twice—until they saw his eyes. Cold, dead, distant.

He had done work for the Rainmaker in the past, and his failure rate was zero. Max was expensive, silent and thorough. Bringing him in to find the Hanes woman would have struck the Rainmaker as overkill a few weeks ago. In fact, he'd taken on Pony to indulge his own good-heartedness. The kid could get this done and make his uncle proud.

"Pony, you're fired," the Rainmaker said.

"Huh?"

The Rainmaker handed him an envelope. "There's a bonus in there for you. Think of it as an incentive not to trouble your dying uncle with your incompetence. Now please vacate the booth. Max and I have business to discuss."

"He ain't gonna waste me?"

"Consider this your lucky day."

"My lucky day. Yeah, sure. Sure." He slid from the seat, making a wide arc around Max.

Max grabbed him by the shirt, twisting the fabric. "Keep your mouth shut, kid, or you'll be lunch for the rattlers I keep for pets."

Pony's Adam's apple bobbed, and his eyes looked like popped rivets. "I ain't seen nothin'. Don't know from nothin'."

Max let him go, and Pony was out the door in four steps.

Max slipped into the opposite seat. The Rainmaker sighed. "Please tell me you have something worth my time."

"You're too good a man, Mr. S. You shoulda cut him loose weeks ago."

"I know." He sighed again. "Have we lost an impossible amount of time?"

Max laid down a bulging manila envelope. "On the contrary. She should be nice and comfy and believing she's got this gig aced."

The Rainmaker relaxed and ordered another drink. For the first time in weeks, he felt confident his operation would once again be making him money.

"What do you have for me?"

Max dumped the envelope, and mail spilled out. "This is hers. I've been picking it up at the house. These provide some interesting connections that should put us in her face in short order."

The Rainmaker leaned forward, excitement on his face. "What kind of connections?"

"Insurance, for one. Her mother had an insurance policy that left a small sum to Kathleen. It's in an account with the company, and Kathleen can write checks against it. These are the account statements through June. I found them at the house. Since the July statement was missing, she must have contacted them about a change of address."

The Rainmaker straightened. "Max, you are brilliant!"

"Yes, I am, Mr. S."

"What else?"

"She had one credit card that hasn't been used. The bank sends zero balance statements. I thought that was curious, because if she's starting out in a new place, it would seem likely she would use a credit card."

"Not if she's as smart as I'm beginning to think," the maker grumbled. "Too easy to trace."

"Lucky, Mr. S. Not smart. If she'd been smart, she'd have ditched Hanes years ago."

"I like your confidence, Max."

Max sniffed. "She'd be coolin' her brains in a county jail now if you'd put me on this right away."

The Rainmaker wasn't convinced of that, but he stayed silent. Indulging Max's ego was preferable to dealing with Pony's incompetence any day.

"We're on the right track now," the Rainmaker said forcefully.

Max sniffed again and continued. "Likely she's working or someone has taken her in. But I did find this." He held up a gas-card statement. "She charged gas in a number of states all headed toward the East. The last place was along Interstate 80 in Pennsylvania. I got some men trying to track her down from there."

"What about the Cleveland area?"

"That's in Ohio."

"Never mind."

"I don't think she's in Pennsylvania, either."

The Rainmaker scowled. "I'm not going to like this. I can tell."

"She sold her car in a town south of Williamsport. She wanted cash, but the dealer refused. He gave her a check, but instead of just leaving with it, she opened an account in a local bank, deposited the check, waited the three days for it to clear, then cashed it and closed the account."

"The woman is beyond brilliant," the Rainmaker grumbled, finishing his drink. "So she hasn't used a credit card, has an insurance account and knows better than to open any local bank account and start writing checks. I need someone like her running my operation."

"She'll mess up, Mr. S."

"My hope is that I'm still alive to see it. How much did they give her for the car?"

"Under two grand."

"Chump change. Damn."

"Now, relax, Mr. S. I've got something else."

"What?"

"Something she cares about more than money. Something that will lead us right to her front door."

By the time Max had finished, the Rainmaker was smiling and ordering a third drink.

CHAPTER EIGHT

KATHLEEN PULLED THE pan of blueberry muffins from the oven and wrapped them in a clean dishcloth to keep them warm. She then gathered her bag and the new sheet music she intended to look through once she got Lisa settled for a morning nap.

She locked the apartment and climbed the stairs to Booth's. It was exactly 8:00 a.m.

He had the door open before she got there.

"I'm not sure which smells better—you or what you have wrapped up."

She smiled. "Why don't you take these. Is Lisa up?"

"No, but *I* could be." He gave her a lecherous grin while taking the warm muffins.

"Really, Booth. Don't you guys ever think about anything but sex?"

"No." He folded back the dishcloth and sniffed. "Unless a lady brings fresh-baked muffins." He plucked one from the pan and took a bite. "Besides, I'm in a great mood. Just got off the phone with Oscar Roanquist."

"Pamela's father?" Kathleen put her bag and sheet music on a table.

"Yep. She called after the Nashville police paid

her a visit at her friend Diana's house. After I talked to you we contacted Nashville. They checked out the Grand Ole Opry for anyone working there with a sister named Diana. Once they had that, all the pieces fell into place.''

"Oh, Booth, I'm so glad. What about the other girls?"

"With Pamela. Oscar and the other two fathers are flying down to bring them home. From what Roanquist told me, they got a healthy taste of life on their own with little money. Apparently Pamela's friend lived in some dumpy one-room apartment, and the girls all had to sleep on the floor. Food consisted of cornflakes and canned beans.''

Kathleen shuddered. "Poor kids."

"But an educational experience. And this time, thank God, a happy ending.''

Kathleen nodded. "What about the boys who were with them in Hartford?"

"They abandoned the girls in some Jersey rest stop. We've got an APB out to pick them up for transporting minors across state lines.''

"Oh, God, don't tell me the girls hitchhiked to Tennessee.''

Booth touched her back, urging her into the kitchen. "Can't say for sure, but it's likely. However they got there, they're okay, and thanks to you, about to be reunited with their families.''

"I'm just glad I knew something worth repeating.''

"So am I.'' He went to the cupboard and brought

down two mugs. "I made some coffee. I just looked in on Lisa, and she's still conked out." He poured coffee, put a carton of cream on the table and straddled a chair opposite her.

Kathleen took a sip and grimaced. "This stuff could be exchanged for the oil in my old car."

"Yeah? Sorry. I can make a fresh pot."

She shook her head. "It just takes some getting used to."

"Down at the station we're used to it tasting like sludge, so I make it the same way here."

"Won't this keep you awake?"

"Naw." He picked up a second muffin and bit into it. "Don't know much about baking, but I'll wager these didn't come from a box."

"No, they didn't."

"Who taught you to cook?"

"My mother."

"She was a brilliant pianist and a great cook."

"She was both and more. She passed away a number of years ago."

He stopped eating, lifted his mug and sipped. "That's tough. You miss her."

"Yes."

"It shows in your eyes. Like you lost a close friend, too."

Kathleen looked at the floor. "You see too much."

He chuckled. "Actually, you're very good at keeping a distant expression—a 'Don't look too closely because I'll run you out of my life' look."

"You don't seem to have a problem probing." She took one of the muffins, broke it in half and took a bite.

"Nope. Too busy trying to figure out why you're running."

Kathleen set the muffin aside, her appetite gone and a sudden tightness in her chest. She couldn't flee—it would be too obvious. Besides, Booth was just looking for some reflex action from her. He couldn't know, or he wouldn't be sitting here this calmly. *Just tough it out.* "I don't know what you're talking about."

He leaned forward and touched the corner of her mouth with his finger, pushing a crumb between her lips. "You're lying, babe."

And for a dangerous moment, she almost nodded, almost blurted out why she was here, why she was so evasive, why she didn't trust cops. But to what end? The only one hurt would be her. Booth might be curious, he might have some sexual desire for her—as she did for him—but ultimately he would do his job and arrest her.

"The thing is, I don't know what you're lying about." He watched her closely, and she made herself return his gaze. "I ran a check on you down at the station."

Kathleen dropped the muffin. "A police check? Like I was some criminal?" She was stunned by his bluntness and terrified of what he might do. She felt her entire body go on alert, her mind scrambling for a way out.

His tone of voice remained casual. "I wasn't going to tell you because I hated that I had to do it." He glanced at her before refilling his mug. "But you *have* acted strangely—the incident when George approached me at the grocery-store parking lot was too odd. Cops get itchy at odd behavior."

She opened her mouth to say something, but no words came. Fear had evaporated all the moisture from her throat. She reached for her mug, then put her hand into her lap. She was shaking too badly.

"So I ran your name through the national computer network."

Her head pounded, and she wanted to run and hide from the anger and horror she knew would be in his expression. She raised her eyes, expecting to see him looming over her.

"It came up zero," he said in easy dismissal.

Relief pumped through her. No one in Wyoming had dug deep enough to find the name Yardley. *Careful,* she warned herself. *Be very careful. You're not home free yet.* Booth might have hit a dead end in one place, but that hadn't ended his curiosity over her behavior.

Time to take the offensive. "Really. I'm offended and irritated that you'd do such a thing just because I don't fit some mode of behavior you expect." This time she rose from the chair.

"I did it to eliminate the possibility in my own mind."

"And did it?"

He shrugged. "Cops deal in facts, and I can't argue with the results that came back."

Her decision on a last name had worked. What name to use had been a real dilemma. She couldn't use Hanes, and she'd considered her maiden name of Brown, but that, too, was risky. So she'd chosen her mother's maiden name, instead. No one in Rodeo, never mind the local cops, knew the name, and obviously the choice had paid off. She felt almost buoyant. But she couldn't let Booth off the hook too quickly. She needed to play this out for a little while longer.

Arranging a serious scowl on her face, she said, "Did anyone ever tell you that you're a devious man? Was this "problem" with Lisa a ploy to get me up here so you could tell me you've been reassured I'm not a criminal?"

"I could have said nothing, babe, but I wanted to be up-front and honest with you. I ran the check three days ago, and believe me, no one was as happy as I was that nothing came back. And Lisa *had* been crying for days." He scowled, then added tersely, "You volunteered to come up here and watch Lisa."

Kathleen scowled. He was right. She'd allowed this, she'd stepped into it. And she had learned she was safer than she'd dared hope. But that didn't mean she could get careless or overly talkative. Booth might have been only temporarily satisfied, or simply decided to bide his time. She hated being so suspicious of him, but she couldn't get past the fact that he was a cop—first, last, and always.

He grinned. "Babe, I love watching you chew on the next approach to take with me." He held up his hand to ward off denials. "Since we were on the topic of your mother, all your sheet music belonged to her, didn't it?"

His sudden change of subject made her mind dizzy. That was her real problem with Booth. She never knew where the most innocent of conversations would lead. "How did you know?"

"The day you played for me? While you were changing clothes to go shopping, I saw the name Loretta Brown written on the covers. I just assumed that was her name."

Of course. Now she felt silly and paranoid. "It was hers. When she left my father, she took only a few things besides me, including her sheet music."

"Do you ever see your father?"

"No. He resented my mother for leaving and resented me for going with her. He made it clear years ago that he wanted nothing to do with either of us."

"I'm sorry."

They were silent for a few moments. Booth reached across and squeezed her hand. "His loss, babe. He's missing out on having an incredible daughter. Siblings?"

She hesitated. It didn't matter. He wouldn't connect her with Clarke, and Gary wanted no part of her for the same reasons her father didn't. "I have two older brothers. But we're not close, either."

"A family in name only."

"For a very long time," she said sadly.

"How old were you when your mother took you and left?"

"Nine."

"Are you serious? How could your old man resent a nine-year-old torn between two parents?"

"You don't know my father. He's very rigid and sees life only in black or white. No gray areas allowed, and God forbid that anything like emotion and caring and forgiveness could ever be part of his life." Kathleen felt a deep sadness swamp her. Her anger had dissipated years ago. "I called him when my marriage was in trouble. He hung up on me. We hadn't seen one another or spoken for years, and he treated me as if we'd had a major battle the day before."

Booth stood and drew her up from her chair. Without saying a word, he folded her into his arms. She lowered her head to hide the sudden moisture that sprang into her eyes. The pain should have left her years ago, but she still felt the sting. Perhaps her inability to put Booth and Lisa from her mind and heart resulted from her own deep need for family connections. She'd never found them with Steve, and she'd been unable to create them by having a child. Yet here was Lisa, motherless and so sweetly attached to her, Kathleen could almost allow herself to believe that she belonged here.

She pressed her face against Booth's shirt, finding a solid comfort that made her wish she could tell him about the rest of her life.

Booth held her tightly in his arms, his voice low and steady. "Do you know that's the most unguarded and straightforward you've been about your past since we met?"

She knew it, had known it even as she talked, but the words had just kept coming. "It's not a pleasant thing to talk about."

"But it tells me something about you. That being open is hard for you, because when you were open in the past, you were hurt."

Kathleen hated that once again she had to dodge the truth. She wanted to blurt out that being open with him was too easy—which was exactly why she'd be in so much trouble if she told him the truth.

"You're right," she said softly.

But even as he nodded, she wondered if this lie was the very worst one she'd ever told him. Not because the truth would get her arrested, but because the truth would take her away from him.

HALF AN HOUR LATER, Lisa had awakened. She was still in her pajamas and finishing up her breakfast while Booth stacked the dishes in the dishwasher. Kathleen lifted the baby from the high chair and put her on the floor, where she promptly used the cabinet handles to pull herself to her feet. She turned back and grinned impishly at Kathleen.

"Next thing we know, sweet pea, you'll be walking."

Booth groaned. "Not yet. I'm not ready. She just started these trips around the furniture a few days ago."

"She's growing quickly and getting more independent."

"And noisier."

At that moment Lisa pulled out a pile of pan lids from a kitchen drawer and dropped them on the floor. She clanged two together. Kathleen handed her a plastic spoon and demonstrated how to hit the lids. In a matter of seconds, Lisa was happily banging with the spoon.

"You're a big help," Booth said, wincing.

"Spoons and lids are part of being a kid."

Booth leaned against the counter, his eyes warm as he watched his daughter. "She is incredible, isn't she?"

"Absolutely. You've done a wonderful job with her."

"She hasn't been this happy in days." He looked at Kathleen. "Do you think she knows she doesn't have a mother?"

Kathleen caught his gaze on her; it was one of both longing and vulnerability. "She has you, Booth. And she adores you. Plus she has a wonderful extended family—your mom and sister and others who love her."

"Yeah, but it's not the same."

Kathleen glanced down at the very contented

baby, at the same time appreciating the importance of a family with two parents. Lisa crawled over to her and pulled herself up beside her chair, then laid her head in Kathleen's lap.

Tears sprang into Kathleen's eyes as she stroked the baby's curls. This was the kind of image she'd fantasized about when she and Steve were trying to have a baby. How ironic that this child should inspire in her such a fullness of maternal love at a time when she couldn't embrace it and treasure it.

"Oh, Lisa, I wish I had—" She cut herself off, realizing almost too late that with a few words she would reveal too much.

"Kathleen?"

"Please don't ask me, Booth."

"It wasn't going to be a question. Just an observation."

"I shouldn't have said anything."

"You wish you had a baby of your own."

She nodded. "But not just to have a child. To have a child in a happy and stable family."

"With two parents who love and honor each other," he said softly.

"Yes."

Their gazes collided and neither spoke. The moment seemed fraught with her old failures now fading beneath the onslaught of new possibilities. Kathleen felt as if her heart had soared into some new unexplored space—a place where she belonged, a place without regret or fear or deceit.

Booth cupped her chin and tipped her head up. "There's that elusive look again."

"I'm sorry. It's just that visualizing ideals is hard when my life is so complicated."

"Maybe I could help if you told me what the complications are."

"They're my problems. I have to figure them out for myself. Please just leave it at that."

He pulled back, his eyes shuttering. Lisa had gone back to banging with the spoon. Kathleen, glad for the diversion, stood and began to put away the lids. "Your daddy wants to go to sleep. How about we find a quiet game?"

"Kathleen?"

Warily, she glanced at him.

"This isn't finished."

She knew he was right, simply because she'd only added to his interest. Somewhere there had to be an end to this. She couldn't hide out for the rest of her life. How could she ever have a life that had any meaning?

Gail would be back in a few days. She'd talk to her, and between the two of them, surely she could find a way out.

Now, she scooped Lisa up and nuzzled her neck, making her giggle. "You're stinky."

Booth grimaced.

Glad for the diversion, she said, "I'll take care of her. Why don't you go and get some sleep.

"You know, sweet pea, I think a bath would be

in order. Then we can read one of the storybooks and take a nice morning nap.''

"Good luck," Booth mumbled. "She's refused to take a morning nap for the past week."

Kathleen tickled her and she giggled. "Your daddy's going to take his nap, and you are going to be a quiet little kitty cat, aren't you?"

Lisa's eyes widened and she pointed to the door.

In a serious voice, Kathleen said, "Bosco is out on a mouse hunt. Maybe later we can find him and you can pet him."

Lisa's grin became a giggle, and Kathleen hugged her close.

Booth touched her back. "You know where everything is? Clothes, diapers, all that stuff?"

"We'll find everything. You go on to bed."

He leaned down and kissed the side of her neck. "Thanks, babe."

Kathleen shuddered, but Booth sauntered away, going into his bedroom and nudging the door almost closed.

"Okay, Miss Lisa Rawlings. Let's get you cleaned up and sweet smelling."

By ten o'clock, Lisa had been bathed and read a farm story about a pig and a rooster, and she was curled up, sound asleep with her blanket and a stuffed toy. Kathleen had straightened up the living room, fielded two phone calls and written down messages—one from the police chief confirming that Booth's request for Saturday night off was covered, and one from Mavis.

"How nice to talk to you, Kathleen. Has Booth recruited you into full-time baby-sitting? He mentioned to his mother that he would love to have you stay with Lisa."

She laughed. "I think Lisa's charmed her way into my life permanently."

"Well, I can't think of a better person to charm. She needs some consistent care."

"We do seem to get along well."

"Booth could do with some care, too," Mavis said with a coyness Kathleen found amusing.

"Why, Mavis, is this a matchmaking attempt?"

"Yes."

Kathleen laughed again, wishing things were as simple as Mavis made them sound. "At least you're honest."

"And hopeful. Have you met Booth's family? I told Janet—that's Booth's mother—about you."

"No, I haven't met them."

"Well, what is that man waiting for?"

"Booth and I aren't serious in the way that would mean family introductions."

"Balderdash. You're friends. Lisa adores you. And Booth's family will, too. Although meeting his father will have to wait. Janet got her week on the Cape, but Doug bargained for his own trip to Alaska. He's wanted to go fishing up there for years, so he and four of his friends left yesterday. Frankly, given his timing, I think he wanted to avoid my annual cookout on Saturday. Has Booth mentioned it? No? I don't know what's wrong with that man's manners, but I'd love to have you come.''

"It's not Booth's fault, Mavis. I've been busy, and to be honest, we haven't seen a lot of each other.''

"You're not letting that kiss the neighbors saw bother you, are you?''

"You know about that?''

"Now don't go getting upset. Talk spreads pretty quickly here in Crosby, like it does in most small towns. There're a lot of us who think it's about time Booth found someone to care for.''

Gossip, Kathleen thought with a shudder. Just what she didn't need.

Mavis rattled on. "Booth needs to have a woman in his life. Angie isn't coming back, no matter how much Gladys Hucklebee would like to think so. She's been very critical of Booth, and frankly, I think it's about time the old crone was put in her place.''

"I met Gladys at the grocery store when I was with Booth and Lisa.''

"Oh, dear, and she wasn't pleasant, was she?''

"I think maintaining Angie's memory is important to her, and anyone who takes Booth's attention from that is a problem.''

"What a diplomat you are. I imagine Booth wasn't quite as kind.''

"Uh, no.''

They chatted awhile longer, and Mavis again issued the Saturday invitation. "Please come.''

Why not? Kathleen thought. What could it hurt? One picnic with people she liked. She was tired of hiding. More than six weeks had passed and no one had approached her, and thanks to Booth, she knew that "Kathleen Yardley" wasn't on any nationwide list of wanted criminals. Yes, she was going to do this just because she was hungry for something normal and fun.

"I'd love to come, Mavis."

"Wonderful. Give that precious Lisa a kiss for me and tell Booth to call me when he has a chance."

Kathleen hung up the phone, fixed herself a glass of iced tea and was about to curl up with her new sheet music when she heard a crash in Booth's room.

She walked quickly to the door. It was ajar, and she peered inside. The room was very dark, and icy cold from the air conditioning.

She stood for a moment considering whether she should go in to see what had happened. As her eyes adjusted to the darkness, she took a deep breath and eased in quietly. Whatever had crashed evidently hadn't awakened Booth. She took two steps sideways when she stumbled on the fallen item—a small table lamp.

Picking it up and setting it aside, she noted Booth sprawled across the bed with a sheet tossed across his hips. Obviously he was naked. She moved to the window where the air conditioner hummed on the left side of the bed. She tiptoed, being careful not to trip on the spread dragging on the floor. Just as she passed Booth's shoulder and reached to turn the doorknob, he grabbed her.

"Oh!" She grappled for balance, but she landed on her back across his warm, rumpled sheets.

One of his hands tangled in her hair, and his leg across hers prevented her from moving. Aroused and making no secret of it, he loomed above her, his eyes amused.

"You tricked me."

"It's the old ploy to get women into my bedroom. Knock something over and they come running. Works every time."

"If I hadn't heard the crash—"

"Let me guess. You thought I fell out of bed?"

"No. I just thought…" What had she been thinking? Had she been curious? Wanting to see his bedroom? Wanting to see him? Wanting this? All of the above, and more. He intrigued and fascinated her; he made her too aware of her loneliness and too mindful of how he had insinuated himself into her life. Not by choice or even by chance, but by the simple, natural attraction between a man and a woman.

He brushed his mouth across hers, lightly and softly, like the fanning of feathers. "Be honest with me, babe. At least about this be honest."

"I feel as if I was asking for it."

"And why shouldn't you?"

"Because I'm not usually that forward and obvious."

"I like you with your guard down."

She slipped her arms around him. "Yes, I imagine you do."

His hand fell to her breast, working open the buttons of her cotton blouse. Her bra was old and plain, not lacy and sexy, and she suddenly wished it were more provocative. But he murmured how pretty she was, then opened the front clasp with a dexterity that surprised her. He palmed her nipple, and instinctively she pressed forward into his hand, her breath coming in a pant.

Booth moved, and she felt his hardness against her lower belly. She touched his chest, sliding her hand across the mat of hair that felt rich and dark and sexy. When he lifted her and rolled beneath her to pull her up so that she straddled him, she went willingly.

"You have too many clothes on," he murmured as he dispensed with her blouse and bra. She sat above him, her knees hugging his sides, wriggling to relieve the pressure that surrounded her lower body.

"I think we put this off for too long," he said, opening her shorts and sliding his hands around her to tug them down.

"Booth, this is crazy. Sex is too serious to just do it."

"Too serious not to do it," he replied. He slipped his hand between her legs, pressed lightly, and Kathleen, to her total horror, felt a surge of arousal that made her hot and wet. "Nice."

She covered her face with her hands. "This isn't like me."

"I'm honored."

"You must think—"

"That you're beautiful, lonely, and sexy without knowing it, and best of all, you just might be attracted to me." Booth held his hand against her, pressing, releasing, and Kathleen felt her response build.

She tried to pull away, but he held her fast.

"Easy. Easy."

"I can't believe this is happening to me."

"That you want to have sex with me? Why?"

"Because it's been so long since I've felt anything like this."

"No one since your divorce?"

"No."

"Your husband must have been a real bastard."

She didn't want Steve here—neither the memory of him nor any sexual comparisons to him. She placed her hands on Booth's cheeks, her thumbs coaxing at the corners of his mouth. She leaned forward, her breasts brushing his chest, and then she kissed him.

He groaned, pressing his palm more urgently against her, finding the most sensitive area, and Kathleen couldn't suppress her shudder. His mouth absorbed hers, their tongues tangling, tastes mingling, and deep inside her body sparkled and bubbled.

Booth felt it, too, for he turned her onto her back,

took off the rest of her clothes and settled between her thighs. His hardness found her softness and slid in deep.

"God, you feel good. You fit around me like you've belonged there for a thousand years."

Kathleen sighed. "You're too good at this."

"And you're too desirable. Lousy foreplay on my part, babe."

"Next time," she murmured, not even thinking about the ramifications of her words. "Right now, this feels too good to stop."

His mouth covered hers as they began the ancient rhythm that increased and took them higher and higher.

"Booth! Booth, where are you? The door was unlocked."

Kathleen froze.

Booth swore.

"Booth?" the female voice came again, closer this time.

Kathleen struggled to get out from beneath him. He rolled onto his side, holding her still, putting his mouth against her ear. "It's my mother."

"Oh, my God!"

"Take it easy."

"Easy? Easy!"

He clamped his hand over her mouth. "Shh…"

He threw the sheet over her, rose from the bed and found his jeans. He had just pulled them on when the door opened and the light from the hallway poured in.

"Oh dear." The older woman looked genuinely embarrassed.

Booth moved forward, blocking Kathleen's view. She'd pulled the sheet all the way to her chin, and if she could have turned to ashes, she would have done that.

"Mom, why don't you wait in the living room? We'll be right out."

"Oh, honey, I'm so sorry." Her voice was shaky. "I called you, and when I peeked in and Lisa was asleep and there was no one around and..."

Booth walked over to her. "I hear Lisa now. Why don't you go and get her up? Kathleen and I will be right out."

"Your father will be furious with me. He's always telling me I walk around with blinders on."

"He's in Alaska, remember? He isn't going to know unless you call and tell him." Booth eased her out the door.

"Even so, I should never have just barged into your bedroom."

"It's okay. It wasn't deliberate, I know."

"Maybe I should leave and come back another time."

"I don't want you to leave. Just give us a few minutes, okay?"

"Please tell your friend how sorry I am."

"I will."

He pushed the door closed, and not until he did so did Kathleen begin to breathe again. Her head was pounding, her ears ringing. She searched around for her clothes. If only he had a back door.

In two steps, Booth was on the bed and tugging her into his arms.

She burrowed there for warmth, unable to stop shaking.

"This isn't the end of the world, babe."

"I've never been so embarrassed, and the worst is yet to come. I mean, what on earth can I say to her?"

"Why don't we just accept that everyone's embarrassed and start over?"

"You're acting as if it didn't bother you."

"Actually, I think it's kind of funny."

Her head popped up. "Funny!"

"My mother is always so cool and so together, that to see her so flustered sort of reassured me that some things do throw her off stride." He grinned. "Besides, she's going to love you. Lisa does, and my mother believes that babies have the best instincts about people."

"Are you crazy? It's not like she caught us having coffee and muffins."

"She didn't see anything."

"She didn't have to, for God's sake. And I have only myself to blame— No, dammit, this is your fault. You knocked that lamp over...."

"Look, it's just a set of bad circumstances, not the end of the world. People do have sex. It could have been worse."

"I can't imagine any way it would have been worse."

"We could have been on the kitchen table."

She shuddered, considering the possibility. Good grief, what was she doing? Rationalizing her actions according to the amount of embarrassment she felt?

"I can't go out there, Booth."

"Of course you can." He pulled her close, leaned down and kissed her breasts, murmuring. "She won't stay long, and after she leaves we can finish what we started."

"Are you listening to yourself?" she snapped, scrambling off the bed and turning the light on. "Maybe it's no big deal to you, but it's a major big deal to me."

She rustled around gathering her clothes, but not finding her bra. Booth stretched out, his head propped on one hand, and watched her.

"Well, where is it?"

"What?"

"My bra."

"You don't need it."

She glared at him so hard, he actually winced. "Okay, okay." He pulled it out from under the covers and handed it to her. She snatched it and turned her back to put it on.

When she was dressed, she peered into the bedroom mirror. Her lips were bruised, her cheeks stained with color, and to her horror she felt frustrated by the interruption. That infuriated her. In all her years of marriage to Steve, sex had always been just okay. She'd never missed it when they went days without it, and when on occasion Steve couldn't perform, she'd never felt deprived. Sometimes she was just relieved when he turned away and refused to talk to about it.

But now, here with Booth, she felt itchy and shaky and out of control.

Booth took her hand. "Come on, I promise this won't be as bad as you think."

"What am I going to say to her?"

"How about that you're going to marry me?"

CHAPTER NINE

WHEN KATHLEEN STEPPED out of the bedroom, Booth was right behind her, his words still resounding in her mind.

Marry him? Sure. The perfect solution when caught having sex. It was ridiculous, impossible and totally out of the question. And even if they'd been engaged, even if his mother had been her new best friend, she would never have wanted to be caught in such a humiliating position. Of course, he hadn't been serious, anyway.

"Sounds like Mom's still in with Lisa," Booth said.

Kathleen stuffed her balled hands into her shorts pockets. "I'll wait here."

Fleeing held great appeal but would have changed nothing. Besides, she and Booth were adults. This might be unpleasant, but Kathleen's mother had taught her years ago that discomfort often prepared the way for insight and wisdom. How that applied here, she wasn't sure, but she certainly felt the discomfort.

Still, when she compared this problem to her other difficulties, it paled. She and Booth had been caught in a private act, not an illegal one, she reminded herself. Mortification was perfectly normal. And the more Kathleen thought about it, the more she realized that this had to be even worse for Booth's mother.

Kathleen recalled being a let-me-die-on-the-spot intruder when she was about eight years old. She'd walked into the barn and caught her brother Clarke and another boy with their clothes mussed and their arms around each other. She'd been confused and embarrassed. Clarke had yelled at her, but later had begged her not to tell. As if she would. She knew her father would have beaten Clarke badly, and she would have felt responsible for tattling.

Kathleen glanced up and saw Janet Rawlings enter the living room, carrying Lisa. Booth's mother was tall and slender with a smooth, unlined face that would have been patrician if not for a slight overbite. She wore a green seersucker suit with a short-sleeved jacket, and Lisa was fascinated by her chunky white necklace. Booth stepped around his mother to stand with Kathleen.

"I'll handle this, babe," he whispered. "It was my fault."

"I could have said no and left the room." Kathleen wasn't about to be a wuss about this. She took a deep breath and seized the initiative before Booth could protest. Extending her hand to Booth's mother, she said, "I'm Kathleen Yardley. You have a beautiful granddaughter, Mrs. Rawlings, and a persuasive son, because I really wanted to hide in the bedroom."

Janet Rawlings looked immensely relieved that Kathleen had brought the subject into the open. "I wanted to run out of the apartment and back to my car. Please forgive me for causing what has to be one of the most horrifying moments in our lives."

"Worse than that time I drove the car into the lake?" Booth asked, smoothly diverting their attention. He took Lisa, who was trying to chew her grandmother's beads, and put her onto the floor. The baby headed straight for the kitchen. In a few seconds she was banging the pan lids.

Janet grimaced at Booth. "Raising you was one horrifying moment after another."

"I can just imagine," Kathleen said.

"Oh, Kathleen, I was so glad when Darlene turned out to be a girl. Another Booth— Well, I'm not sure I would have survived."

"Darlene was no angel," Booth said defensively.

"Darling, compared to you, she had a halo," his mother replied. "I got gray very young."

Booth chuckled and Kathleen laughed, and the earlier awkwardness slipped away.

The maternal pride in her glance at Booth revealed to Kathleen that all Janet's worst moments had been worth it.

"She had no vision when it came to fast cars and how guys like to drive them," Booth said.

"It will be interesting to see your expansive 'vision' when Lisa's a teenager," Kathleen said.

Janet laughed. "If he hasn't scared away every boy who finds her attractive."

As if on cue, Lisa appeared. Using a nearby chair, she pulled herself to a standing position, teetered for a moment and then took a single step all on her own.

"Is this her first step?" Janet asked, looking at Booth. At his nod, she clapped her hands in excitement. "Oh, Booth, get your camera. Kathleen, isn't this exciting?" She sailed over to Lisa, who promptly took two more steps, then teetered just as Booth snapped two shots. Janet scooped her up and hugged her close. Lisa, however, was having nothing to do with being held. She'd walked on her own, and she obviously wanted to try out this new-found accomplishment.

The three of them watched as she teetered and tottered and mastered the distance between the chair and the couch. Each time, they all clapped, and Lisa giggled and clapped for herself.

"Just wait until Mavis sees you, you little imp." Janet glanced at Booth. "You did invite Kathleen to Mavis's picnic, didn't you?"

"Mavis invited me," Kathleen said, pleased to be part of this special time with Lisa.

Booth scowled. "When?"

"Before I went into— Uh, she called earlier to talk to you."

"Did she say about what?"

"She was vague. Something about a suggestion of yours that was passed on to the right party and that he would call you."

"Sounds mysterious," Janet said.

"I do admit to being curious," Kathleen added. Booth remained silent.

"Guess that means he isn't telling," Janet said to Kathleen, clearly indicating this wasn't new.

"Hey, what can I say. I'm good at keeping secrets."

The next half hour was spent exchanging stories about Booth, with Kathleen being deliberately vague about her own past. About her music, though, she was enthusiastically open. And when she mentioned trying to find an apartment large enough for her piano, Janet asked, "You're moving?"

"Yes, my stay with Gail was never intended to be permanent. She's been in Missouri with her family. She called and said she was bringing her sister back with her for a visit. The apartment will be crowded for the three of us, so I decided to find a place of my own."

"One big enough for your piano," Janet mused. "Booth mentioned that you play beautifully."

"You did?" Kathleen asked, pleased by the compliment and somewhat surprised that Booth had discussed her with his mother.

He shrugged. "It was one of those times when Mom and I were trying to get Lisa quieted down. I mentioned that if you were home, you could put Lisa to sleep with your playing."

"Thanks a lot—I think."

"You know what I mean," Booth grumbled.

Kathleen grinned at him. While they'd been talking, Janet had been thoughtfully silent.

Finally she looked at Kathleen, her face animated. "I might have just the place. Booth, you remember the Stokers? They have that lovely carriage house that overlooks the lake."

Booth rolled his eyes, saying to Kathleen, "Sophie Stoker sings opera when no one wants to listen and collects bad splashy canvases from struggling art-school dropouts."

"Booth, really, that's unkind."

Booth shrugged. "She's very naive, Mom, and she has too much money to spend on artists who should be working for a living instead of conning her into supporting them."

"She's kind and generous. And I'm only too happy to remind you that it was Sophie who helped the police catch those art thieves last year."

"Can't argue with that, but she's still too naive for a woman her age."

Kathleen intervened. "I think she sounds fascinating. You say she has a carriage house, Mrs. Rawlings? It must be expensive."

"Please call me Janet. Actually, it's not that costly. She and her husband, Percy, are rather precise about tenants. They are both very much into the arts and spend a lot of time visiting out-of-the-way museums looking for undiscovered artists. They don't advertise the carriage house because they're particular about who lives there. It's been empty for a year or so, and when the Stokers do rent, it's always a referral. Their goal is to provide nice surroundings for someone in a creative field without charging an outrageous rent. Sort of like a scholarship in progress. A pianist would be perfect.''

She glanced at Booth, who was stretched out on the floor, with Lisa crawling over him. "Why didn't you ever mention Sophie's generosity to Kathleen? Then again, why didn't you tell me she was looking for a place to live?"

"Actually, I haven't discussed moving with Booth," Kathleen interjected.

But Janet continued, obviously excited by her own suggestion. "Sophie leaves me in charge when she's away, and if I'm lucky enough to find a candidate, she's given me authority to rent the place. Booth? You knew all that."

"She could stay here," he said blandly.

Kathleen stared at him. "That's the first time you've mentioned that." Marriage and now this? Why?

"She can't live here, Booth."

Booth gave his mother a long, indulgent look. "Mom, I'm a big boy, and while I don't want to upset you, who lives here is my business."

Janet said to Kathleen, "He thinks I fuss and treat him too much like a kid."

"You do. I love you and respect you, but I run my own life."

"I didn't mean she can't live here because you're not married, I meant because you have no room for her piano."

Kathleen nodded. "She's right."

"Let me get this straight." Booth got to his feet, a frown darkening his eyes. "You would have moved in here with me if I had room for a piano you don't even have?"

"It's in storage, but it's one criterion for deciding where I want to live."

Kathleen knew she was being pulled along like one of Lisa's toys on a string, and she would no doubt regret this later, but for the moment Booth's suggestion enticed and intrigued her. "Then again, maybe I *could* stay here for a few days. It would help Gail out."

"Plus the carriage house will need to be made ready. Since it's been empty for some time, it will need airing out and cleaning."

Booth wasn't listening to his mother. To Kathleen he said, "Why in hell didn't you say something?"

"You never asked me," Kathleen said primly. "I'm hardly going to walk in and say, 'Do you want me to come and live with you?'"

"So if I'd been able to read your mind and had asked, you would have said yes?"

Thank God you can't read my mind. "It certainly would have been an option."

"'Would' have been?"

"On a temporary basis, yes. But now, with this suggestion of your mother's, I want to take a look at the carriage house. It sounds ideal."

"I think I just lost out," Booth grumbled. "And I didn't even know I was in contention."

He was right, and her change of heart was abrupt, but she was weary of her circumstances and felt more secure than she had in weeks—especially since Booth hadn't found her on the national criminal computer. And her feelings for Booth had found a steadier footing. She liked him, she desired him, and as for staying with him for a few days, well, she simply wanted to. "I've decided it's time I started living my life my way."

"Amen."

"Well," Janet said, "this sounds like some crucial decisions have been made. And you'll love the carriage house, Kathleen." She glanced at her watch. "How about going over now? That is, if you don't have any other plans."

"We do," Booth said.

Kathleen knew exactly what he was talking about—finishing what they had started. But this was an opportunity that might not come again. Kathleen didn't want to miss it. "Booth, this won't take long."

"It's already taken too long."

"You could come with us," Janet said.

He sighed. "No, thanks. I've got some calls I have to make."

Kathleen got her canvas handbag, made a stop in the bathroom and returned a few minutes later. Lisa had found a magazine and was happily tearing pages. Booth had poured himself a mug of coffee; Janet was on the phone.

Booth stepped close to her, his voice low.

"You're not going to change your mind? You are going to stay here for a few days?"

"I won't change my mind. But I'm curious why in the bedroom you were going to marry me, and out here I just got a live-in invitation."

"Living together isn't as scary."

Kathleen stared at him for a few moments. What would he think if he knew the truth?

"I might have surprised you," she ventured, watching him closely.

"Yeah, you might have. You've been doing that since I met you."

She laid her hands on his chest, feeling the heat beneath his T-shirt. "Living with you, even for a short time, is pretty serious stuff."

"Never asked a woman to do that."

"Not Angie?"

"Nope. Her parents would have been horrified. Believe me, it's tough being in love with the town angel."

"She must have been wonderful."

"She was. But she was also human. It's just that no one but me seemed to know it."

"Well, after finding me in bed with you, your mother certainly knows that I'm nothing like Angie."

"She likes you. Trust me, she never would have mentioned Sophie's place if she didn't. My guess is that catching us in bed made you very human, and by coming out and facing her—well, she was impressed."

"In the meantime—"

"You're going to sleep with me."

"You could be a gentleman and take the couch."

"Not a chance."

"We might not be any good together."

"We're gonna burn the sheets, babe, and you know it."

Kathleen shuddered, too aware of the return of that clawing need deep within her. She'd never been so conscious of her sexuality, and with Booth, that had become something she both welcomed and feared.

Janet hung up the phone. "I called Sophie's just to make sure the place was indeed still available. Lotti, Sophie's secretary, said to come ahead. Oh, Booth, I almost forgot why I stopped by here in the first place. I had a call from Gladys. She's upset with you, thinks you're not doing right by Lisa and wants to talk to me."

"Tell me you said no," Booth said with a scowl.

"I told her to stop over on Tuesday afternoon. She's lonely, and she adored Angie."

"She's a nutcase." Booth stalked across the room and back again. "I don't want her in your house, Mom. Kathleen and I ran into her, and she was weird and hostile. There's nothing she can say to you that I want to hear."

"But what excuse can I give her? I can't just say don't come over."

"How 'bout saying *I* said she couldn't come over."

"It just seems so cruel and heartless," Janet insisted, fretting. "She's all alone, and you know how Angie took her under her wing."

"Angie never learned how to say 'Get lost.'"

Janet sighed. "I can't argue with that. She was just too good to everyone."

Kathleen began to feel uneasy. Compared to Angie she was a reckless intruder filled with dangerous secrets.

"Let me handle her, Mom."

"If you're sure. And promise me you won't be nasty and overbearing."

"I'll be clear and to the point."

Janet agreed, kissed Lisa, who had hauled in a dozen of her lids and was happily piling them one on top of another, and said to Kathleen, "Ready?"

"All set."

Booth stopped her before she could get out the door. "She'll be right with you, Mom."

Janet went on down the stairs, and Booth slid his hands into Kathleen's hair.

"You messed up my plans, babe."

She leaned back against the wall, her forefinger sliding along his chest. "In the past hour, you seem to have taken over my life."

"I want you."

"It's all going so fast, Booth. You're not giving me time to think."

"You could have said no to the carriage house."

"I should have said no to you."

"You won't." His hands slid down her arms,

came back up to cup her breasts, his mouth opening over hers as if he'd been born to kiss her. "You won't because you can't."

He was right. She wanted this. She wanted him and their plunge into a passion that promised breathtaking fulfillment.

"You're too good at this, Booth."

"Damn right."

Then he kissed her again, deeper, his hand moving down her body to settle at the apex of her thighs. Kathleen felt as if she'd been blown in a thousand different directions, every one an exquisite point of new pleasure. She floated in a realm of desire she'd never even known she could experience. His mouth, his tongue, his taste were wild sensations, raw and primal and hot.

A tremendous clatter made them spring apart. The tower of lids that Lisa had been building had fallen and scattered. She started to cry; Booth sighed.

"Later, babe." He released her, went over to the baby, reached down and swung her up into his arms. "Shh, it's okay. We'll build them again." He knelt on the floor and showed her how to stack one on top of the other.

Kathleen, her breath choppy, her heart hammering, grabbed her handbag. Taking advantage of the distraction, she slipped out the door.

THE CARRIAGE HOUSE rose from behind a profusion of tangled wisteria and huge bushes of pink hydrangeas. Its windows sparkled in the late-morning sun. Fashioned of brick, it was a square single-story with a shale roof that gave the structure substance and grandeur. Built at the end of the nineteenth century during the golden era of wealth and privilege, it had once housed horse-drawn carriages.

Still in place were the huge doors that slid on brass rails and were dressed with heavy brass hardware. The living quarters had been restored to blend with the original, but the doors now opened at the touch of a button to reveal a spacious room with hardwood floors.

Kathleen could already picture her piano against this backdrop of lush summer light and color. Other rooms opened off the larger one—two bedrooms, a modern kitchen with every convenience, including a stack washer and dryer, a bathroom with a tiled walk-in shower and plenty of light from a glass door that opened onto a private garden.

Kathleen was glassy-eyed by the time they returned to the immense living room.

"This is an incredible place."

"It is."

"I know you spoke of Sophie's generosity, but honestly, Janet, as much as I'd love living here, I know I can't afford it."

"Will your piano fit?"

"Perfectly."

"And Lisa would love the garden."

Kathleen had no trouble envisioning the toddler

picking flowers and walking in the grass. "Yes, she would."

Janet eyed her the way one woman connects with another. "Booth has spoken of you a few times when he's stopped by the house, and of course Mavis mentioned your late-night rescue of Lisa."

"I'm just glad I heard her," Kathleen said, curious about what Booth might have told his family. "I understand his father is in Alaska."

Janet rolled her eyes. "It's a male thing, or so Doug told me. He and three of his friends flew up there, rented a cabin where I'm sure no one will bathe or shave and they'll spend the two weeks subsisting on unhealthy food and too much beer. They asked Booth to go, but he had a couple of investigations he didn't want to leave. And the plans were made a month ago, when Booth was still trying to find a permanent sitter for Lisa."

Kathleen's admiration of Booth climbed. There was something endearing about a man who put his child before two weeks with the guys.

"I know this isn't my business," Janet said, "but I had the sense that you really didn't want to move in with Booth for an extended time. Am I correct?"

Kathleen turned to watch the wedges of sunshine that glimmered through the trees. The question caught her off guard. "Booth can be very persuasive. But, no, I don't want to simply live with him. I like to think that we're friends—maybe more than that. I find him fascinating and understanding, and I like his 'Protect your own' attitude." She smiled.

"And he's very determined when he wants something."

"Yes, he is that," Janet murmured.

"I do adore Lisa, and I've loved taking care of her on occasion, but I don't think it's good for her to become too attached to me. Right now my life is complicated, and trying to plan isn't always easy."

Janet was staring at her oddly, and Kathleen leaned down to brush some grass off her sneaker. She was rambling and she knew it; she also knew that the burden she was carrying was becoming unbearable. She wanted to be free, to be totally truthful with Booth, with his mother—with all the kind people she'd met in Crosby. She needed to allow herself a life without fear of the consequences.

"Then perhaps the carriage house is a good place to be while you straighten out all those complications."

Oh, God, if only it were as easy as finding a new place to live. She glanced up at the sky. "Crescendo blue"—a color her mother always said was the applause of nature. Her best, her most vibrant, a blue given to mortals to remember on the cloudiest of days.

Kathleen looked back at Janet. "It is a serene and beautiful place. But the rent— Janet, I'm afraid—"

Janet named a ridiculously low figure.

"That's less than Gail is paying!"

"I told you that Sophie's motive is altruistic, not financial."

"I have to be honest, Janet. At the moment, I'm working in a restaurant and not spending as much time on my music as I'd like. I feel as if I'm not really as serious as Sophie would expect."

"Well, of course you're not," Janet replied. "You don't have your piano. Once that's here, you'll be right back in the world of music."

Kathleen felt her eyes fill. It was all so incredible, and looking around, she wondered how she could have been so blessed. It was like discovering a place that had previously only existed for other people. Running from a frame-up for Steve's murder seemed like something from a time warp. Here, she felt safe—safer than ever before. At last she could send for her piano, which had been in storage since last winter, when Steve had lost his temper and smashed the music stand.

She'd waited until he'd gone to work to call the storage company to come and get it. Later, she realized that at some level she'd worried more about her piano than about herself. But her music was all she had that was entirely hers—a legacy from her mother—and she wasn't going to let Steve destroy it.

When he asked what she had done with the piano, she said she'd given it away. For that, he'd called her stupid for not selling it, but she'd simply nodded. What he said didn't matter, and how he'd felt about her was of little consequence. She'd already been making plans to leave him, file for divorce and start a new life in a new place. Then she'd have her beloved piano shipped to her. His unexpected death—the murder—and her flight to save herself had changed her plans and her life.

Now was the time for a new life. And this was the place. Because no one knew where the piano was stored, she felt safe in sending for it. As they toured the grounds, Janet urged her to call that afternoon about having the piano delivered. Sophie would be home the following week and the instrument should be on the premises.

Later, back at her apartment, Kathleen called the storage company in Casper. Yes, they would ship it in the next few days. The storage and shipping were payable C.O.D. And when the clerk told her the cost, she was thankful she hadn't spent the money she'd gotten from selling her car in Pennsylvania.

When she got off the phone, she nodded to Janet. "It will be here next week."

"Wonderful." Janet stood staring out the front window. "I wonder if I should mention this to Booth."

Kathleen stood. "Mention what? The piano?"

"No, no. That car across the street."

"What car?"

"The big fancy one. I saw it earlier in the week when I stopped by to see Booth, and now again today."

Kathleen studied the car, trying to quell her rising

panic. "It doesn't look suspicious," she said, unsure whom she was trying to convince.

"It looks out of place. This isn't a fancy-car neighborhood."

"Perhaps someone's visiting a friend."

"Perhaps." Janet shrugged. "Nevertheless, it doesn't hurt to have these things checked out. There are children playing here, and I know a lot of those awful drug dealers drive big fancy cars. Booth would want to know about anything that looks suspicious."

Suspicious. Was it possible she'd been found? Or was she leaping to a huge paranoid conclusion?

Janet promised to call the following day with a time to get the keys for the carriage house and sign the lease.

After Janet left, Kathleen stood at the window for a long time. There was something about that car. Something...

She quickly left the apartment and walked down the steps, making her way toward the cream-colored car with tinted windows. She passed by it, turned and passed by it again. She glanced at the license plate, her heart praying it wouldn't be a Wyoming tag.

It wasn't, but it was just as bad. Georgia plates, and suddenly she knew why she was uneasy. The vehicle looked just like the one that belonged to the Southern woman who had admired Lisa while Kathleen had been waiting for Booth at the grocery store.

Kathleen folded her arms against her body, feeling icy and numb. She desperately wanted to believe it was a coincidence. But what if it wasn't? If the woman was connected with the murder, or was an undercover cop sent to hunt her down, then what was she waiting for? Why hadn't she made a move?

The questions knotted inside Kathleen. Just when she'd felt safe. Just when she'd begun to believe that maybe she could have her life back. Just when she'd wanted to be with Booth, it looked as if she had to run again.

She turned to go back to the apartment and crashed right into Booth.

CHAPTER TEN

HE GRIPPED HER SHOULDERS, steadying her. "What's wrong? You're pale and shaky."

Think. Think. "Your mom saw the car and was worried that it didn't belong around here," she said, the words rushing out, sounding lame and forced.

"So you came out here to ask the bad guys what they were doing polluting the neighborhood?"

"She was worried."

"I know. That's why she told me. That's why I came out to take a look." She felt his gaze boring into her. "But why did you?"

"I was curious."

"That was stupid."

She jerked back. "Don't call me stupid!"

For a second he looked puzzled by her reaction, then he drew her close again, his voice soft. "I didn't call you stupid, Kathleen. I said what you did was stupid. If you believed there was a problem with the car, you should have come to me."

But she wasn't ready to yield to his judgment. There'd been too many years of Steve telling her what to do, how to think, when to act. It had set her teeth on edge, and she was astonished by how quickly the same kind of irritation had surfaced now. ''Really. So you can be the cop to the rescue? The cop who gets all the bad guys and saves all the good guys?'' *Stop!* she urged herself. *Stop!* But the words still came. ''Did you bring your gun? Are you going to wave it around? Does that make you feel brave?''

He stared at her, his eyes flitting past her panic and assessing her hysteria. ''Babe, I want you to take a deep breath and relax. I'm not going to shoot anyone. All I'm going to do is take down some general info and the plate number. I'll have it run through NCIC. That's the nationwide computer system for finding fugitives, hot cars, people with outstanding warrants against them. If there's any illegal or criminal connection with the car, they'll have it. It'll probably come up clean. I'm just making sure.''

Kathleen's breath was lodged in her throat. ''I'm sorry.''

He stared at her as if trying see inside her. She braced herself for questions, but he released her, then reached into his pocket and took out a scrap of paper and a stubby pencil. He moved to the back of the car and jotted down the plate number, then moved to the driver's side and recorded the vehicle identification number that was near the windshield.

Kathleen stood very still, feeling snared by her own carelessness and having no idea where she should escape to. Living at Gail's had been so safe. She'd had a friend and ally who knew the circumstances, a place to live and a job. It had all been working out, all within her control, until Booth.

Now what? If she'd only maintained her distance. Her instincts had been telling her from the moment she'd learned he was a cop not to get involved. But no, she'd allowed herself to be charmed by him and by Lisa, to be seduced by her own inner longing for peace and comfort and love. More depressing was the realization that she would have to walk away, let him go and never see Lisa again. Kathleen hadn't realized that until Booth and Lisa, her soul had been slowly starving to death.

She now faced an impossible choice. If the plate number belonged to some criminal connected with Steve's murder, Booth would probe deeper. And once he started down that path, it wouldn't take him long to put the pieces together. Once he learned that Steve's wife was named Kathleen, and that she was a fugitive, it would be all over. On the other hand, if he ran it and nothing came up, it might only mean that the bad guys were too smart to possess or drive something that could so easily trip them up. Even the best-case scenario wouldn't end this now. Booth wasn't going to shrug and walk away. He would insist on knowing why she'd reacted, overreacted and God knows what else.

"Kathleen?" He was slipping the pencil and paper into his pocket.

Then again, if she could stall…

But how could she stop him from making a phone call? Eventually he would do what he intended. And if it turned out that the car and Steve's killer were connected, she was cooked. She had only one alternative. Prepare to leave quickly and silently.

Booth cupped her chin and lifted her face. "What is going on in that head of yours?"

Confusion. Terror. Desire. She licked her lips. "I want to go to bed with you."

She made herself stand firm. She wanted him, and she wanted him before he learned the truth and hated her. His astonishment at her admission made her smile, so rarely had she seen him rattled.

He narrowed his gaze. "A provocative answer to my question, that's for sure."

"That was the plan, wasn't it? You didn't forget?"

He didn't look pleased. "No, babe, I didn't forget."

But he didn't take her arm with any passionate urgency. He simply leaned against the car's front fender and watched her, obviously waiting for her to make the next move.

Kathleen shivered. She wasn't good at this. Seduction was foreign to her. She'd be humiliated if he laughed. Complicating things even more was a burst of shame for her behavior. It cheapened what they had and made her seem coarse and out of character. "I shouldn't have said what I did."

"It's not what you say, Kathleen. It's what you're trying so hard not to say that makes me uneasy."

"You're imagining things."

"I don't think so."

"Why is it all right for you to make sexy suggestions, but it's not okay for me?"

"Look, forget I said anything. Are we going inside or are we going to stand out here and fence all day?"

He took her arm and she pulled away, walking quickly to the apartment building and up the steps.

Booth caught up with her in the entrance.

"Come upstairs with me," he muttered.

"No."

A shadowed coolness dusted through the space between them. She wanted to press her cheek against him, she wanted to run away, and she wanted to fling herself into his arms and tell him everything.

Instead she leaned against the wall, watching Bosco slink out from under the stairs. She opened the door to Gail's apartment and the cat scooted inside.

"Kathleen, I admit you are the most evasive and fascinating woman I've ever met. That little performance out there was no aberration. Since you don't seem inclined to tell me what you're hiding, then maybe we can find some common ground in bed."

"Just like that? You give the order and I'm supposed to obey?"

"It's not an order." He sighed. "I thought you

wanted to have sex. You just asked me two minutes ago. Or were you lying?''

''No. I wasn't lying.''

He glanced at his watch. ''I'm on duty in a couple of hours.''

''I have to work tonight, too,'' she said, feeling a new sense of panic, a loss of control over everything. This wasn't the way she wanted their lovemaking to be. Suddenly it felt contrived—not romantic and exciting. ''Maybe we should wait.''

''Is that what you want?''

She scrubbed her hands down her face, her thoughts so chaotic, even she wasn't sure what she wanted. One thing, though, was true. ''I don't want you to hate me.''

To her distress she felt her eyes fill with tears.

Instantly Booth hauled her against him. ''Hate you? Kathleen, I don't know what's going on with you, but I do know I don't want to take advantage of you or seduce you into something that you aren't sure about.''

She rested her head against the wall, her eyes still moist, a smile curving her lips. ''You seduce me when you walk into a room.''

Booth caught his breath. ''I won't tell you what you make me want when you walk into a room.''

She tipped her head to the side, a fullness filling her heart. ''Tell me.''

''No way.''

She giggled. ''Is it dirty?''

He lifted an eyebrow. ''It's a guy thing.''

Before she could ask him to expand on that, he took a step down and caged her against the wall. She brought her arms up and curled her fingers around his forearms as if they would steady her. She turned her face and kissed the inside of his right elbow. Her tongue touched his skin.

"What do I make you want?" she murmured.

"Persistent, aren't you?"

"Yes."

"You make me hot, babe."

"I want you to want me so much you forget everything else."

"Done now. Done a week ago..." He leaned down, brushing her mouth, covering her lips with moisture, with the taste of him. "And I promise no unexpected interruptions."

"Lisa?"

"Mom has her. She wanted to show off her new walking ability to Darlene. I'll pick her up in the morning."

"I didn't see them leave."

"Because you were too busy checking out the car. Any minute, I expected you to pull out a fingerprint kit." As her eyes widened, he added, "You do have to admit, your curiosity was over the top."

"I didn't know it was a crime to be curious," she replied as he slung an arm around her neck and they walked up the stairs.

Inside his apartment, he closed and locked the door. Then he went to the phone.

"Booth?"

"This will just take a minute." He punched out some numbers.

"Can't it wait?"

He turned around, gave her one of those dark intense looks and covered the mouthpiece before saying, "Want me that bad, huh?"

In response, she opened the buttons on her blouse and let the garment slip off. Booth stared, and his expression delighted her.

"What?" he responded to whoever answered, but he was still staring at her. "This is Rawlings. I got a plate number I want checked out. Is Frank on duty? I'll wait." His gaze was on her as she moved slowly toward him. He leaned his shoulder against the wall, shifted his body, his expression lazy and languid.

Kathleen felt shy and wild at the same time. This was new ground for her, and she couldn't have imagined herself doing it just weeks ago. Booth had given her back the confidence she'd lost during her troubled marriage. Doing this with him was okay, and one of her walls of mistrust crumbled.

When she dispensed with her bra, he dropped his head forward and swore. "Hold on a minute," he said into the phone.

She was close now, and his breathing became heavy and ragged. "Come here," he said.

"Promise to touch me?" she asked, wondering where all this boldness was coming from, but loving it.

"You're killing me, babe."

He did indeed look as if he wasn't going to last much longer. She took the few steps needed to reach him, and was rewarded with his hand around her neck and his mouth covering hers. He hauled her closer, crushing her bared breasts against his shirt.

She pressed against the zipper of his jeans and was rewarded with the hot evidence of his arousal.

He anchored her close, his hand cupping her breast and palming her nipple into pebble hardness. She nibbled at his neck, brushing his chin and jaw with kisses.

"Yeah, Frank," he said, his voice husky and raw. "I got a Georgia plate I need you to check." He gave the series of numbers and letters and then swore in disgust. "Terrific. How long is it going to be down? Never mind. I'll handle it when I come in at five."

"What's wrong?"

"Computers are down. Some system screwup somewhere. They've been out for a couple of hours, which means a backlog."

"That's too bad," she said, feeling as if she'd escaped execution.

He lifted her off her feet and into his arms, lowering his head to kiss her. "I think we can find a way to fill up the time."

She slipped her arms around his neck. "You're very persuasive."

"You're very sexy," he murmured as they entered the shadowy bedroom. He kicked the door closed, crossed to the still-rumpled bed and lowered her to the floor. He plunged his hands into her hair, kissing her deeply. She clung to him, as if sustenance and hope could be found in their union.

He buried his face in her neck, his body shuddering against hers, his breathing ragged. "How do you do this to me, baby? How do you make me want you so much?"

His muffled questions caught her by surprise, showing a need and vulnerability that touched her heart with newfound joy. Never had she believed she possessed such erotic allure. Her whole body felt alive and throbbing as her mouth explored and possessed, hungry to give and to take.

With one blazing kiss, he had managed to evaporate her past and her problems into the dustbin of yesterday. She pressed against him, her breasts aching, her thighs restless, her body slick despite the chill in the room.

He pulled back, releasing her. "No...please don't leave me."

He bent and kissed her neck and breasts. "Not a chance." He sat on the bed and tugged her between his legs. His hands ran up her sides, then slid to her back, over her bottom, and urged her forward. His mouth brushed her breast with tantalizing slowness. Pleasure rolled through her womb, but when she tried to guide his mouth to her other breast, he pulled away.

"Booth, please..."

"Tell me what you want."

"I want you to kiss me and love me and make me belong to you."

Booth went still, certain every bone in his body had just dissolved. The afternoon light arced across the cream of her breasts, making the nipples appear a deep rose. He took each one into his mouth, laved it and then watched as the moisture changed the color to rich wine. He felt as if he were indulging in a feast of discoveries. He found a place on her side where she was ticklish, a small mole on her hip when he lowered her shorts. He found skimpy lacy panties that revealed more than they hid, and he found a pleasure point on the inside of her thigh that made her quiver.

He brushed his thumb across it, watching her, suddenly realizing she'd only just discovered the tiny spot's existence.

"What are you doing to me?" she asked when he touched it again and then lowered her shorts and panties.

"Tell me what you feel," he whispered, urging her close to the bed as he stretched out across the rumpled covers. He brushed his hand across the spot again and watched her shudder. "Kathleen?"

She clasped his hand and pulled it to her breast. "You make me light-headed and dizzy and achy and..."

He touched her between her thighs, pushing his fingers into the rich, damp heat.

Her hands fisted and unfisted, her body rising and lifting, hips coming forward, knees touching the edge of the mattress, her hand locked around his wrist. "Oh, Booth..." Her eyes were wide, the pupils dilated. "This has never happened.... I can't stop...can't wait...."

"Baby, let go. I want you to come."

She did, calling his name, over and over again in a way Booth knew he would never forget. This wasn't just sexual release; this was new and fresh and so mystifyingly innocent, Booth was at a loss for how to respond. He hadn't experienced or even wanted the responsibility of innocence in sex since the awkwardness of the teenage grope-and-hope. Yet here he was at thirty-six, fascinated, delighted and honored by something as basic as a woman climaxing for him.

Her expression was dazed, and for an impossible moment he wondered— No, it couldn't be. She'd been married; surely the bastard had given her pleasure.

Booth moved, bringing her forward. He laid her on the bed, absorbing her provocative sprawl. No inhibitions, no false modesty or guilty blushes. She bloomed before him like a dewy rose, soft and velvety and intoxicating.

Booth's own body felt as if someone had released a trip wire. He was imploding with lust and fire and a kind of scorching heaviness that shot through his groin. He was hard beyond arousal; he was hard even in his subconscious.

Getting his clothes off took herculean effort, and

still she lay sprawled before him, a veritable banquet just for him.

Finally he was naked, and she looked at him with such wonder, such desire, he felt heat stain his cheeks. She grazed her mouth along his thigh, and her fingers, like a delicate glove, curved around him and drew him to her.

He groaned. "Don't."

"I want to taste you."

"Kathleen." And before he could stop her, her lips kissed him and drew away; skimmed and retreated, feathered and kissed, and then, when he thought he could take no more, her mouth enveloped him.

Time stopped. Desire vibrated hot and raw and frenetic. Control abandoned him. There was only Kathleen and her mouth and her hands and this moment of insanity and wonder. He hung on the brink of every man's fantasy, using what shred of control he still possessed to pull away.

"No. No, Booth. I want to."

"I know." Before she could protest anew, he slid his hands beneath her arms and lifted her back and onto the bed. Coming down on top of her, he slid into her as if they'd done this a dozen times. Her hips lifted to meet his thrusts, and with her mouth locking on his, her arms tightly around him, he reached his own release.

Booth rose up enough to stare down at her tangle of hair, her luminous eyes, her heated cheeks, her swollen mouth. "You're the most delicious creature I've ever seen."

He collapsed across her and she held him, her fingers light on his back. They lay like that, as their breathing slowed. The phone rang, but neither moved. A car roared down the street, but neither got up to glance out the window. Voices drifted upstairs, and Kathleen recognized one of them as Gail's, but she didn't stir except to kiss Booth and ask, "So when do we do this again?"

He looked down at her with amusement and a trace of intoxicating greed. "You just about killed me."

"I climaxed twice."

"You did, did you?"

"Yes, and it was wonderful. You're wonderful and we should have done this days ago." She stretched like a satisfied cat, and Booth decided he'd been given a gift far beyond good sex—he'd been given her heart.

He tried to roll away from her and was delighted when she refused to let him go.

Nipping at her mouth, he said, "There's no law saying we can't make up for lost time."

"I'd love to, but you have to go to work and so do I."

"Afterward."

"I don't know if I can wait that long," she said.

Booth clenched his teeth, then murmured, "What have I have created?"

"It's never been like this for me. Never."

He kissed her deeply but didn't say what he guessed she wanted to hear—that it had never been as good for him, either. Though it was true, something silenced him. Booth had been a cop for too long to ever completely capitulate. He knew Kathleen intimately, trusted her with Lisa without any hesitation, but something still held him at bay. And whatever that something was, she was doing her best to keep it hidden.

CHAPTER ELEVEN

"ARE YOU SURE WE haven't missed anything? Like the refrigerator or the bed?" Booth grumbled as he watched Kathleen add extra diapers and another change of clothes for Lisa. The baby was standing in her crib, glaring at him with an unhappy pout for putting her there.

Since she'd taken that first tottering step two days ago, she'd been walking like a demon; Booth was going crazy trying to keep her contained in one spot for more than twenty seconds. The crib had become a lifesaver.

"Always better to be prepared," Kathleen said, tucking in another bib.

"The cookout is only for a few hours. You've got enough stuff for a week in the woods."

She shuddered. "I hate camping."

"So do I."

"Then it's a good thing we don't have to sleep in a tent tonight, isn't it? Why don't you take Lisa down to the car. I already changed her. I'll get the rest of the stuff and pick up a sweater I left at Gail's."

The two women had spent most of the previous day together, catching up, with Kathleen taking

Gail to show her the carriage house. The place would be ready for her to move in in a matter of days, but in the meantime Kathleen was staying with Booth, who'd observed the women's closeness with a kind of wonder, because the two didn't seem a whole lot alike.

Gail was blunt, and too acerbic, judging by the snatches of conversation he'd overheard when he'd gone downstairs to retrieve his mail. And he'd heard a couple of cracks from Gail reminding Kathleen that relationships with cops were bad news. His ears had pricked up, then, and despite feeling sneaky, he'd listened, hoping that Kathleen would mention her reasons. But all she'd said was, "Booth is different." That, of course, pleased him, but still left the question unanswered.

By the time Kathleen had returned to his apartment, Booth had pushed Gail out of his thoughts. He wouldn't have Kathleen with him for very long, and he sure didn't want to spend the time discussing a woman who obviously didn't like him.

Now, Booth shouldered the diaper bag as Kathleen glanced around, tapping her finger against her cheek.

"Oh, no, you don't. No more. And we're going out together. If I leave you up here, you'll be packing Angie's clock collection." He lifted Lisa from the crib. She immediately grinned and squealed, grabbing her favorite blanket. Booth rolled his eyes, asking himself how one twenty-pound baby could require so much junk.

In the living room, Kathleen slid another small bag over her shoulder, then picked up her handbag. In her free hand she carried a folder of sheet music.

Booth eyed the folder. "I don't think Gail's piano will fit."

"Very funny. Mavis has a piano and she asked me if I'd bring some of my music. She said you'd mentioned to her that I played."

He shrugged. "Don't remember. I could have."

"It just seemed like such an odd request." She hesitated, then set the sheet music aside. "It is odd. I'll leave it here. We have enough stuff."

"Better take the music. If Mavis asked you to bring it, she wasn't kidding."

"But maybe she was just being polite."

"Or she'll be annoyed that you didn't."

"Hmm, all right." She retrieved the music folder. "So, are we all ready?" she asked, tickling Lisa's pudgy leg and then glancing back as Booth urged her out of the nursery. "I wonder if—"

"I rented a truck? No. Let's go before you think of something else."

Booth followed her downstairs. Kathleen stopped at Gail's, and Booth went on out to the car. He got Lisa into the child carrier in the back seat, checked for the cream-colored car and noted it was gone.

The plate had come back clean. The vehicle was registered to a Mason Knight of Savannah. Booth had Knight's name checked for any outstanding warrants, but didn't even come up with an unpaid parking ticket. He'd called a retired bounty-hunter friend in south Georgia to ask him do some digging around—probably a waste of time, but his gut hadn't been satisfied. His pal had assured Booth that if there was anything to be found, he'd find it.

The car had been parked in the same place the previous night when Booth had come home from work. The fact that it was missing today could mean something or nothing. In the meantime, he had no cause to do anything official. But Booth had taken note of Kathleen's relief when he'd told her the plate was clean. He had kept his own expression bland, tossing out the information as if her over-the-top reaction a few days before hadn't lingered in his mind. It had been too similar to her reaction that first night about hating cops.

Pieces weren't fitting together, but without being direct with her, and risking her closing down, he'd decided to let the issue drop.

The past few days had been crazy—moving her things into his place, juggling their schedules so that someone would always be available to care for Lisa, making arrangements for Kathleen's move into the carriage house and the arrival of her piano on the following Tuesday. And Booth wasn't all that pleased that she'd be moving out almost as soon as she'd moved in.

He liked having her with him. He liked having her there when he came home, having her in his arms before he was through the door. They could talk about anything. Kathleen had admired and asked questions about Angie's miniature clock collection. Someday, Booth told her, he wanted to give it to Lisa as part of her mother's legacy. He'd packed most of Angie's possessions away in anticipation that someday they'd be given to Lisa. The clocks, however, had remained displayed exactly the way Angie had placed them—where they could be enjoyed. Kathleen offered to buy a glass case for them, where they would be safe, but placing them in a case bought by another woman made him uncomfortable. He knew it was asinine, but he couldn't do it.

"It's better that they stay where they are," he said to Kathleen. "They've been displayed that way since she started collecting them, and, well, it's just difficult to make a change."

"I understand," she said quickly, and busied herself doing something else.

Booth left the issue there, but he was insightful enough to recognize that his hesitation had cut her out. She'd immediately withdrawn. Perhaps on some level he was putting limitations on his involvement with Kathleen, balking at a relationship he hadn't been prepared to jump into. He'd made no promises or suggestions about the future. Nor had she given any indication she wanted anything beyond what they already had.

And as if Kathleen were as aware of his thoughts, she was adamant about the move to the carriage house. Living with him would generate talk in the neighborhood. Then she'd mentioned his job with teenagers; he was a role model for good behavior, whether he liked it or not.

He hadn't liked it, and he'd told her so, but she wouldn't budge. The fact that his mother had agreed with Kathleen and then chastised Booth for not appreciating what a wonderful and principled woman Kathleen was, hadn't helped his case. Even his wild and ditzy sister had been impressed.

Booth didn't mention that he and Kathleen intended to continue their sexual relationship whether she lived with him or a thousand miles away.

He'd figured he'd gotten past any more comments or lectures on his relationship with Kathleen until he'd run into Gail the day after she returned home with her sister, just before Kathleen took Gail to see the carriage house. Kathleen had mentioned she'd be staying with Booth for a few days, then shifted all the emphasis to her future home. Gail had nodded and smiled and saved her acid for Booth.

While Kathleen had taken a sleeping Lisa upstairs, Gail had swooped down on Booth like a tornado funnel. Without any preliminaries, she'd warned him that if she learned he had sexually coerced Kathleen, he'd be roadkill.

"I'm a cop with a kid, for God's sake, not some scum from a back alley," he'd snapped, immediately wishing he'd escaped with Kathleen and Lisa.

"Right, a *cop*," she'd retorted, as if there wasn't much difference. Gail was tall and gangly with hair the color of canned salmon. She had a jutting chin that reminded Booth of a female lieutenant from his days at the police academy.

Lt. Patsy Plockmader could bull's eye the haunches on a buffalo nickel from two hundred yards with one eye closed, and she could peel the bark off a tree with her bare hands. How she did the latter had been a mystery, but she threatened to do the same to any recruit who made her training program look bad. No one had crossed her. Gail had a similar "I'll peel your ass" look. He probably might have accorded her a grudging respect for her fierce loyalty to Kathleen, if something about her attitude didn't bother him.

"Don't tell me. You don't like cops, either."

She'd shrugged. "Kathleen has her own reasons, and all of them are valid. I don't have anything against you personally, just cops and macho types, in general."

"I'm not dating you."

"I wish you weren't dating Kathleen!"

"Kathleen's an adult. She can make her own decisions. She's smart, and she's the most cautious woman I've ever met," he'd argued, not liking that he had to defend himself when he hadn't done anything wrong. "She can take care of herself."

She'd leaned forward, and Booth had thought she was going to grab a handful of his shirt. Instead she'd just snarled, "Cautious or not, she's my friend, buster, and she's too damn good, sweet and vulnerable for her own good. If it weren't for—

Never mind. You just make sure you don't hurt her. She and I have had our fill of bad-tempered men.''

That unexpected comment had given Booth an opening he didn't pass up.

''Like Mason Knight?'' he'd asked, watching her closely, hoping the name would garner a reaction. Any reaction.

''Who's Mason Knight?''

''From Georgia.''

''Never heard of him.''

''Good.''

She'd peered at him suspiciously. ''Are you asking me if Kathleen was once involved with a guy named Mason Knight?''

''Was she?''

''No.''

''Then we can both rest easier, can't we?'' He'd turned and walked away, leaving her staring after him. He was both pleased he'd escaped with the last word and disappointed that the name-drop had yielded nothing. At least Kathleen hadn't lied to him, but that still didn't explain her overreaction to the car.

Leaning against the Explorer now, he watched her emerge from Gail's and mentally counted the hours he'd have to wait before he could make a valid excuse to leave Mavis's. Kathleen wouldn't be staying with him much longer, and he didn't want to waste the time in a crowd of people.

''You look rather thoughtful,'' she said, loading in the tote of toys and the diaper bag. She placed her sheet music flat on the floor and away from the food she'd already packed.

"I'd rather be making love than traipsing off to some boring picnic."

She climbed into the back to rearrange a few items, and he had to clench his hands to stop himself from pulling her against him.

She scooted out and dusted her hands together. When she looked up at him, he knew his dark glasses hid the depth of his need for her.

She laced their hands together. "I want you, too. All the time. And that scares me."

"Babe, we could skip this."

"We need to do something besides make love."

"Why?"

She grinned. "So we can think about how good it will be when we do."

"I don't need to anticipate and neither do you. We know it will be great."

"Your mom wants to show off Lisa to everyone."

"So we can drop her off, then find a nice private spot where I can ravish you."

"You did that an hour ago."

"Seems like it was days ago," he grumbled. Booth felt time was running away from him. He wanted her with him for more than a few days; he wanted her...forever? Too extreme. So what *did* he want with her?

She palmed his cheek, her hand feeling warm and inviting. He snagged her wrist and tugged her against him. "Somehow you've managed to blow my life apart, babe. I can't stop thinking about you or wanting you."

She brushed her mouth across his, her tongue dancing along the inside of his mouth for a few seconds. She had learned how to tease just enough to make him crazy.

"We're going to be late," she whispered as she pulled away. "We can finish this later."

In the Explorer, Booth glanced back at Lisa. "What about it, kiddo, should we keep her around?" Lisa clapped her hands and laughed, kicking her chubby legs. "I think that was a yes."

Kathleen laughed. "Good thing. Without her approval, I'd be history."

THE COOKOUT WAS IN full swing by the time they arrived. The cake and bowl of fruit salad were placed on a table on the cool side of a redwood deck. Booth left most of the stuff in the Explorer, figuring they could get it when needed. Lisa was immediately stolen away by her grandmother. Kathleen was introduced to relatives, friends, a litter of brand-new puppies and enough food and games to exhaust the most enthusiastic picnicgoer.

Booth was dragged into a game of softball that Kathleen and some of the other women watched. Darlene, Booth's sister, arrived late on the arm of her fiancé and flashing a huge diamond ring. Kathleen recalled Booth saying his sister spent all her time getting engaged and was known around town as the local jeweler's most frequent customer.

Darlene Rawlings bounced rather than walked, wearing a green checked sunsuit and a brown Stetson that had a green-and-yellow scarf woven through the brim. The tails of the fabric fluttered down her back, catching the breeze. Her smile was vivacious, her grip on the man with her possessive.

When she spotted Kathleen talking to Janet, she whispered something to her boyfriend and skipped over. She resembled Booth in that she had the same sensational green eyes.

"You gotta be Kathleen," she said enthusiastically.

"And you gotta be Darlene."

Darlene slipped her hand through Kathleen's arm. "We have to talk."

"Definitely," Kathleen replied, liking her immediately. Suddenly she felt secure and fortunate to know such terrific, openly friendly people. It was such a change from the closed, insular life she'd lived in Wyoming.

Darlene bent her head close to Kathleen's. "First we get ourselves a couple of mudslides, and then I'm gonna tell you just how to handle my brother."

A few moments later, the two women were lounging on matching chaises on the deck, sipping the cold potent mudslides. The sun was high and warm; the sounds of laughter and baseball and children squealing spiraled around them, making the summer day all the more special.

Booth slid open the screen door, saw his sister and tried to retreat.

"Oh, no, you don't," Darlene said, leaping up and grabbing his arm.

"No lectures, muskrat."

Instead she scolded him for not introducing Kathleen to her sooner.

"We've only been seeing each other for a short time. Besides, when did you become the benchmark for family introductions? The last time I saw you, you were clinging to Barry, now it's— What's his name?"

"Gavin Bryson. And it wasn't Barry, it was Larry."

Booth peered at her hand. "I will say this. The stone is bigger. Sure it's not a zircon?"

Darlene gave him a friendly punch. "You are so nasty. I picked it out myself, and Gavin promised me matching earrings for my birthday."

Booth looked at Kathleen. "Fat chance. Her birthday is in October. She'll never make it."

"I'm very serious about Gavin," she said with a sniff, then grinned. "At least for a while."

Booth rolled his eyes. "I'm going to get a beer. I see Darlene is feeding you mudslides. Careful, they're potent."

"And yummy. I've never had one."

"Leave it to my sister to further your education," he muttered.

Darlene kissed his cheek. "Run along. She's

staying with me so I can tell her all your flaws and shortcomings.''

"That should take all of three seconds.''

She leaned close to Kathleen, talking in a stage whisper. "Trust me. I know enough to get him arrested. Run along, big brother, us babes are gonna dish the dirt.''

He dropped a kiss on Kathleen's mouth. "Yell when the shit gets too deep, and I'll come and rescue you.''

Kathleen played along with Darlene. "Oh, I don't know. It sounds pretty interesting to me. Especially the 'arrested' part.''

He managed an offended look that was about as deep as a wading pool.

Kathleen loved all the sibling teasing. It was so obvious that Booth and Darlene loved and respected each other enough to toss out barbs with easy assurance. Each knew the rules, the comfort levels and the permissible degrees of mockery.

Kathleen whispered, "I'll see you later.''

"Behave yourself, Darlene. No dirty jokes.''

Darlene laughed and tossed her arms around Booth's neck. "You look so good and so happy and I love you bunches.''

He tweaked her nose. "You, too, muskrat.'' Booth sauntered off, with Kathleen admiring what she'd begun to think of as the sexiest, most lethal walk she'd ever seen. He joined three other men, and they headed toward the barrel of iced beer.

Darlene said, "You know, you've accomplished the impossible in snagging Booth."

"I don't think he's quite snagged."

"Oh, he is. He just doesn't know it. Angie was cool, I liked her, but she was so perfect that poor Booth has been forced to stay married to her long after she died. Never has dated anyone here in town. Not once. And now to be with you, and bring you here and not give a damn what anyone thinks… Not that anyone is critical. Unless it's Gladys Hucklebee." She glanced around as if the woman were hiding there to spy on them. "She isn't here, is she?"

"I haven't seen her."

"Bless Mavis." Darlene took a long swallow of her drink. "I think your being with Booth is terrific."

"Actually I think it's pretty terrific, myself. You have a wonderful family."

"Sure wish Dad was here to meet you. He's a lot like Booth. Laid-back and thoughtful. Mom and I are more gregarious, and Dad rolls his eyes a lot. He wanted Booth to go with him on this fishing trip to Alaska, but Booth didn't want to take the time off work. Personally, I think he didn't want to leave Lisa. He always feels he doesn't spend enough time with her."

"He certainly is a proud and devoted father."

Darlene nodded, then took a sip of her drink. "So where's your family?" she asked bluntly.

It was the most direct and unexpected question that Kathleen had had about her past in some time.

"We're sort of scattered. My mother passed away a number of years ago, and I haven't seen my father since I was about nine."

"Bummer. No husband and no kids, huh?"

"No. Two brothers. One I haven't seen in years, and the other is in California."

"Okay. So why are you here? I mean, it's cool for Booth, but this ain't exactly Boston or Hartford. Excitement in Crosby is when two dogs pee on the same fire hydrant."

Kathleen giggled, probably too long. The drink was already making her silly. "I have a college friend who lives here."

"You're just visiting? But you have a job and you're moving to that cool carriage house."

"I like it here and I decided to stay."

Darlene shrugged, gave an enthusiastic wave to someone passing by, and added, "Well, that's as good a reason as any."

Kathleen took another sip of her drink. It was cold and potent and delicious. "So tell me about Booth's arrest record."

Darlene sat forward on the cushioned chaise, anchored her drink between her legs and started counting on her fingers. "Well, here's one that I thought was really cool. One September he stole some beer kegs from a storage room. He'd bet some guys that he could lift three of them into his pickup in three minutes. It was pretty tense for a while, cuz

Mr. Beasley—he was the owner—showed up un-expectedly. But Booth waited. That's the thing about him, he's patient when most guys would be itchin' and hoppin'. Poor Beasley, he never did fig-ure out how those kegs were where he'd left them when he went in to take a leak and gone when he returned.''

Kathleen laughed, which only encouraged Dar-lene to tell more. Most of the stories sounded like mere pranks and mischief. A half hour passed, and Kathleen was about to get up when Darlene launched into the last story.

"There was the time he and two girlfriends were caught naked in the mayor's pool. Dad had to do some fast talking about that, cuz they'd gotten through some elaborate security system that was connected to the police. Dad being the chief and all made it look suspicious.''

"So how did Booth do it?''

"He figured out the coding and jammed it. It didn't do any damage, but proved that if a kid could get into the pool area, then a burglar could get into the house.'' She took a long swallow of her drink. "He's always liked to prove he could do things that were supposed to be impossible. If he can't figure it out, he waits and studies and examines it from every angle until something triggers something else and he's got it. Guess it's like loving a challenge. Tell him he can't, and he's determined he can. Kathleen, are you okay? You look a little pale.''

She managed a thin smile. "I'm fine.''

"Let me get us fresh drinks." And before Kathleen could protest, Darlene had scooted off the chaise, hugged a passing guest and gone over to the makeshift bar.

Kathleen sat transfixed watching a volleyball game that was going on some distance away. She had to be crazy to be here, to be with Booth, to have let all of her past slip to the side as if it were no longer relevant. *"He waits and studies and examines it from every angle until something triggers something else and he's got it."* Here she was, yearning to get started on a new life, but realistically she was still in danger, still living with a time bomb.

Booth was just biding his time, looking, watching, waiting until some unfiltered word or passing comment lit up all his buttons and pushed the pieces he already had into a whole picture.

She took a deep breath. *Okay, stay levelheaded. Don't go off on some tangent. Get through today, and then....* But suddenly she realized she'd trapped herself. The lease at the carriage house and the arrival of her piano had created joyous anticipation but now they felt like millstones, capable of drowning her.

Darlene returned, handed Kathleen a second mudslide, and the subject shifted to local gossip and Darlene's latest engagement. Thirty minutes later, Kathleen had finished her drink, deciding that her earlier alarm was probably unwarranted. When Booth swooped down and kissed her, murmuring that he hoped she didn't take all of Darlene's exaggerations seriously, Kathleen said no.

"How many of those things did you drink?" Booth whispered as he led her across the slope of lawn and away from most of the guests. Lisa was still entrenched amid various aunts and cousins, and had them all wrapped around her finger.

"Just two. I feel floaty and relaxed and—" She looked at him and swore his face drifted by and returned before she could blink. "Did I say something to embarrass you?"

"Of course not."

"Still like me?"

"Big time."

"I still like you."

"Good."

"Are we going to bed?"

"I only wish." Then he dropped a quick kiss on her tingly mouth. "Later. Now we're going to walk and get you sober. Mavis is looking for you." In the distance came the sound of someone banging on a piano.

"The piano?" For a second, she scowled. Then, "Oh, God, she wants me to play, doesn't she?" She stopped walking, eyes wide, hands coming up to her cheeks. Then she took a deep breath. "Do I have to?"

"Nope."

"You're always so agreeable."

"Yep."

She danced a few steps ahead of him and turned

around, her swirling sundress revealing her tanned legs. In the next instant she was in his arms. "I'll play on one condition."

"Okay."

"You have to kiss me." She hiccuped and then giggled.

He drew her close and kissed her, deliberately, provocatively and filling her with an assurance of deeper, sexier kisses to come. His mouth was more dizzying than the drinks she'd had.

"I have a condition, too."

"What?"

"Promise me you'll always be as happy as you are right now."

She went very still, her eyes shimmering, her hands climbing up his shirt to slide over his shoulders. It was okay. Everything was okay. Nothing could be wrong when it felt so right. "Will you sit beside me when I play?"

"Yes."

"Then I'll be happy."

CHAPTER TWELVE

AN HOUR LATER, totally sober and more than a little unnerved, Kathleen was in exactly the place she'd tried to avoid for months—the center of attention. Her audience, which had begun as just Mavis and Janet and a few stragglers who had come in from the deck to listen, had grown to include the entire cookout guest list. With all of them gathered around the gleaming baby grand, and Booth seated on the slippery bench beside her, Kathleen felt as if she'd been thrust into the spotlight of a sold-out private concert.

Her fingers moved across the keys more naturally than they had in weeks, and she surprised herself by how easily she slid into the role of performer—professional, accessible, and glorying in her ability to give her audience what they wanted.

Sheet music gave way to memory and the complex chords she'd learned from her mother. Favorites were requested as she moved effortlessly from the classics to songs from *The Sound of Music,* to rock, to hits from the eighties, finishing with a request for Jimmy Buffett's hit "Margaritaville."

All the while Booth sat beside her, sliding out of

her way as her hands moved up and down the keyboard.

The applause after the final song was loud and enthusiastic, with two encores requested. Someone placed a glass of iced tea in her hand, and Lisa toddled over to bang on the keys, making everyone laugh.

"Where did you ever learn to play like that?" an overperfumed woman asked, triggering more questions and comments from the others.

"Are you sure you're not a professional?"

"Do you give private lessons? My niece has gone through three piano teachers and my sister is desperate."

"I can't believe you're not with some group."

"Are you a Juilliard graduate?"

"You're so versatile. Most pianists are really good in only one or two areas, but you seem to have mastered them all. Have you ever been a church organist? Our congregation is in the process of interviewing if you'd like to stop by."

Kathleen was overwhelmed. Offers, praise, questions—she answered them, and thanked everyone for their enthusiastic comments. After months of being so closemouthed and careful, she found herself chattering like a freed woman after being gagged in a closet.

She told them how her mother had loved music and that her ability at the keyboard had brought in money after she and Kathleen's father separated. She told of her mother's belief that everyone should know how to do something so well that if necessary they could earn a living at it. It was this last comment that had more than a few people looking at her with curiosity.

She didn't have an answer beyond the truth. And she couldn't tell them that. Instead, she sidestepped the issue. "After your enthusiastic comments, I will certainly consider playing in a professional capacity in the future."

Booth eased her away then, and the crowd began to drift back outside. The food was ready, and soon the conversation changed from Kathleen to other topics. She and Booth fixed themselves burgers, added spoonfuls from many of the salads and sat down at one of the picnic tables.

Booth excused himself to check on Lisa, who was perched in Janet's lap and making serious headway into a bowl of peach-and-gelatin salad.

"Mom, I can take her," he said. "You've had her all day."

"She's fine. I'm spoiling her and loving it. Go and enjoy Kathleen. And since the crowd around her was so huge I couldn't get close enough to say this directly, please tell her I think her playing was sensational."

"Yeah, she's talented, isn't she?"

"More than that. She's gifted. And the beauty is that I don't think she knows it."

Booth repeated the conversation to Kathleen, leaving her mouth agape at the word "gifted."

"Your mom is a sweetheart, but I think it was because the guests chose familiar songs."

"Nope."

"Nope?"

He shrugged. "That's what I said."

"You think I'm gifted? Oh, Booth, I could kiss you."

He grinned and leaned forward. "Anytime, anyplace, anywhere."

"I won't take that literally, since we're in a public place."

"I'll take a rain check."

She slipped her hand around his arm and said, "I'm so glad I came here. It's been a terrific day."

Booth squeezed her fingers, raising them to his mouth. He placed a kiss in the center of her palm and folded her fingers around it as if to preserve it for all time.

"Uh, excuse me."

Kathleen straightened and turned. Booth extended his hand. "Eric, good to see you. Kathleen, this is Eric Carmody, Mavis's son."

Of medium height, he wore stark-white tennis clothes that were pressed and immaculate. He was almost pretty in a cordial way, with a slight five-o'clock shadow and resolute features. He wore a wedding ring and carried a piece of sheet music in his hand.

"How nice to meet you," Kathleen said. "You requested 'Margaritaville.'"

"I was hoping you wouldn't remember."

"I never forget requests for great songs."

He lowered his voice. "I like Buffett, but I'm supposed to be more serious about music."

Kathleen nodded mock seriously. "When someone gives you a hard time, you tell them there's room for innovation and greatness beyond the classics and the lofty composers. What moves a person and speaks to their soul is what defines excellence whether it's a Gregorian chant or Buffett."

"Very well put," Eric said, smiling. "I'll remember that."

Kathleen glanced at the sheet in his hand. "Is that another one of your favorites?"

He glanced at it as if he'd forgotten he was carrying it. "Actually, I don't think I need it. I brought it in the hope you might play it for me, but after that medley I think I've heard enough."

Booth interjected. "He heads up the music department at The Swanhill Academy. It's a small private school west of here—"

"I've heard about it," Kathleen said, puzzled and curious as to where all of this was going. "In fact, I passed it the other day on my way home."

"You've heard of it? From anyone in particular? Forgive me for asking, but the school is small and underfunded. Most times when I mention it, I get blank stares, so I'm curious. I know you're fairly new in town, and Swanhill isn't one of the area's points of interest."

"That's too bad. There's an understated elegance just in the building itself. I heard about the school from a friend, Gail Morgan. She told me about a scholarship program you offer. She's encouraged some of the kids from the Powell Street Center to apply."

Eric nodded, and glanced at Booth. "I'm impressed. I wasn't prepared for her to be so knowledgable. I assume you haven't said anything."

"No."

"Said anything about what?" Kathleen asked, suddenly uneasy.

"My mother said you were good at keeping a secret. She was right."

"Secret about what?"

Booth lifted his beer bottle and added, "I wasn't entirely sure you'd come to a decision immediately."

"I did need to hear her play, and when Mother suggested this rather informal approach, I liked the idea. Less pressure on Kathleen, and less on me to take action. Now, having heard her, I don't think there's any problem. There is the usual paperwork—job application stuff—but I'm confident the board will be as pleased and excited as I am."

Kathleen looked from one to the other, feeling invisible.

Booth grinned at her.

"What am I missing?" she asked, although she'd filled in most of the blanks with her own name.

"Guess it's time, Booth."

"This is all yours, Eric."

While logic told her she was overreacting, her

body wasn't listening. Kathleen's heart began to pound and a dozen terrifying possibilities burst through her—from some diabolical trick to set her up, to a brilliant police operation orchestrated by Booth.

Booth knew that her music was the one area where she was vulnerable, where she tended to talk when she should shut up. She'd certainly done that just moments ago in the house. And my God, hadn't she called to have her piano sent?

Her breathing felt reedy, and she wondered what else she'd done that was careless or foolish. She couldn't talk herself out of a sense of entrapment, of being blindsided, and fought off the urge to panic.

"...piano at the academy."

She blinked. "Excuse me?"

"I'm offering you the position of teaching piano at the academy."

"Teach? At Swanhill?"

"Yes."

She looked at Booth. "I don't understand."

Booth put his arm around her and said to Eric, "I think she's overwhelmed. Babe, Eric is serious. The academy has an opening in the music department, and he's offering you the position."

"But why?" she asked.

Eric blinked as if he had misunderstood the question. "Because you're a fine pianist with a tremendous range and an ability to connect with your audience. Our students will learn from you, and that is the whole purpose of teaching, isn't it? I'm just stunned that you haven't been snatched up by one of the big music schools.''

She opened her mouth to say something, and then to her horror her eyes filled with tears. Relief. Awe. Gratitude. "Oh, my God.''

"I think she is truly stunned by the offer, Booth.''

"Kathleen?''

She swiped the back of her hand across her eyes. "I've just never heard of anyone getting that kind of position in such a casual way.''

"Actually, it's been in process for a while. Booth mentioned your name to my mother after he heard you play—''

"Eric, don't—''

But Eric waved him off. "Look, I know you didn't want your name mentioned, but you deserve credit for your part.'' He winked at Kathleen. "In fact, he's called a few times to see if I had you under consideration. No, correction, he called so many times, I was beginning to wonder what he expected to get out of it.''

"Dammit, Eric.''

"Of course, I know now,'' Eric said, ignoring Booth's dark expression. "It was because you were so good. And when I told my mother I'd be here today, she came up with the idea of you bringing some music and playing. It would give me a nice way out if you turned out to be— How should I say this…?''

"Tone-deaf and unable to play 'Chopsticks'?"

"Well, that's a little rough, but yes."

She glanced at Booth. "And you set all of this in motion?"

"I made a phone call to Mrs. Carmody after I heard you play at Gail's place."

"I didn't know you were interested in the staffing of music academies," she said in a flat, cool voice.

She knew by the flash in his eyes that she sounded sharp and irritated. And on one level, she was. Her relief was profound, while at the same time she hated that she'd been so easily taken in. She'd been careless and trusting when she should have known better. Booth was a cop, and from her own experience cops were experts at secrets and sleight of hand.

"I'm only interested in you. And because I'm no expert— Look, this isn't complicated. It wasn't a conspiracy, no one was trying to embarrass you. I thought you were good, you obviously enjoyed playing, so I made a phone call. Period."

Eric shifted his feet uneasily as Booth talked. Finally Eric took a few steps back, saying, "Let's leave it this way, Kathleen. If you're interested in the position—and I profoundly hope you are— please stop by my office at the academy one day next week. We'll get the paperwork done and set a date for the board to hear you play. As I said earlier, this is more a formality, just reinforcing your credentials for the position. Now, if you'll excuse me,

I'm going to indulge in some dessert." He extended his hand to Booth. "Thanks. She's a jewel."

"Yeah, I thought so, too."

Kathleen smiled. "Thank you. I'm honored at being offered the position."

Eric walked away, and Booth sat back down to eat. Kathleen didn't.

"Why didn't you tell me what you did?"

"Because all I did was make a phone call. I had nothing to do with you being offered the position."

"I don't like surprises."

"Yeah, I noticed."

She knew he was angry because of her unexpected reaction. On one level it would be wise to just let this go, but at the same time, her insides were as unstable as loose mercury. "I'm not a child, Booth. I can take disappointment."

"Would you have been disappointed?" he asked, swinging around to look at her. No smile like before, no warmth in his eyes, no saying he only wanted her to promise to be happy. "The way you're acting, you'd think I'd arranged to have you arrested for imitating a pianist."

"You're angry."

"You could say that."

She ducked her head. "I know I don't sound very grateful, but I like to know what's going on."

"Really. Now I wonder why I didn't figure that out?" He pushed his plate aside. "I mean, considering the way that you've kept me up-to-date in what's going on with you. The mistress of hidden information dumping on me for keeping something quiet because I had no idea of the outcome? There's a hell of a lot of irony in that."

"Booth, please…" She touched his arm, but he pulled away.

"Maybe I should have gotten your hopes up, and then if it hadn't worked out, I could have said, 'Tough luck, kid. Them's the breaks. Guess you're doomed to spending your life waiting tables.'"

"You wouldn't have done that," she said softly, beginning to feel disgusted by how ungrateful and downright nasty she'd sounded. She also realized the pointlessness of having a relationship that wasn't honest. Her instincts that first night had been the right ones. Why, oh why hadn't she stuck with them rather than allowing herself to want him and need him and to love— No! She couldn't. She wouldn't. She didn't.

Turning away so he couldn't see the color of despair blotching her cheeks, she said lamely, "I know you meant well."

But Booth was having none of it, and Kathleen cringed at the bite of contempt he tossed back at her. "No, goddammit, you don't know that at all. Once more, you don't believe anyone wants to do anything for the simple reason that it's the right thing to do. There always has to be some ulterior motive. You're skittish and wary and terrified of something. Oh, don't sweat it, babe. I'm not asking any questions, because I know damn well I'll get no answers, or if I do, it will probably be a freaking lie.''

She backed up, feeling as if she'd been slapped. "I've never lied to you," she said. She hated the mere thought of it, which was why she'd been so evasive. She had reasons—solid, her-future-depended-on-them reasons—and they had less to do with him than with protecting herself and safekeeping their relationship.

Booth was too honest, and if he knew the truth, he would have to follow it to its logical conclusion—he'd have to arrest her, hold her for extradition back to Wyoming. That, she couldn't bear to contemplate.

Now he took her by the shoulders. "Kathleen, we're never going to work anything out between us with you living in some secret world you won't let me into."

Wearily she said, "You don't understand."

"And you won't help me to."

"I can't."

"Not you *can't*. You *won't*. And, babe, there's one hell of a difference between the two. That's the gist of it, isn't it? You won't today, or tomorrow, or next week."

She said nothing.

At her silence, he asked a little louder, "Isn't that true?"

"Yes!"

He stared at her for a long time, then shrugged when it was obvious that was all she was going to say. "Guess I should chalk that up to progress. Not a lot, but some. Maybe I should have shaken you down weeks ago. Whatever it is you won't tell me, you've locked it up and decided it's too powerful for anyone else to help you with."

Kathleen barely heard him. She was losing him, feeling him slip away, and there wasn't anything she could do about it.

He continued, his tone growing more sarcastic. "Now, if I'd been smart, I would have realized you'd freak over an unexpected turn of events, but in my rather limited capacity for figuring things out, I actually thought you'd be—uh, dare I say it?— happy about teaching at the academy. So, since seeing you happy and content was what I had in mind, it seemed wise to keep my mouth shut when I couldn't guarantee that outcome."

She turned away from his words that were like tiny knives. Gathering her dishes, she put them in a nearby receptacle, then slung her canvas bag over her shoulder. Her sheet music peeked out of the top, a grim reminder of how badly this day had turned out through no one's fault but her own.

"I don't have anything more to say, Booth."

He swore, but it wasn't vicious, merely frustrated. "I'll get Lisa and her things and meet you at the car."

In the next few minutes Kathleen said her goodbyes, stopping especially to thank Mavis.

"You were wonderful, my dear. I'm so glad Eric offered you the position."

"Yes, I am, too."

"Booth was so excited when he called me and suggested I mention you for the academy. I think he felt a bit like a talent scout who had made the discovery of a lifetime."

"He only heard me play once."

"Apparently it was enough. Then again, I think he had more invested than just an ear for good playing. He obviously adores you, and, you know..." She lowered her voice, drawing Kathleen aside. "I shouldn't be saying this, but, well, it needs to be said. You're the best thing that could have happened to Booth. Angie was very self-sufficient, very controlled. She never needed help, never asked for help, and despite all of Crosby viewing her as a paragon, and always reminding Booth how lucky he was to have her, I don't think Booth was all that happy. Oh, he loved her, he respected her, and little Lisa will always hear only the best about her mother, but when I saw Booth with Angie, he never looked as relaxed and content as he's been since he met you."

"Oh, Mavis, what a sweet and generous thing to tell me." Kathleen hugged her, feeling as if she'd been given some rare insight into Booth, while at the same time realizing it had come too late.

"Now, you run along, and when that piano arrives and is all set up, I want to come over and hear you play."

"Yes." But it was the only word she could say around the huge lump in her throat.

In the next few minutes, Lisa was strapped into her car seat, the back of the Explorer was packed and Kathleen had slipped into the passenger seat.

In all that time, Booth said nothing.

They drove out the tree-lined drive, the late-afternoon sun dipping low and promising a spectacular sunset.

Kathleen felt the distance between them and thought about their mutual teasing about going home early to make love. She turned and watched the scenery pass by, thinking that, like her relationship with Booth, the summer day had come and touched her, giving her joy, and now it was gone.

CHAPTER THIRTEEN

"WHAT ABOUT THE PIANO?"

"You're gonna love this, Mr. S."

"Wait, Max. Start at the beginning."

In a Victorian-style room in the west wing of the Old Faithful Inn, deep in Yellowstone, the Rainmaker was enjoying a snifter of brandy and a manicure while savoring the news that his problems were almost over.

On the telephone was Max.

"So let me have it again, Max. This is just too sweet not to repeat."

"We've finally hit pay dirt in that mail I've been collecting from her house. There was a flyer from a storage company thanking Hanes's old lady for her business and prompt payment. They trust that she will continue to store her oversize valuables with them."

"And what valuable item has she stored with the Wyoming Storage Company?" the Rainmaker asked, feeling like the straight man in well-rehearsed routine.

"One piano. Back in the early spring."

"And what did you do?"

"I called them and posed as her brother, told

them I needed some information on her piano because I wanted to purchase one exactly like it for
my wife.''

"And they gave you what you needed?"

"They gave me some, but getting an address for
the broad was going nowhere."

"You should have come up with some other
ruse. A relative would know where she is."

"I told them I'd moved and lost her letter with
her new address. The last one I had was the Wyoming address. The broad on the phone said she'd
go check with her supervisor. When she came back,
she said she couldn't give out personal information,
and then she said something very interesting about
the piano."

Which was exactly were the Rainmaker had in-
terrupted and asked Max to repeat the information.

"What about the piano?"

"It was gone."

Rainmaker choked on his brandy. "Gone? Gone?
As in lost? Mistakenly sold?" This was not the interesting and satisfying conclusion he'd expected.
Huffing and sputtering, he snapped, "What the hell
kind of storage place is this? How could they lose
a piano?"

Max chuckled. "Not to worry, Mr. S. I tore into
that like a wild wolf with a hind quarter of beef. I
ranted and raved on how they'd lost my sister's
piano, and how I'd sue them, and then the broad
got her supervisor on the line. He was wheezin' and
yappin' about how I had it all wrong, the piano

wasn't lost, and then he spilled the info. The piano was shipped per the owner's request to Connecticut. The guy reeled off the address and told me I could check for myself. The delivery is set for Tuesday.''

The Rainmaker straightened, his smile returning, and waved away the nubile young woman buffing his bluntly cut nails. "Tuesday? That's in a few days.''

"Yes, sir.''

"Max, this is perfect. This is freaking perfect.''

"Yes, sir.''

"I'll make the necessary arrangements. You've been superb, Max. This deserves a bonus.''

"I'd like to do one more thing.''

"Not necessary.''

"Mr. S., if you'll forgive me for disagreeing, I think this will take care of the bitch in such a way that your plans for her to go to the slammer will go forward without any more unexpected escapes.''

"Okay, let's hear it.''

Max explained, his voice so diabolically calm that the Rainmaker was pleased Max worked for him, instead of the other way around. By the time Max was finished, however, the Rainmaker was nodding. A smoothly executed arrest with as little fanfare as possible would, of course, be accomplished. After all, who was going to argue with a Wyoming sheriff bringing in his deputy's killer? But having Max leave an opening presentation would definitely show the displeasure of the Rainmaker in a very personal way.

Smiling at the trembling manicurist, the Rainmaker gestured for her to return, then said to Max, "Make it good."

"Oh, not just good, sir. Spectacular."

BY TEN ON TUESDAY morning, Booth was cranky and grumpy and not at all in the mood to think about how his life had been turned upside down by one woman.

And not just any woman, but one who made him hard and happy and frustrated and confused. Just who in hell was Kathleen Yardley, anyway?

Booth had been examining that puzzle at various levels of his consciousness since the night he'd come home and found her in the rocking chair holding his sleeping daughter. Not once had she directly answered it.

She'd overreacted, she'd clammed up and she'd dissembled. My God, she'd bobbed and weaved with quicker moves than a wily target avoiding a sharpshooter.

Bad enough that he'd spent the past few nights with little sleep, but Kathleen had refused to share his bed. He'd awakened this morning finally prepared to eat some crow, to apologize, although he didn't know what in hell for. But whatever it took, he intended to get things back to the way they'd been before Eric had made his offer.

Yet, when he came out to the living room, the sheet she'd used for the past few nights on the couch was folded on top of the plumped pillow beside a note saying she was moving to the carriage house.

"So you don't want to face me or talk to me, huh, babe?" He crumpled the note and tossed it into the trash. "Just swell."

Booth kicked the couch and cursed. Shoving his hands through his hair, he made himself consider his options.

He wanted to drive over to the carriage house and demand an answer about what in hell had happened between them. But he couldn't even do that, thanks to Gladys Hucklebee. He'd assured his mother he would deal with whatever off-the-wall reasoning the woman had for visiting her today. Of one thing he was sure: he intended to see that it was her last visit.

Maybe afterward he'd go see Kathleen, but then he had to go to work, which meant he would have to ask his mother to keep Lisa. He assumed, rather grimly, that Kathleen wouldn't be coming back.

Dammit.

Booth got Lisa up and sat her in the high chair. "Well, princess, it looks like it's just you and me." He tickled her belly and she giggled.

He went to the coffee maker and poured a mug, then spilled some dry cereal onto the chair tray for Lisa. She kept looking at Booth, then pointing toward the bedroom. "'Leen. 'Leen."

Booth stopped and looked at her. "What did you say?"

"'Leen."

"Lean? What are you talking about, Lisa?"

"'Leen!" She scrunched up her face in obvious frustration.

Booth sighed, resting his hands on his hips, realization finally dawning. "'Leen as in Kathleen? Is that it?"

She grinned, calmer now. "'Leen."

"She's not here, princess."

Her lower lip trembled.

"Ah, sweetheart, don't cry." But Lisa began anyway, and Booth knew then that Kathleen had not only wreaked havoc on his life, but on his daughter's, too. And not just ordinary, lousy havoc, but a life-changing havoc, by removing her affection and caring. That was the problem, he thought. She'd become too much a part of their lives.

He distracted Lisa by turning on the small TV to one of the cartoons. "Look, there's that silly bunny. He's jumping and hopping, and look, he's going to make that kitty run." Lisa clapped her hands and giggled, forgetting for the moment that Kathleen was gone.

Booth took another swallow of coffee. He could either feel sorry for himself—which was tempting but unproductive—or he could go out to the carriage house and tell her he understood she wanted to live there, but he wanted her back in his life, in his bed. A small voice inside muttered, *But back for what?* An affair? Continuing what they'd started? And what happened when good sex was no longer enough?

Hell, he hadn't had it long enough to imagine it not being enough. He rubbed his knuckles over his eyes. One thing at a time. Deal with Gladys Hucklebee, go to work and then tomorrow, when he wasn't as edgy, he'd go and talk to her and get this all straightened out.

The phone rang and he answered, hoping.

"Booth, I got some news," Lou Deasley, his bounty-hunter pal from Georgia, said without preliminaries.

Hope collapsed. "Make it good."

"Man, are we in a foul mood or what?"

"Foul and nasty and getting worse. Make me happy."

"Hey, buddy, I only dig it up, I don't promise rewards. First off, this Mason Knight ain't as rich as the car would indicate. He and his wife own a detective agency."

Booth brightened instantly. "Are you serious?" At his friend's affirmative, he muttered, "Well, I'll be damned."

"Now, before you go into high gear, hear me out. It's not on any five-star list. More like one phone and a few old cameras. They mostly follow straying husbands and boyfriends, but recently their lawyer resolved a lawsuit brought by one of their clients claiming Mrs. Knight had acted in an unprofessional manner when she had an affair with one of the straying husbands."

"Doesn't sound like she's one of the brightest bulbs in the attic."

"They swear it didn't happen."

"Uh-huh."

"Anyway, the Knights settled rather than lose their shirts and their business. But the suit took its toll. Unprofessional conduct doesn't sit well down here, and they went a number of months without the phone ringing."

"So what were they doing up here?"

"That I don't know," Deasley said. "I did some checking around but couldn't find any connection to Connecticut, much less Crosby."

"Run across the name Kathleen Yardley?"

"Nope. Nothing even close."

"Terrific," Booth muttered, discouraged again.

"Hey, I said I couldn't guarantee rewards."

"Yeah, but thanks for this. It's more than I had, but now that I have it, it's just one more piece that doesn't fit."

"There is one other thing. Their home mail is being held at the post office, and their newspaper isn't being delivered."

"Vacation?"

"That was my reaction."

"But in Crosby?"

"Maybe relatives?"

Booth sighed. "I checked around the neighborhood, and no one knows of anyone having company from Georgia."

"Mind if I ask why the interest?"

"A woman I know had a very strange reaction

to the car, and then she was too quick to change the subject when I asked her about it.''

"This Kathleen?"

"Yeah."

"Maybe she had an affair with old man Mason."

"I can do without your sarcasm."

Deasley chuckled. "Hey, dead ends ain't nothing new to you or to me. Chalk this one up and move on."

"Ever the philosopher."

"Hey, Booth."

"What?"

"You bangin' this Kathleen?"

Booth bristled at the term. He'd never been squeamish about describing sex. He'd "banged" a few women in his time, and they'd banged him right back. But not Kathleen. Whatever he'd had with Kathleen, it was too special to be described in street language.

"She's not the type."

"Hey, whatever greases your skids."

"Thanks for your help, buddy. Ever need a favor, give me a call."

He hung up, poured himself some more coffee, then realized he was going to have to bathe and dress Lisa since Kathleen wasn't here. "Okay, princess, let's get it done."

By the time he had his daughter clean, diapered and dressed, his shirt was soaked from splashed bathwater and the floor was covered with baby powder where Lisa had grabbed and waved the open container that Booth had left too close to her. His elbow stung from knocking the door closed and hitting his funny bone.

Feeling dragged out, he settled Lisa in her crib for a nap, kissed her, packed up the overnight bag for her to stay at his mother's. Then he dropped wearily into a living-room chair. He knew exactly why dads weren't created to be moms. It was too exhaustingly complicated.

About four hours later, at a little past two o'clock, Booth bundled Lisa into the car seat and drove to his mother's.

Janet opened the front door, relieving him of her granddaughter. "Where's Kathleen?" she asked, nuzzling the baby and anchoring her possessively in her arms.

"She's busy at the carriage house." Booth saw no reason to go into detail. He placed the overnight bag on the staircase to go upstairs. "Would you mind keeping Lisa tonight?"

"Of course not." Then she glanced at Booth and her smile shrank. "You should be helping Kathleen. Good heavens, Booth, where is your gratitude?"

"I told you I would be here today to deal with Gladys."

"You prefer Gladys to Kathleen?"

"I'm not making a choice." But he had to ask himself the same question. Why wasn't he at the carriage house with Kathleen? Maybe, just maybe, he was avoiding the inevitable confrontation.

His mother wasn't letting go. "After all she's done for you with Lisa...and I thought you really cared about her...." Her voice trailed off as if she wasn't sure what more to say, then she straightened and added bluntly, "At least I certainly had that impression when I visited last week." She nailed Booth with a stern look to remind him she expected her son to be as honorable as he'd been taught. "In my opinion, she's the most positive thing to happen to you and Lisa in months."

Booth stayed silent. He agreed, which again had him wondering just what had gone wrong? *Wait a minute,* he thought, feeling bruised and contrary. *She's the one who walked out, not me.*

His mother frowned, stepping close to him. "You don't look very well. Tired and cranky."

"And royally pissed and not in the mood to be reminded of my bad manners or Kathleen's good points."

"My goodness, you *are* touchy." She was staring at Lisa and scowling.

Booth didn't miss the scowl. "Now what?"

"You have her shirt on backward."

"It's on, isn't it?"

"But the buttons are supposed to go at the back and the lace at the front. Come on, sweetheart, Grammy will fix it. Your grampy never did very well when it came to dressing your Auntie Darlene, either. Guess these Rawlings men just don't know how to dress babies."

Booth rolled his eyes and leaned down to Lisa. "Tell Grammy you don't care."

"'Leen."

Janet blinked. "'Leen?"

"First word. Just this morning."

"Oh, sweetie, can you say it again for Grammy?"

"'Leen."

His mother hugged her. "I wonder what she means."

"What else?" he said wearily. "She's talking about Kathleen."

Janet Rawlings looked at Booth and then at Lisa and back to Booth. "Very interesting."

"Doesn't mean a thing."

"Of course it means something. You just haven't allowed yourself to figure out what." Booth started to say it was too damn late for subtle meanings, interesting or otherwise, when Janet glanced out the window. "Oh, and there's Gladys. Good Lord, what is all that stuff she's carrying?"

It was Booth's turn to scowl. The "stuff" was in wrinkly faded grocery sacks bearing the name of a store that had closed more than ten years ago. Gladys the pack rat. He recalled Angie telling him that she had boxes and boxes of old mail that she cut and used for scrap paper, a shoebox full of pencil stubs, and four hundred dollars she'd found in an apron pocket where she'd tucked it in 1985 when there'd been a spate of burglaries in her neighborhood.

"Mom, why don't you take Lisa out to the sun-porch. I'll deal with Gladys."

His sister sailed in, smelling like grape bubble gum and looking about twelve with her hair in braids. "I'll take her. Where's Kathleen?"

"That was what I asked and nearly got my head bitten off," his mother said, handing Lisa to Darlene and touching the baby's shirt. "Kathleen would have put the buttons in back and the lace in front."

Booth had had enough. "What the hell is this? The woman isn't attached to me like my right arm."

"Are we in a bad mood?" Darlene asked.

"Your brother isn't having a good day."

"I'm having a fabulous day."

"Did they have a fight?" Darlene whispered to their mother while peering at him. She drew closer to her mother and cradled Lisa a little tighter.

"Probably just a lovers' spat. She's at the carriage house."

"And he's here all edgy and snarly and looking very unhappy." Darlene raised an eyebrow, then touched her tongue to her upper lip, a habit she displayed whenever she thought she had the upper hand with her brother. "This is not the highway to happy endings, Booth."

"Oh, for God's sake."

"No, this isn't good at all. And Kathleen is such a cool lady. I mean, what did you do to her?" But without waiting for him to say anything, she rolled on. "Mom and I will be glad to keep Lisa while you go and apologize. A private apology with the lights low and the music soft works every time."

Booth glowered at Darlene, then gripped the door handle. "Better make tracks, muskrat, or Gladys, the self-appointed moral police chief, will be lecturing you on your shorts and skimpy top."

"Get me outta here." And she disappeared with Lisa, making the baby giggle.

Booth took a deep breath and pulled open the door, delighted by Gladys's surprised look at his presence.

"Well, well, fancy seeing you here."

"I used to live here."

"And it's too bad you don't anymore, instead of going off and doing sinful things with a loose woman. My poor Angie is barely cold in the ground."

Booth narrowed his eyes. "Gladys, stop insulting Kathleen."

"The truth will be very enlightening," she said mysteriously.

Janet stepped between the two of them and invited Gladys inside. "Whatever have you brought? Not that collection of recipes you've been telling me about."

"I did promise you those, didn't I? Another time. These are some newspapers I found. I've been looking for days because I knew there was something in them that was important."

She trundled into the house, heading for the

kitchen, the scent of musty tweed and camphor wafting in her wake.

Booth looked at his mother. "Recipes?"

"She mentioned some old apple recipes of her grandmother's, and I wanted to look through them for the cookbook the church is putting together for a fund-raiser."

"Giving her a good excuse for a return trip."

"Now, Booth, she is odd and cantankerous, but you're the one who has the problems with her."

Booth rubbed his hand across the back of his neck. "Let's go and see what's in the bags, but I'm telling you right now, I don't want her anywhere near Lisa."

"I understand."

He glanced at the ceiling. "Thank you, God."

By the time they reached the kitchen, what had looked like bags of randomly stuffed newspapers had been emptied, with the tabloid pages spread out on the table and continuing onto the counter. Gladys stood to the side, rocking back and forth like a preening mistress of ceremonies secure in her presentation of the scandal of the year.

She watched Booth, giving him the eerie sense she was about to pronounce judgment. She wore a boater with limp ribbons and clusters of dusty pansies weighing down the brim. Its outdated whimsy actually softened her face, but Booth was in no mood to notice. The woman was weird.

"What do you have here, Gladys? These are all

grocery-store tabloids,'' Janet said in a friendly tone.

"Where the real news is," she replied.

"Yeah, I've been following all those space-alien scoops."

She turned and glared at Booth. "You won't be talkin' so sure when you take a closer look. The one there on the end of the counter. Start there."

Humor her, he thought, barely glancing at the screaming headlines—until he got to the one she indicated.

Wanted Woman Escapes Wyoming Statewide Roadblock. Then in a smaller caption: What Went Wrong between a Deputy Sheriff and His Lovely Wife That Made Her Shoot Him?

Booth drew closer, and when the name Kathleen Hanes, beneath a grainy photo of a man and woman swam up at him, he stared in disbelief.

"Kathleen?"

Gladys snipped, "So you do recognize her. I knew when I saw her with you that there was something familiar about her. So I went home and began looking through all my papers. It took some time, but I knew I'd seen her face."

Booth stared, looking at one, and then the next and the next. The stories were dated June, and typically salacious and sensationalized, but he couldn't get beyond the gist of them. Kathleen was a fugitive, wanted for murder.

Janet came closer, gasping when she comprehended what she was seeing. "There has to be some mistake."

Booth felt as if he'd been sucker punched. The headlines screamed, the pictures bled through the text with painful clarity. Photos of Kathleen and her husband, Steve, on their wedding day, a picture of Steve Hanes when he was sworn in as deputy sheriff, and a discomforting shot of the murder scene, hours after the fact. There was a splash of photos of police cars around a simple white house with brown trim that squatted amid flats of sagebrush. A pine forest on one side of a nearby barn reached hopefully into a canyon of clouds. A flag hung limply from a pole in the front yard.

If not for the cop cars, it would have looked idyllic—Middle America where the flag was still saluted and lemonade served on hot summer afternoons.

Booth had never been to Wyoming, but he associated the state with cowboys, endless stretches of highway and hundreds of miles between one town and the next. The Kathleen he knew didn't fit in Wyoming, and for damn sure she didn't fit the tabloid portrayal of a wanted killer.

"Booth?" His mother had gripped his arm, and he could feel her body shaking. His own felt numb. "What can all this mean? There has to be a mistake. It is a mistake, isn't it?" Her eyes were wide and worried. "Isn't it?"

Booth slipped an arm around his mother and gave her an encouraging hug.

"My newspapers don't lie," Gladys said.

"But they exaggerate," Janet said, her voice breaking. "And they make things up. Why, some of these very papers have been sued for false reporting."

"It's the truth!"

Booth released his mother. "Well, I'll tell you what, Gladys," he said, bearing down on her. "I'm a cop, and if anyone would know any of this stuff, it would be me, and I don't know a thing about it. And if Kathleen were some dangerous gun-waving fugitive, her picture would be plastered all over television and in newspapers with more credibility than these rags you read."

By the time he finished, Gladys was hugging her empty bags to her chest. "Just 'cuz you don't like it don't make it a lie."

Booth glared at her. "You know what I don't like? You. I want you to take your goddamned newspapers and your goddamned warped perceptions and get the hell away from me and my family."

"Janet," the old woman sputtered, "are you going to let him talk to me that way?"

"Yes, Gladys, I am." Janet gathered up all the papers and put them into one of the bags and handed them to her. "I feel sorry for you, Gladys, but I can't let you hurt people I care about. And that includes Kathleen."

Booth turned his back and walked out the door. He felt dirty, slimy and angry. At Gladys for dumping on him whatever twisted piece of truth there was in those tabloids, and at Kathleen for not trusting him enough to tell him. He wanted to believe it was all some made-up tale for juicy-gossip purposes, but there were some details he couldn't ignore. Her separation from her father and brothers, her mother's death and the fact that Kathleen was an accomplished pianist who had given lessons the first few years of her marriage. The story supported what he knew about her, despite her vagueness about where she'd come from and about her past in general. And it answered the question of why she feared cops. God knows what Hanes had done to her to deserve being killed, but Booth would bet his own years in law enforcement that their marriage hadn't won any blue ribbons for happiness or quality of life.

In the distance he heard the front door close and then his mother's approaching footsteps.

She touched his back. "What are you going to do, Booth? I know you can find out very quickly if there is any truth to this nonsense."

"Yeah," he said quietly. Now he had the right name to run through NCIC, or he could call the Wyoming State Police, or he could ask Kathleen directly. All three possibilities lay in his belly like rat poison.

"You don't want to know, do you?"

No! But a hard-assed denial was a position he couldn't defend. His silence would become complicity. Withholding evidence could cost him his job; it would damage his reputation for integrity, and to what end? Gladys would make sure her tabloids landed on the chief's desk, and she'd relish the moment.

He turned and kissed his mother's cheek, then stepped past her.

She caught his arm. "Where are you going?"

"Downtown. I have to check this all out."

"Booth, are you going to have to arrest her?"

"If this is all true, yes."

CHAPTER FOURTEEN

AT 1:15 A.M. ON Wednesday morning, after he left police headquarters, instead of going home, Booth turned into the drive that led to the carriage house. The early morning was warm and humid; the night sounds of crickets and the faraway barking of a dog were overwhelmed by the rolling tones and chords of "Memories" from *Cats*. Kathleen's piano had arrived, and she was obviously in her glory.

Getting out of his car, Booth stood in the darkness listening. He could vividly imagine her fingers sweeping across the keys, her face expressing the intensity of the music. He was struck by how badly he wanted her, and at the same time by how furious he was that he'd opened the door that had brought her into his life in the first place.

It wasn't rational, it wasn't objective, it wasn't even marginally imaginative, but the dichotomy defined the murky seesaw of his thought processes over the hours since reading Gladys's tabloids.

He shoved a hand through his hair, rubbed at his eyes and cursed his unending exhaustion. He hadn't been home since Gladys had made her presentation. He'd been on the phone, checking police files, digging through every possibility he could think of for some hint that all the evidence he was coming up with wasn't true. He desperately needed to find a hole in the story—one hole that would reveal some screwup, either massive or minor.

And he hadn't.

He walked up to the front entrance of the carriage house and found the screen unlocked.

Booth snorted in disgust. She was alone at one in the morning in a desolate area on the outskirts of Crosby, and she hadn't locked the doors? Careless or stupid or foolishly innocent about intruders. Booth applied the latter instinctively. And naiveté just didn't fit the profile of someone who'd blown away her husband. That was his problem. The facts he'd gathered about the Steve Hanes murder were pretty condemning, but his gut or his heart wanted desperately for there to be another explanation. He wanted to find that hole.

He wanted that explanation from her, and he wanted it tonight.

He opened the door and stepped inside. Light and music flooded the air as he turned the corner into a massive room with a gleaming hardwood floor. Centered perfectly on a round burgundy carpet beneath the exposed oak ceiling beams was a baby grand piano.

Kathleen sat on the bench, looking fragile and small, as if she'd been a forgotten last performer at a music recital. She faced away from him. Her back was ruler straight, her hair loose and tumbling around her shoulders. She wore an oversize sweatshirt and her legs were bare. Her equally bare feet worked the foot petals furiously.

Booth stood still, the music enveloping him as he wanted to envelop her. His body, weary just minutes ago, was now tense and alert. Every moment of uncertainty drifted away, every testy conversation they'd had no longer mattered, every instant of mistrust was reduced to ashes and dust.

Nothing mattered to him but now and her and...

Then he moved up behind her, swiftly and silently. In the deepest part of his being, his restraint released into lightning and heat, becoming a thundering swell of need and anticipation. He brought one hand around to cover her anticipated scream of alarm, and at the same time he used the other to turn her to face him.

For a second she froze, and Booth's mouth covered hers. She pushed at him, grabbing handfuls of his shirt. Booth felt the scrape of her nails through the cloth, and sweat broke out across his belly. Then her resistance collapsed into a moan and he tasted her hunger, drank in her thirst.

He straddled the bench, not once lifting his mouth, plunging his tongue even deeper while he lifted her across his thighs. That was when he knew she wore nothing beneath the sweatshirt.

Positioned so that her body was glued to his, he moved his hands under the shirt, gripping her hips, bringing her even closer. He slid his palms up her sides, cupping and circling her breasts.

She broke the kiss and tipped her head back, staring at him, her eyes pools of allure.

"What are you doing here?" she whispered.

"This is what I'm doing here." His mouth devoured hers once again.

She gasped, her fingers tangling in his hair. "But it's over between us."

Booth suckled her breasts, then buried his mouth in her neck. "Then climb off, babe, and I'll go away."

She closed her eyes and he counted the beats of silence while his body hummed hotter.

"You know I can't."

"I was counting on that. Come here."

Her arms slid around him, their grip tight and unrelenting; her mouth moved over his with a hunger he welcomed and devoured.

She kissed him deep and deeper still, then sank back, her breath rushing, her gaze hot with passion. Booth reached for her, but her hands went to his jeans, one tugging at the belt while the other moved over him so possessively he nearly lost control.

She slipped off him and stood staring, looking as if she'd wanted this moment as much as he had. Then, as if this were their last chance to be together, she tugged him from the bench and onto the floor. She slipped off her shorts, then pulled her sweatshirt over her head.

She was naked and aroused and shaking with her power over him. Booth blew out the breath he'd been holding, got his pants open and barely below his hips before she'd sunk down on top of him. The dark heat of her tore through him as she moved and swayed and held him. Nothing mattered beyond the next erotic moment.

Neither spoke. Neither needed to. As their bodies tangled, bathed in the light from the lamp beside the piano, Booth settled into a different realm than he'd ever known. Hypnotic, mystical, saturating. Her body lifted and settled and lifted and settled again. He gripped her hips, whipped his head back, his teeth clenched.

His climax pounded through him, rushing, racing, rolling forth in a bone-wrenching renewal. He held her so tight, so close, she became a part of him, making him unsure whether his grip was to keep her from falling or himself from dying.

Kathleen came in a sweep of heat and pleasure, her body arcing and then falling in a boneless heap across him.

They lay replete, their bodies sweaty, satiated but still quivering with a wild savagery.

Finally she rolled off him, but he didn't move. He didn't think he ever would again.

"I didn't know you were coming."

His eyes still closed, he grinned at the double meaning. "I didn't, either."

"This doesn't change anything."

"Everything is already changed."

She reached for her sweatshirt and pulled it over her head. Booth watched, unmindful of his own clothes. She stood, stepping out of his reach.

He knew she was nervous and uneasy. "I still have some things at your place. I'll get them tomorrow. Today was just too busy."

"Yeah, busy for me, too."

She gave him an odd look, then added, "I had to give notice at the restaurant, do the paperwork for Eric, and then the piano arrived a few hours ago. I have your key, and as long as you're here—"

"Forget the key and the itinerary," he said, annoyed that she was acting as if he were already out of her life.

She stared down at him, and he made his face relax. One thing he didn't want was an argument.

"You come here in the middle of the night, catch me off guard and we have sex, when we haven't even been speaking to each other for the past few days. Something is going on."

"Well *something* certainly was."

But she didn't laugh and she didn't smile. She planted her hands on her hips and glared down at him. "You took me by surprise."

"Uh-huh. You were wet the second I touched you."

"Music arouses me."

Booth winked. "I'll remember that."

She narrowed her gaze, started to say something and then shut her mouth.

Booth rolled to his feet, fastening his jeans and dragging his hands down his face. He could still smell her, and the scent stirred his gut anew. "So when did the piano arrive?"

"About eight o'clock. The driver called and said his Vermont delivery unloaded faster than he'd expected and he'd like to deliver the piano so he could get a good night's sleep and start back tomorrow."

"Back to where?"

"To where he came from." She folded up the sheet music and placed it inside the hinged bench.

"And where was that?"

Without looking at him, she again ducked the question. "You sound like a cop."

"I *am* a cop. Where did the driver come from, and where is he driving back to?"

He saw the dance of indecision in her eyes, the beginnings of panic.

"Kathleen, it's not a hard question."

"Why does it matter?"

"Because you're stalling and tap dancing and refusing to answer me."

"It came from Wyoming," she snapped. "And if you don't believe me, I'll show you the packing slip."

"I believe you."

"Then if you're through with your questions, I'd like you to leave so I can go to bed."

"How about you? Where did *you* come from?"

She stared at him, her fingers gripping the folds of her sweatshirt. In that moment she looked like a small defenseless child, and Booth hated himself for the questions he'd already asked and for the tougher ones still to come. He didn't much believe in miracles, but in that moment he would have welcomed one.

"You know, don't you?" she asked in a defeated whisper.

"I know."

Her cheeks paled, her hand fluttering up to her mouth before she dropped it to her side. "So why are you asking all these questions if you already know the answers?"

"I want to hear it from you."

"What? A confession?"

"Is that what you need to do? Make a confession?"

"No!"

"Okay. Then why don't you just tell me who you really are, what happened in Wyoming and why you're here. And give me at least one truthful reason why you hate cops."

"Why are you doing this? If you know everything, then what does anything I have to say matter?"

"What you have to say matters because you and I just made love, and if you can trust me enough to be a lover, then I want to know why you can't trust me enough to tell me the truth."

"Because I can't!" She nearly screamed the words. "Do you hear me? I can't! I don't trust anyone, and if you came here thinking that having sex would lure me into making some damning confession, I'll tell you right now, Detective Rawlings, it's not going to happen. And that's what tonight was all about, wasn't it? Is this the way you usually work? Or did you make an exception for me?''

"I want to make an exception of you, Kathleen. But I need your help.''

"My help? That's a joke. You want me to make it easy for you. Well, I won't.'' She crossed to the door, then turned and marched back. "You want the truth, Detective, well this is my truth. I put up with my husband's abuse and the put-downs and the terror. I gave up my piano, my life and my heart, for God's sake. I protected him because I loved him, and I thought he loved me—he said he did. And we wanted children, and I wanted my marriage to be forever. I didn't want to run away the way my mother had to. I wanted to make it work. I thought it was just me, that I wasn't doing things the way I should. The town loved him and respected him. He was a cop sworn to uphold the law and keep the streets safe. But it was my home that wasn't safe, because he lived there. I was a fool— a stupid, blind fool.'' Tears shimmered in her eyes, and when he reached for her, she backed away, waving her hands to keep him at a distance.

Booth spoke softly. "You weren't stupid, Kathleen. You were committed to honoring the vows you'd made.''

But she glared at him, her eyes suspicious. "You're a cop.''

"And you're still running. You can't run forever.''

She tipped her head to the side, her eyes glittering with resolve. "Yes, I can. I learned something with you. I never should have let you become my friend."

"Did you kill Steve?"

She went very still, swaying and shaking, before folding her arms around herself.

Booth moved closer, and she shrank back.

"Talk to me, baby. Give me a reason, an explanation, something I can use to help you. Did he beat you up that day? Did he threaten you? Was it self-defense?"

"You believe them," she said as if she'd just lost her last hope.

He took her shoulders and shook her gently. "Kathleen, I have a lot of police facts, reports and opinions stacked on my desk at work. I've just spent the past eleven hours going over them so closely I have them memorized. According to all of them, you're a fugitive. The facts say I should arrest you and notify Wyoming. I want you to give me a reason why I shouldn't do that."

"You want me to prove to you that I'm innocent?"

"I want you to tell me the truth. Did you kill him?"

"No."

"Not self-defense?"

"No."

"And not premeditated?"

"No."

"Then why are you the prime suspect?"

She threw her hands into the air, her head fell back and she laughed. "Why? Why? Because I was his wife. I was there. I had a motive and everyone in the sheriff's office said I did it. Isn't that the way it works with cops? A consensus of opinion—she's got a good reason so she's guilty. And of course poor beleaguered Steve was always the real victim. And you want to know why?" Sarcasm laced her voice as she continued. "Because I had the audacity to go to a safe house to get away from him. Because I didn't give him a baby and had the nerve to mention to a friend that Steve wouldn't accept that the fault was his, not mine. Because I wanted to destroy his macho image of tough guy who made his wife do as she was told. You know the old cop rule— 'If you can't handle your wife, how are you gonna handle the criminals?'"

Booth tried to take her in his arms, but she pushed him away.

"But you know how to handle me, don't you, Booth?"

"Kathleen..."

"That's what tonight was about, wasn't it? That's what it's always been about. Turn her on and you can get anything you want. I said I didn't do it, but do you believe me? Of course not. I knew you wouldn't from the very beginning, and all your soft smiles and gentle tones now aren't going to convince me otherwise. You want me to make a full confession and make your job easier? Or are there more cops waiting out there in the bushes for your signal to come in with guns and tear gas?''

Booth reined in the words he wanted to fling at her. He'd bungled this badly, and he wasn't sure if he was furious with her for her offensive tack or if his fury was self-directed. He knew better than to handle a case where he was emotionally involved. He should have given all the details to another detective and let him deal with it. But he couldn't now.

''If you're not going to arrest me, I want you to leave.''

''So you can disappear?''

''You're in charge, Detective Rawlings. If you're worried about that, then arrest me.'' She held out her wrists. ''Bring any handcuffs with you?''

''You're enjoying this, aren't you?''

''As much as you are.''

Then he looked at the piano. This was the source of her happiness, her joy. Not him, not even her freedom or her innocence. She'd risked discovery by sending for it. He'd listened to her play, watched the contentment bloom within her like spring after a long winter. Just as it had set her free emotionally, it would also hold her here physically. At least for a little while.

He had some time. Maybe only until she could make arrangements to have her piano returned to storage, but a few hours, at least.

He knew he was procrastinating, and he knew he was taking a huge chance with his career and his future if he was wrong. But Kathleen as killer-turned-fugitive was impossible to reconcile with the woman he knew, the woman he loved. He wanted to go through those police reports one more time.

"I'll be back tomorrow."

"No. I don't want you to come back tomorrow. I don't want to see you again."

"Tough." He turned and started for the door.

"Booth, wait." She grabbed his arm and halted him. "What are you going to do?"

"Since you don't want to answer my questions, I'm going to try to find someone who will."

"You're going to call Wyoming, aren't you? You're going to tell them you have me."

He could read the terror and panic in her eyes. "Do you honestly believe I'd do that without warning you?"

"I don't know. I don't understand why you're walking away and not doing anything."

Because I fell in love with you. But he didn't say it. He knew she'd read it as a ploy to manipulate her, and he couldn't blame her for that conclusion. At the moment, her trust of him was bobbing around the zero mark. Using what was still new, scary and fragile as a way to hold her—hell, he couldn't do it.

"Lock the door."

"I don't understand."

He cupped her neck and drew her close. The kiss was soft and bland, more friendly than passionate.

Kathleen didn't respond, but she didn't push him away, either.

"I'll see you tomorrow."

And he walked out into the night, got into his car and drove away.

Kathleen stood in the coolness of the dark until the sound of the vehicle had faded. She stepped back inside, closed the screen door and locked it.

Her head ached and her thoughts were a jumble of confusion. Why hadn't he arrested her? Did he believe she was innocent or was this some kind of trick? She didn't know. If this were Steve, then trick would be the obvious answer. But this was Booth, and as he often had in the past, he rattled her perceptions and mixed up her feelings.

He was coming back tomorrow, but she didn't intend to be here. She'd leave all the information, and she'd leave him her statement of what had happened, but she couldn't face him tomorrow. She didn't have the strength or the will to resist if he asked her to trust him. She wanted to, but she was too scared, too used to being blindsided and lied to.

She went into her bedroom and dragged out the box of newspaper articles Clarke had sent to her. Also in the box were all the papers she'd taken from her car before she'd sold it in Pennsylvania. They'd been in a desk drawer at Gail's, and she'd swept them into the box when she'd moved to Booth's.

She put all those aside, and for the umpteenth time she went through the articles. News reports gathered from the police left no place for her innocence. Someone had killed Steve, and thanks to a very cooperative sheriff's department, she'd been accused and convicted even before a charge had been filed. It was obviously a frame-up, but why? And since she'd had no witnesses, hadn't been anyplace where someone could vouch for her—

My God!

She grabbed the pile of papers she'd shoved aside and went through them. Old gas receipts, a wrinkled map, outdated car registrations—and then she found it. The speeding ticket. Given to her by a Wyoming state trooper almost a hundred miles from home. She held it under the light. It wasn't the original, and some of the printing was light, but the time and place were clear. No way she could have killed Steve, for he'd been murdered when she was being stopped for speeding a hundred miles east of Rodeo.

She swung around in a circle, hugging herself, feeling as if some inner floodgate had opened; all the tightness of the past few months flowed out. She put the ticket back in the box and remembered Booth's advice. She skipped past the piano on her way to lock the door.

"Ah, she dances, too."

She stopped and froze at the strange voice coming out of the darkness. Booth had been gone less than half an hour.

The figure came farther into the light. First she saw the ax and then she saw the man. Big, dressed in black and silver. Behind him was another figure, shrouded in the scent of cigar smoke.

She was so scared her mouth refused to open. He was going to kill her and she didn't even know who he was.

"Relax, doll baby, this isn't for you. You're already claimed." The other man stepped into the light, grinning and aiming a gun at her. The first man lifted the ax and brought it down on her piano.

Then she screamed.

CHAPTER FIFTEEN

A HAND CLAMPED OVER her mouth, and the gun jammed into her ribs. She struggled, arching back, trying to kick, fighting for her freedom as she watched the destruction of her most prized possession.

The man with the ax walked over to Kathleen, taking a long strip of nylon rope from the man with his hand over her mouth. He then reached down and grabbed first one ankle, then the other, yanking so hard it felt as if her hip and leg joints had separated.

Within seconds she found herself facedown on the floor with her feet tied together, her mouth gagged and her hands tied behind her. Her head was forced around so she had to face the piano. When the chopping began anew, she squeezed her eyes closed and wished she could block her ears.

The other man, the one with the gun and the cigar, returned to the shadows. Obviously he didn't want her to see him, or he'd been told his turn came second. *Destroy the piano, make her watch and then kill her.*

Kathleen couldn't scream, she couldn't move, she couldn't fight; and when the noise finally stopped, she waited for the other man to do something. Inside her head a demon cackled. "Your turn."

Nearby she heard their voices, low and muted; the two were plotting the next step. She couldn't run. She was helpless, left to await whatever new horror was planned for her. She kept her eyes squeezed tightly closed. She couldn't look at the remains of her piano; the sight and sound of its end would be forever blazoned in her mind.

That was what hurt so excruciatingly—the deliberate cruelty. The same delight in savagery that Steve had so often displayed toward her. A jubilee of inflicted pain and terror.

Ironically, the place where she lay tied on the floor was where she and Booth had made love. If she pressed her nose into the carpet, she could smell him, feel his body envelop her; she could blank out the nearby rubble. She almost wished for insanity or amnesia or numbing shock—any harbor of denial would be better than the present reality.

She couldn't win. She hadn't been able to run far enough. And did it really matter? It wasn't as if anyone cared, as if there were anyone she needed to protect. She had no children, no family, no place where she belonged. For a while she'd pretended she had a bond with Booth, and she'd opened her needy heart to his daughter. Yet at the same time, she'd judiciously guarded her spirit, and she'd maintained her mistrust. To have ignored either would have made her too vulnerable and therefore destroyed the tiny world she'd created.

Turning, she winced anew with inner pain. The men hadn't told her their names or where they had come from or who had sent them, but it was obvious that they'd been waiting for her piano, waiting for the right time. It was clear to her now that being caught had been inevitable. This wasn't random devastation; she'd been found and the point was to break her spirit as thoroughly as they'd dismembered her piano.

How they'd succeeded in tracking her down, she didn't know, but the sheriff or his minions would get her eventually. Wistfully, she regretted her silence and stubbornness with Booth. She should have told him the truth a long time ago. She closed her eyes, weeping for all her mistakes, all her lost hopes, the family she'd found with the Rawlings— all she'd treasured and couldn't keep.

Then the voices stopped and she strained to hear, but there was only silence. Had the men gone? Had the one with the gun been there only to make sure she didn't run? Was there no intent to kill her?

In one small crevice of her soul a sprout of hope came to life. Maybe. If she could talk to Booth. He wanted her to tell him her story. Not the story from Wyoming. Not the story the Rodeo police had. Her story.

Yes, if she could see Booth. He was coming today. He'd said he would come back. Yes, he would come....

When the hand closed over her arm and rolled her onto her back, the face looming over her sent her terror level to a new high.

The voice had a mesmerizing silkiness. "It's all over, Kathleen."

The pitted face was too familiar with its muddy brown eyes and deep pouches beneath. He took the gag from her mouth, untied her and hauled her to her feet. Kathleen's knees buckled from the numbness in her legs, and he dragged her to the bench, forcing her to sit down.

She stared at him. His face and neck were fleshier, his belly saggier, and she concluded that her flight from the frame-up might have taken a toll. For some bizarre reason she wanted to laugh. Sheriff Buck Faswell had always prided himself on being fit, an example of mental toughness and physical stamina. It was obvious that doughnuts and weekend beer and gambling feasts had prevailed.

"How did you find me?" she asked, her voice a husky squeak.

"Brilliant police work plus a couple of timely tips." He laughed then, and she turned away. He'd had bacon and pancakes; she smelled the remains on his breath.

Brilliant police work would have found her weeks ago. More than likely he'd gotten lucky. The arrival of her piano and the arrival of the two men were too close not to be connected. "Tips like the delivery of my piano?"

"You mean that pile of kindling?" He pulled a

toothpick from his mouth and picked at his teeth. "Stupid move, Kathleen."

Which meant that her piano delivery was a tip. "Or brilliant."

"Huh?"

"It got you here," she muttered, enjoying his gathering frown. It felt good to knock that sanctimonious smirk off his face. The smarmy grin of a dangerous man, not of a man on official business.

He'd come personally to get her. First to destroy the piano and then kill her. A legitimate sheriff would have notified the Crosby police that they had a fugitive in their town. Probably the two men had flown from Wyoming to Boston or Providence and then driven to Crosby. No stop at the police department, as any honest law-enforcement officer would have done. He'd come straight to the carriage house after eating his pancakes and bacon. Probably at the Silver Lining Restaurant, she thought with some irony.

It occurred to her, too, that he was totally out of his element. This wasn't Rodeo, where he was king and deal maker; there were no deputies here to back up his bullishness. Kathleen assumed that if he didn't deliver her back to Rodeo, he'd be in major trouble with whoever wanted her to take the fall for Steve's death.

The sheriff snarled a string of expletives about her being a smart-ass broad who thought she could hide from the law. Then he pointed his gun at her, gesturing with the barrel that she should go into the bedroom. When she remained in place, he shoved the barrel into her ribs and pushed her with his free hand.

She gasped at the arrow of pain that zigzagged from rib to rib. She doubled over, moaning, mostly to gain time. He no doubt assumed she'd pull some hysterical trick like begging or pleading. In fact, if she'd thought either would have worked, she wouldn't have hesitated.

He gave a sideways glance at the rubble that was once her piano. "Max didn't waste his talent."

"He neglected to tell me his name." But she filed the name "Max" away in her mind.

"Dead eyes."

"What?"

"That's what Steve called him. 'Dead eyes.'"

"Steve knew this monster?" Even as she asked the question she realized how ridiculous it sounded. Of course Steve would know him. One lowlife usually had no trouble finding another one.

"Sure. Max takes care of business. Like a programmed machine."

"And who programmed him to destroy my piano? You?"

"Naw, I don't care about that stuff. He and the Rainmaker made that deal. I just want you back in Wyoming and in jail for Steve's murder. Trial will just be a formality. Evidence all points your way, Kathleen." He chuckled, obviously enjoying his attempt to be official.

"The evidence is as phony as you are, Sheriff," she said boldly, knowing that it was true.

He closed in on her, his lip curling into a smirk. "We all know you did it."

"By all, you mean the Rodeo sheriff's department?" she retorted, gaining courage with every word.

"Can't beat witnesses like cops for credibility. Let's go."

But she didn't move. "They couldn't witness what I didn't do."

"You talk too much."

"I want to know who shot Steve."

"Yeah? Well, we'll find a mirror, and when you look closely, you'll find a skinny-boned woman named Kathleen Hanes." He laughed then, a sound that had all the humor of fingernails on a blackboard.

Kathleen sucked in a breath, determined. "Who shot Steve? Was it you? One of the other deputies?"

"You think I'm gonna tell you that?"

Kathleen clamped down on her excitement. He'd as much as admitted she'd been set up. Now if she could just bluff her way into getting him to say more. "What if I said I knew who the real killer was? What if I told you that I overheard you and Cory talking while Steve lay dead on floor?"

He paled, then turned a dark red. "You weren't there. You'd been gone for hours."

"But I came back."

"You're lying."

"How else would I know that you and Cory were there?"

He looked flustered, as if he needed someone wiser to tell him what to do. "What did you hear?"

"That Cory killed Steve."

He sputtered. "Cory? That mealy-livered coward couldn't set a wolf trap by himself. Job like that goes to the best man, and that ain't Cory. Gotta have a man who knows how to handle himself."

"You?" She whispered the challenge, easing it out as if it were the most powerful word in existence.

He cocked his gun.

"It was you," she said very softly. Maybe in the back of her mind she'd known all along. Steve had told her that Faswell liked money, liked to gamble, was always looking for new ways to pay his gambling debts. When he had cash, he liked to flash it and hang out with guys who played just beyond the edge of the law.

Faswell glared at her. "Hanes talked too much. Blabbin' like a drunken bum to people he had no business talking to."

"So you killed him to shut him up."

"He was a drunk who couldn't stay silent. The Rainmaker's operation is too smooth and too cash-rich to get screwed by a talkative drunk. I got sent to do the job because I'm the one who could get away with it. Just like I'm the one who's gonna take you back. Gonna get a lotta C-notes for bringing you in, Kathleen, baby, so you're sucking at a dry hole if you think I'm gonna let you get away this time.'' He rocked back on his heels a bit, his chest puffed out with self-importance.

Her newly discovered knowledge combined with inner grit gathered momentum. ''And just what reason do I have to do as you ask, Sheriff? To save my own life? According to you, I'm going to prison. Hardly a pleasant future to look forward to. To stop you from killing me? Go ahead. Right now I'm not terribly sure what I'm living for, anyway. Surely not this nightmare I'm in.''

He started shaking his head, amusement softening his face. ''I'm not going to kill you, and you're going to return willingly with me to Wyoming. And what's even better, you're going to forget this incident and our conversation.''

He was so calm, so sure, new terror stole into her mind.

''What? No questions? No show of bravery? No innocent outrage?'' He chuckled. ''Poor Kathleen. She has Steve's killer complete with confession and she isn't going to tell anyone.'' He moved closer to her. ''Want to know why?'' She wanted to say yes, but she didn't want to give him the satisfaction.

''I believe one is named Clarke and on his way to becoming some star in Hollywood. And the other is named Gary.''

''My brothers?''

''Got guys waiting to take them down if they

don't see me with you, and you singing like a birdie.''

"My God."

"This is the big leagues, Kathleen. Too much of the Rainmaker's operation is at stake to lose out because one female refuses to confess. We go back, you tell your story as it should be told and your brothers stay alive. Now move on into the bedroom."

Defeat covered her like a suffocating blanket, and she moved slowly as Faswell told her what to do. Why had she ever thought she could win? There were no witnesses, no handy hidden tape recorder—it was just the sheriff's word against hers. And who would believe her? She'd run and she'd hidden and by doing so, had acted guilty. And now even her brothers were in danger.

A few minutes later, in her bedroom, she remembered the speeding ticket. It was her only proof that she couldn't have been at the house when Steve was killed. The speeding ticket meant her freedom. She had to hide it so that the sheriff wouldn't know.

"Would you mind waiting outside while I change clothes?"

He laughed. "You think I'm stupid? No way I'm gonna chance you climbing out the window." He pushed her toward the clothes she'd been unpacking. That now seemed like eons ago. Then, for good measure, he shoved the chair near the window. "Get dressed. Put them jeans on." He sat down, stretched his legs out and aimed his weapon at her.

His gaze surveyed the room and came to rest on the box where she had dropped the ticket. Before she could stop him, Faswell dragged it toward him and fished through the papers while Kathleen held her breath. *Please, don't let him find it. Please!*

Her heart fell when he did, and just as instantly, rage burst inside her.

She flew at him, trying to seize the flimsy paper, but he knocked her aside. She fell against the footboard of the bed, immediately got back on her feet and went after him again.

This time he gripped her wrist and snarled, "Back away or I'll break your arm." He yanked and twisted until she began to lose focus from the pain.

He tore up the ticket, put it in a small china dish and lit a match to it. Kathleen squeezed her eyes closed and fought the roll of nausea that gripped her.

"You thought I didn't know about the ticket? Found out weeks ago. But being a good guy, I got it fixed for you. You got a nice clear driving record."

Kathleen sank down on the bed in defeat.

He peered at his watch. "Get dressed. I want to be out of this place in ten minutes."

She turned so he wouldn't see her tears. Her options had all run out.

"BOOTH RAWLINGS?"

"Speaking."

"Detective Booth Rawlings?"

"Who is this?"

"Name is Mason Knight. You don't know me, but I've been watching Kathleen, and you should know she's been caught."

Booth gripped the phone, signaling to his sister to finish tending to Lisa.

"Caught by who? Where? And what in hell are you doing watching her?"

"Take it easy. I'm on your side. I'm out at her place. There's a man with a gun. My wife is working her way around to try and get inside—"

"Don't do anything, and tell your wife not to," Booth ordered. "I'll be right there."

Booth dropped the receiver in the cradle, told Darlene to take Lisa to his mother's and headed to his bedroom. "What's going on?" she shouted after him.

He took his .357 from the closet shelf, pulled on a denim jacket to conceal it and grabbed his car keys as he headed toward the door.

"Booth?" His sister stood holding Lisa, her eyes wide and worried.

"Take her and go back to Mom's. I'll call later."

"Is Kathleen in trouble?"

"Yes."

He raced down the steps and climbed into his Explorer. He fired the engine, jammed it into first gear and sped down the street, leaving the scream of peeling tires behind him.

The six miles from his place to the carriage house

passed while his mind raced from fury at himself that he'd left her alone to fury at her for being so damned stubborn. That was quickly followed by terror that whatever the hell was going on, he'd get there too late.

He swung into the drive, then jammed on the brakes. *Okay, cool it, get it together. You're not going to help her by barging in like some sweat-soaked rookie.* He called for backup, emphasizing no sirens, no lights.

Booth parked the sports-utility vehicle so that anyone trying to leave would have to drive through it, over it, or smash down the ten-foot privacy shrubs planted in thick dense rows.

He got out, silently closed the door and moved forward. That was when he saw the expensive cream-colored car with Georgia plates. Either Kathleen had some mysterious guardian angel or the Knights were two kooks with a lot of time on their hands.

Mason Knight was crouched down by the right front tire, making Booth think of a redheaded frog in horn-rims. His wife, wearing a billowy pink dress and dangling earrings, looked oddly flamboyant for a morning of spying in windows. She grinned at Booth as if they were old roommates. Something familiar about her caught at his memory. In her hand was a camera with a heavy strap and a long lens.

Booth ignored his inner questions for the urgent ones. "Where is Kathleen?"

"He's making her get dressed."

"Is she okay?"

"Seems to be. Someone chopped up her piano."

"What?"

"Looks like an ax did the job."

Booth felt his stomach turn with a sickening twist. "She's okay, not hurt or cut?" he asked again, needing to hear it one more time.

"Didn't appear to be."

"I'm going to take a look."

Booth moved along a row of wisteria, spotting a rental car that had been camouflaged by the curve of a stockade fence. He was familiar enough with the layout of the carriage house to guess which window belonged to the bedroom. He held his weapon tight against his side and moved slowly and silently.

The window was open and he heard the unfamiliar Midwestern accent.

"Hurry up," the man snapped.

"I am."

"I don't have all day. Our plane leaves in a few hours."

Booth moved closer to the window, plastering himself against the shingled side of the house.

He considered climbing in but quickly nixed the idea. The man would hear him, and it would be too risky for Kathleen. He ducked beneath the window casing and made his way around to the door just as he saw his two backups emerge from the drive. He signaled them, and one sprinted silently across the lawn.

Booth said, "Kelly, I'm going to try to get inside. He has Kathleen in the bedroom."

"Something just came in," Kelly whispered. "You know that deputy named Cory that you talked to? He just called back and said that he couldn't keep quiet any longer. Kathleen was stopped for speeding about hundred miles from her house on the day of the murder. The time is so close as to make it impossible according to the autopsy report for her to have been even in the vicinity of Rodeo. Cory said the sheriff learned of the ticket and got it expunged from the record. I got in touch with the Wyoming state police and they assured me that if a ticket was issued, they would find it. I just called in, and the officer who stopped her remembers her and has turned over his own logbook."

Booth felt such a drain of relief, his knees were shaky. "I think I'm beginning to believe in miracles."

"Or you got the hole in the case you've been looking for."

Booth grinned. "Yeah."

Kelly went back to join the other officer, circling around so that one of them covered Booth and the other could go in through the window once Kathleen was out of the bedroom.

Inside, Booth saw the piano, the pieces scattered and flung across the room. His first thought was gratitude that it was the piano and not Kathleen, but the vandal had probably planned it that way. Whoever he was, he'd deliberately left her alive to witness it and make her understand that she was in danger of the same kind of treatment if she gave them trouble.

Booth positioned himself and his weapon, using his hand to push aside the debris. One of the other officers entered the house and flattened himself by the door. From the bedroom exit, neither cop could be seen.

A minute passed.

Three minutes.

Then six.

Finally Kathleen came out wearing jeans and that same sweatshirt. A canvas bag he'd seen her carry before was slung over her shoulder. His first thought was that she'd taken ten times more things when they'd gone to the picnic. The man behind her held his gun mere inches from her spine. It took all Booth's control not to shoot the slimy bastard. She made a wide path around the butchered piano, and Booth noted she kept her gaze down, as if looking for something.

The man hesitated as if he thought it might be a trick when she stopped by the bench. Kathleen lifted the top of the hinged seat and removed a handful of sheet music that Booth remembered had belonged to her mother.

Booth crouched, sweeping his hand across the floor.

Come on, babe, come on. Just a few more steps. Just a few more.

He waited, his patience at the limit, his fear real.

She was too vulnerable, and with this bastard ready to do anything to make sure he left here with her, Booth knew his own timing had to be utterly precise.

Kathleen continued slowly, the bag on her shoulder slipping, and when she reached to adjust it, the sheet music slipped from her arms to the floor. When she knelt to retrieve it, Booth moved.

With the lightning strike of a rattlesnake he flung a handful of wood splinters into the man's face.

"Yow!"

While the man scrambled to get the stuff out of his eyes, Booth darted forward, and his boot caught the weapon, sending it high and wide. It hit the floor with a thud and slid a good ten feet away.

The man swung around and came at Booth, head-butting him. Kathleen screamed and the other officer pulled her to safety. Booth fought with the man, rolling and gaining an advantage, then losing it only to gain it again.

Finally he wrestled the man onto his belly and yanked his hands around and pinned them.

"Hey, man, you don't know what you're doin'. I'm Sheriff Buck Faswell. I came to take the Hanes woman back for trial. She killed her husband."

"Yeah? Then how come you didn't notify the Crosby police?"

"I was goin' to, but I didn't want her to get away. Been after her for weeks."

"Too bad you wasted the trip, because she isn't

guilty of anything except ignoring a speeding ticket.''

Faswell twisted around and looked at him sharply.

''Bingo,'' Booth said, enjoying the drain of color from Faswell's face.

''No way. There ain't no ticket. I, uh— Someone looked after it.''

Booth took even greater pleasure in his next comment. ''You might have fixed it locally, but the state police have a record. You're cooked, Faswell.''

The two other officers got him cuffed against his continued protests. Kelly asked, ''Booth, what about that couple outside?''

''Send them in.''

''You sure?''

''Yeah. If it hadn't been for them, Faswell would have taken Kathleen.''

As he talked, Kathleen was circling the carpet, examining the broken instrument. She came to a stop at the place where they'd made love.

Booth walked over and cupped his hand around the back of her neck. ''Babe, I'm so sorry.''

''It's so painful to look at, it's like part of my heart was cut up.''

Booth turned her so that she couldn't see the rubble. ''You know, most women would have been so relieved that the guy wielding the gun was in custody, they'd have rushed into my arms.''

She looked up at him, her eyes a little glassy, the

events of the past hours just beginning to take their toll. "I knew you'd get here in time."

"Yeah? And how did you know that?"

"I just knew. In my heart I knew."

Her trust filled him with joy. It supported his own instincts about her innocence, but then it had gone even further—it guaranteed her freedom.

"Bet you never thought you'd be grateful you got stopped for speeding."

She shook her head. "To be honest, I'm more grateful for you and Lisa."

Booth let out a deep breath he wasn't aware he'd been holding. "Are you sure you're okay? You look a little shell-shocked."

Then she began to sag and Booth gripped her, drawing her into the security of his arms.

"I've wasted time, Booth," she said in a reedy voice. "I wasted opportunities to tell you the truth instead of hoping if I hid long enough it would all go away. Even that speeding ticket. I'd been so furious when he stopped me, because I was on my way back to get my sheet music. I threw the ticket into the glove compartment. Then when I sold the car in Pennsylvania, I took all the stuff out and tossed it into a box and never really sorted through it. I just found it." She shuddered.

"It gives you an airtight alibi, babe. I'll go with you back to Wyoming to get this cleared up."

She looked up at him, her expression telling him how relieved she was that she didn't have to return alone. "The sheriff killed Steve," she said flatly.

"He told you that?"

"Yes. He and some others are involved in some cash-rich operation. Steve was in on it, too, but he talked too much, and so the sheriff shut him up by killing him."

"You said 'cash-rich operation.' Drugs?"

"I don't know. Max was the name of the man who destroyed my piano. No last name. Someone called the Rainmaker was also involved."

"Well, I'll be damned."

"You know them?"

"Max could be anyone, but the Rainmaker... Well, I've never had any contact with him, but I've heard of him. He used to be a lawyer who billed for more time than he worked. Served some minor jail time, then disappeared. Heard a report about a year ago that he was setting up a drug-import business from Mexico and looking to expand throughout the West. His real name was Nash Varney, but he liked to call himself the Rainmaker because of all the money he made—first for his law firm and then for himself. From what I've learned from the Wyoming state police, some kind of fly-in import of drugs had been going on, but the operation had closed down over the past few months. Apparently the Rodeo sheriff's office had come under some criticism from citizens for not following up on tips about suspicious lights they'd seen. After Steve was killed, the focus all shifted to finding and arresting you."

Kathleen was staring up at him, her mouth slightly open, her eyes wide. "You know all this?"

"Babe, I'm a cop. One of the privileges of being one is that I can ask questions, get answers and then take those answers to the next level. The state police out there are honest and professional, and they want to know about bad cops so they can get rid of them. They are not interested in putting innocent people in prison."

"When you say it, it all sounds so logical. But from where I was it was frightening. All I knew was that the police in Rodeo wanted to frame me to save the real killer. I didn't know why until now." Kathleen scowled. "And they would have locked me up without a backward look."

"Probably."

"So I was right to run."

"You should have confided in me. We could have gotten this straightened out weeks ago. If Faswell killed Hanes, then the Rainmaker had him by the short hairs. My guess is that the sheriff had to do what he was told or face the Rainmaker's wrath—perhaps the guy with the ax who took out your piano." Booth paused as she absorbed it all. "If the sheriff did as he was told and killed Steve, he'd be off the hook with the Rainmaker, but they needed someone to blame. You were perfect. They made Steve's murder look like a domestic squabble that had turned violent. The Rodeo police painted that scenario and made you look desperate. You shot him and ran. It was almost perfect."

"All set up, even to the point of the Rodeo police testifying against me. I'd be convicted because I had no witnesses and the murder case would be closed. But it wasn't really about anyone believing I did it. It was all about protecting some sleazy guy's drug-running and distribution operation."

"You were the ideal patsy, babe. No family around. Very few friends, if any. Isolated, and with Hanes's history of knocking you around, they had the most logical person—a wife who retaliated. What they didn't figure was that you were too smart for them."

"More like too scared."

"Maybe, but also clever and careful and aware. You didn't do things to call attention to yourself."

"Until I sent for my piano."

"Yeah. That kind of thing was the break they were waiting for."

She slipped into his arms, resting her head against his chest. "You know, it's weird. Its arrival exposed me but also saved me."

"Saved you for me. And for Lisa."

She leaned back. "Booth, I've been so horrible to you."

"Yep, you have."

For a moment she looked worried. "But you know it was because I was afraid. You were a cop, and an honest cop wouldn't hide a fugitive."

"True, but an honest cop who was in love with the fugitive would have stuck by her no matter what she was charged with."

Her eyes widened. "In love? You're in love with me?"

"Uh, excuse us?" Mason Knight and his wife stood a few feet from them, obviously uncomfortable that they'd intruded. Kathleen stepped away from Booth, answering his main question about the Knights. "The grocery store. You're the woman who stopped to admire Lisa."

"Actually, we were following you. Mason didn't want me to speak to you, but I never could resist babies, and watching you with little Lisa, well, it reminded me of my own grandchildren."

"Della May?" Mason Knight addressed his wife. "I think they want to be alone, so let's get the explanation made and head on out."

"You're right. Go ahead. You tell them."

He stepped forward. "Your brother Clarke called us weeks ago and asked us to keep watch over you. Apparently he couldn't stop worrying about you. We met Clarke when me and Della May were doing some consulting on a picture in Hollywood. Anyway, we agreed. Gave us a chance to look at some new surroundings and get paid at the same time, so we drove up here to Crosby. We made some inquiries and learned you worked at the Silver Lining. We tried to stay far enough away so no one would get suspicious, but then Della May approached you at the grocery store."

"Clarke sent you to watch over me?" she asked, making that question the only one that really mattered.

"Yes."

"I thought you were sent by the people who wanted to frame me." She swallowed hard.

Booth stepped forward and offered his hand to Mason. "I owe you an apology, Mason, and I have to say this relieves my mind. You two were the pieces of this puzzle I couldn't fit anyplace."

"Well, it's all solved now." To Kathleen, Mason said, "Call your brother. He'll want to know that you're okay, that you've found a new life here and that you're happy."

"I will. Thank you."

Mason and his wife said goodbye, once again leaving Kathleen and Booth alone.

"I want to meet your brother. This is a guy who thinks ahead and knows when to act."

"Yes, he does, doesn't he," she said, pride filling her voice. "Just like you." She tipped her head to the side. "Before they came in you said you loved me."

He grinned. "You look as surprised as I was when I realized it."

"When did you know?"

"Probably that day you came to the grocery store with me. Gladys pissed me off more than usual when she tried to make the relationship we didn't yet have into something dirty. I hadn't even thought about anything permanent, and she was already condemning us. But last night I knew for sure."

"But that was when you said you knew the truth about me."

"No, babe, when I knew the truth about us. If you didn't care about us—Lisa and me—you would have never dug your roots in so deep here. Renting the carriage house, sending for your piano, taking the position Eric offered at the school—those aren't the actions of a murderer hiding out from the law. Those are the actions of a woman who wants roots and a home and a chance to be happy." He went on to tell her about the tabloids and making himself check out the story himself. "At that point, I knew there was more to it than Gladys's newspaper stories. I also knew that whatever the truth was, you weren't some husband killer. I knew there was a hole, and there was. The speeding ticket."

Tears brimmed in her eyes. "I've been so afraid to admit my feelings for you. Of course I adore Lisa. She's so precious and wonderful. But you. You scared me and intrigued me, and I wanted you but I didn't want to want you because I was so afraid—"

Booth silenced her with a long, deep kiss. "Tell me you're not afraid to love me."

"No, I'm not afraid of that. Not anymore."

He kissed her again, and together, arms around each other, they walked outside into the morning sunshine.

EPILOGUE

Two months later

"SHH. I THINK THEY'RE COMING."

"I hope all the cars are hidden."

"They are."

"And everything is exactly the way Booth ordered it?"

"Exactly."

It was mid-September, the air filled with the crispness of a beckoning autumn. The Rawlings family and friends were gathered at the carriage house awaiting the arrival of Booth and Kathleen.

They'd returned to Wyoming, where Kathleen had cooperated fully with the authorities and been officially cleared of any pending charges in her husband's death. The sheriff and those officers involved had been charged with conspiracy, bribery, assisting in an illegal operation, drug dealing and murder. Max and the Rainmaker had been arrested, and the abandoned airstrip used by the drug-carrying planes had been broken up to prevent further use. Kathleen's statement about the conversation she'd overheard between Cory and the sheriff was supported by Cory, who cooperated fully. He wasn't charged with any direct involvement, and in fact, was praised for coming forward about Faswell trying to fix the speeding ticket.

From Wyoming, they'd gone on to Hollywood so Booth could meet Clarke and Kathleen could tell him officially that he was the best brother in the world.

The return to Crosby and the carriage house had been Booth's idea.

"But there are only a few pieces of furniture," Kathleen said as she climbed out of the Explorer.

"Knowing my mother, she and Darlene had most of the stuff from my apartment moved while we were gone. Besides, the most important piece is there. The bed."

She grinned. "Hmm. Guess we can make do."

"For a hundred years or so."

She slipped her arm through his as they made their way up the path. Booth reached out and opened the door, gesturing for her to go first.

No sooner had she stepped over the threshold than Lisa came running out, her arms outstretched. "'Leen! 'Leen!"

Kathleen lifted her into her arms. "Sweetheart, what are you doing here?"

Booth groaned.

Then everyone else popped up in quick succession and yelled, "Surprise!"

"Oh, Booth, I'm sorry," his mother apologized. "But she saw your car and she just got away from me."

Kathleen was laughing and hugging the toddler while greeting everyone else. Lisa wriggled to get down and Kathleen complied.

A tall, strikingly handsome man with deep hazel eyes came forward and grinned. Kathleen had met Doug Rawlings before she and Booth had returned to Wyoming. When Doug had heard about the frame-up, he'd called a Wyoming attorney he'd known since college and arranged to have him represent her.

Putting an arm around Kathleen and shaking Booth's hand, he said, "It's good to have you back home again. Both of you."

"It's good to be home," she said, her eyes glistening with wonder and happiness at such a show of support and love.

Booth touched her back, urging her forward.

She whispered, "This is all wonderful, but what's the occasion?"

"Look," he murmured, turning her toward the room where her piano had been. "That's the occasion."

Kathleen looked and blinked, sure that it was some kind of illusion. A brand-new dark mahogany grand piano stood in the center of the room, its keyboard gleaming ivory and black. The bench was pulled back, sheet music rested on the stand.

"Oh, Booth," she said, her hands coming up to her face.

"It's from everyone. They wanted to do it, and I told them you'd be thrilled."

She turned to the crowd, her eyes damp, her voice cracking. "What can I say? I'm simply overwhelmed."

Doug, Janet, Mavis, Darlene and Gail all stepped forward. "We love you, Kathleen, and we want you to stay and be part of our lives and part of Crosby."

Silence filled the room, but for a few sniffles and some throat clearing.

Finally Kathleen said, "I can't think of anywhere I'd rather be."

"There's some sheet music on the stand," Mavis said. "Would you play the song for us?"

Kathleen took Booth's hand and walked over to the massive instrument. She ran her hands over the wood before sliding onto the bench. Booth stood beside her.

She reached up and opened the sheet, but instead of sharps and flats and chords, the words "Will you marry me?" were written in big letters.

Kathleen stared, her throat so tight she couldn't speak.

Then she swung around and flung herself into Booth's arms. "Oh, yes, yes, yes!"

Booth held her, kissing her, looking deeply into her eyes. "Look, Lisa has something for you."

Kathleen glanced down. The little girl held a tiny box, and at her father's urging she got the lid open and presented the ring.

Everyone clapped and Lisa giggled. Booth took the ring and slipped it on Kathleen's trembling finger.

"You're incredible," she murmured to Booth, staring at the diamond solitaire.

He leaned closer. "I have a question, though."

She raised her lashes and looked at him. "Hmm?"

"How do we get rid of all these people so I can take you to bed and show you how much I love you?"

"I think they all got the message."

And sure enough, they all excused themselves, with Janet Rawlings taking Lisa. "We're having dinner at our house. If you two want to join us, you're welcome. If not, we all understand."

In the quiet that followed once everyone had departed, Booth lifted Kathleen into his arms and carried her into the bedroom. And there in the sweetness of love and commitment, they found their own promising "forever."

HARLEQUIN SUPERROMANCE®

GUARANTEED
★
PAGE-TURNER!

THE ENDS OF THE EARTH (#798)
by Kay David

To protect her nephew, Eva Solis takes him and runs to a tiny village in the remotest part of Argentina. No one will find them—or so she thinks. Then a tall stranger arrives. And he seems to be watching her every move. Now Eva knows that the problem with running to the ends of the earth is there's nowhere else to go.

Be sure to watch for this and other upcoming
Guaranteed Page-Turners!

Available August 1998 wherever Harlequin books are sold.

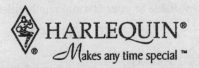

HARLEQUIN®
Makes any time special ™

MEN at WORK

All work and no play?
Not these men!

July 1998

MACKENZIE'S LADY by Dallas Schulze

Undercover agent Mackenzie Donahue's
lazy smile and deep blue eyes were his best
weapons. But after rescuing—and kissing!—
damsel in distress Holly Reynolds, how could
he betray her by spying on her brother?

August 1998

MISS LIZ'S PASSION by Sherryl Woods

Todd Lewis could put up a building with ease,
but quailed at the sight of a classroom! Still,
Liz Gentry, his son's teacher, was no battle-ax,
and soon Todd started planning some
extracurricular activities of his own....

September 1998

A CLASSIC ENCOUNTER
by Emilie Richards

Doctor Chris Matthews was intelligent, sexy
and *very* good with his hands—which made
him all the more dangerous to single mom
Lizette St. Hilaire. So how long could she
resist Chris's special brand of TLC?

Available at your favorite retail outlet!

MEN AT WORK™

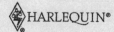 

Look us up on-line at: http://www.romance.net   PMAW2

HARLEQUIN SUPERROMANCE®

DEBORAH'S SON

by award-winning author
Rebecca Winters

Deborah's pregnant. The man she loves—the baby's father—doesn't know. He's withdrawn from her for reasons she doesn't understand. But she has to tell him. *Wants* to tell him. She wants them to be a family.

Available in October
wherever Harlequin books are sold.

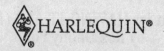

HARLEQUIN®

Glamorous, hot, seductive...

THE AUSTRALIANS

Stories of romance Australian-style guaranteed to
fulfill that sense of adventure!

September 1998, look for
Playboy Lover
by **Lindsay Armstrong**

When Rory and Dominique met at a party the attraction was
magnetic, but all Dominique's instincts told her to resist him.
Not easy as they'd be working together in the steamy tropics
of Australia's Gold Coast. When they were thrown together in
a wild and reckless experience, obsessive passion flared—but
had she found her Mr. Right, or had she fallen for yet another
playboy?

*The Wonder from Down Under: where spirited women win
the hearts of Australia's most independent men!*

Available September 1998 at your favorite retail outlet.

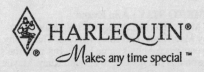

HARLEQUIN®
Makes any time special ™

COMING NEXT MONTH

#802 YOU WERE ON MY MIND • Margot Early
The Midwives
Ivy's a midwife; she understands the mystery of birth,
the wonder of babies. But she hasn't got a baby of her
own…has she? *She doesn't know.* Who was she before the
accident, before she became Ivy? Then, unexpectedly, she
learns that she was married and actually had a child, and
she knows she has to go back to Tennessee, back to her
family. *Even if she can't remember them…* The first book
in Margot Early's stunning new trilogy, THE MIDWIVES.

#803 CLASS ACT • Laura Abbot
"Is *this* all there is?" That's what Connie Weaver—teacher,
divorced single parent and lone caregiver to her own elderly
and difficult mother—wonders when she's presented with
her fortieth birthday cake. Thanks to the demands of work
and family, she doesn't have time for anything else, leaving
her with only memories of the idyllic summer she spent
with the one man who might've changed all that…and
who's about to walk back into her life.

#804 RIDE A PAINTED PONY • Carolyn McSparren
Guaranteed Page-Turner
You never lose people on a carousel, Nick Kendall tells
Taylor Hunt. *They may go out of sight for a while, but they
always come back.* His words are what Taylor is counting
on as she and Nick are drawn into a world of intrigue,
danger, betrayal and passion. *Ride A Painted Pony* by
Carolyn McSparren will keep you on the edge of your
seat. You may never look at a carousel in quite the same
way again!

#805 HOME TO STAY • Ann Evans
Fort Myers, Florida, simply isn't big enough for
Abby MacAllister *and* Riley Kincaid. That's why it's been
ten years since Abby's come home. But now she's back for
a reason that has nothing to do with Riley. Maybe she won't
run into him before she returns to Boston and her busy law
practice. Fat chance! Because Riley Kincaid has moved into
the house next door.